I0676377

Sydney's Child

By

Jenni Roussell

Dedication

To my dear friend Helen
        For your ongoing help and sage advice
    Thank You JR

Copyright 2023 - All rights reserved

Sydney's Child

The names, characters, and incidents portrayed in it are
the work of the
authors imagination. Any resemblance to actual persons,
living or dead,
events or localities are simply coincidental.
Jenni Roussell asserts the moral right
to be known as the author of this work.
Copyright 2023 Jenni Roussell

Chapter One:

March twenty-five, 2020, *Ten thirty in the evening less than two hours before the Government's impending lockdown to fight the Covid19 pandemic spreading across the world.*

'Sydney Martin?' the tall dark stranger called, setting down his bags on the veranda of the old homestead. The lights were on in the house and the front door open. Inside the TV blared. Nobody answered, a horn beeped. He turned and waved the officer goodnight as the patrol car drove off. Turning back to the open door about to call out again, he noticed a small boy in pyjamas standing in the doorway, his little face flushed. Standing beside him stood a Jack Russell terrier with tail wagging welcomingly.

'Is Sydney Martin home? Can I speak to her, please? Will you get her for me, please?' Is this kid thick or just being obtuse? The boy stood blocking the half open doorway looking unimpressed, then he opened his mouth and yelled, 'M-u-m!'

Fletch Carter stood feeling decidedly unwelcome. He'd been travelling since six this morning from the South Island. It had been a case of hurry up and wait all day, as the airlines scrambled to get people home before the midnight curfew.

'Finn where are you?' an irritated female voice called. The young boy turned, and the voice stood in the hallway in front of him.

'Oh, who's this?' she asked. 'What can I do for you?' Placing her hands on the boy's shoulders she bent affectionately towards him, saying quietly, 'Finn your warm chocolate is on the bench.' She looked up at Fletch.

'I'm looking for Sydney Martin, are you Ms Martin? He asked. 'The police officer who drove me said Sydney Martin lives here.'

Fletch watched the woman's expression become irked.

'Constable Ryan Murphy knows very well who lives here. Yes, I'm Sydney Martin. Who are you?' She stood shifting her weight from one bare foot to the other, revealing her shapely legs. A baggy plaid shirt covered her to the edge of her fraying denim shorts. Thick dark hair hung in wisps around her face, the rest pulled back in a messy ponytail.

'I'm Fletch Carter, your brother's business partner,' he said brightly, offering extended hand. A confused expression covered her face. 'Oh no, he hasn't told you, has he?' Fletch said sounding exasperated as she ignored his outstretched hand.

'Is he expecting you?' Her head spun, she knew her brother lived in America, California to be precise, where he had been busy trying to finish a movie. 'Before the world goes to hell in a handbasket,' according to the email he sent her just days earlier. She had not heard from him since.

'No, Perry's still in America busy winding up the shoot and as I've been in the South Island scouting for filming locations for our next venture, he told me to high tail it up here and stay in his house during the lockdown. This is his house the police officer confirmed it.'

Sydney scoffed and Fletch stood staunch. Looking at him, he appealed, rugged, obviously he'd been around the block a few times. Although his features were attractive his expression seemed belligerent. The scar above his eye not alone, as another sliced right through his lip. Both were old giving him a certain gravitas, something about his bearing made him commanding, like a soldier perhaps? It made sense thousands of Americans serve in the Military.

'This place belongs to the Martin family trust, which is Perry and me, and I live here. He never told me you were going to join us,' Sydney said annoyed. Perry was often vague, but this took the cake, inviting a complete stranger to join her and Finn to stay on their isolated rural property during lockdown.

'Please ma'am, it's been a long day. Could we discuss this inside maybe?' he sighed.

'I don't think so, not until I've checked you out. I mean you obviously don't know my twin well.' The stranger gave her a rueful smile as she spoke. 'Perry never mentioned a partner. He did say something about being involved in a new venture.' Sydney's frowned and she stood hands on hips.

Fed up and not wanting to spend all night on the front veranda Fletch dredged the archives of his tired brain trying to bring up every small piece of trivia Perry had ever shared with him.

'I know your parents were killed in a boating accident in Queenstown during his early years at Television New Zealand.' That didn't convince her. 'He said you were doing legal studies and then you got a job with some high-flying law firm.'

Sydney cringed. 'Typical' she sneered; her brother had made her sound like she's some hot shot lawyer. Because he's ashamed of her, she felt sure.

'Back then I worked as a legal executive, a para legal, the flash name for a dogsbody secretary. I haven't worked for Winthrop and Associates since before Finn was born.' Curiously her voice sounded weak and a little bitter.

'Perry also told me you keep a spare house key in a stone with a large hole lasered into it and a black rubber bung keeps the key in situ. He said it's in the circular garden in front of the house underneath the birdbath,' Fletch said, relieved, he didn't have to scramble around in the rose bushes looking for the key in the dark. 'Perry also said you had an account at Pain and Kershaw's in Martinborough. I emailed them a grocery order and they said they would deliver it tomorrow as I had missed today's deliveries.'

Sydney stood worrying her bottom lip in thought.

'Why did Ryan...er Constable Murphy drive you out here?' she turned slightly as young Finn joined her on the veranda.

'Because I couldn't get a taxi at the bus stop in Martinborough. When I told him my story, he seemed pretty amused.' Then as though a light bulb switched on, he added, 'I think you two have history, right?' He watched her bemused expression as she held open the door.

'Come in, let's just say Ryan and my twin are mates from way back.'

Chapter Two:

What self-respecting parent would call a cute, feminine, little imp of a girl, Sydney Georgina Martin? Georgina and Sydney Martin did passing the curse of their own beloved parents on to their only daughter. Fortunately, apart from their name and a very spirited personality, everything else her parents passed on turned out to be an asset.

When Sydney graduated secretarial college with her diploma as a Legal Executive and applied for a job in a law firm everyone expected she'd do well. Nobody appeared surprised when she landed the plum position of personal assistant to Timothy Winthrop. An up-and-coming barrister, Tim's career steered a fast track to celebrity, due to his distinction in successfully defending the accused in a widely publicised murder case. The man, who preferred to be called Tim, enjoyed a flamboyant delivery in the Courtroom. Even if he never opened his mouth, he had such presence sometimes he played the powerful 'say nothing' card.

A strapping man over six feet tall, he looked as though he could easily go twelve rounds in the boxing ring with Mike Tyson, until he opened his mouth and delivered the smooth rhetoric of a polished criminal barrister. He dressed like an advert for Esquire magazine's best dressed man of the year.

When the efficient spitfire called Sydney joined the firm of Winthrop and Associates, she soon made her mark. The senior partner Grant Winthrop, Tim's father thought her the best person Tim could ever have as his PA. But it took him Grant a good year to admit it. Tim's manner came across as arrogant rather than confident and it never fazed her. The consummate professional, Sydney ignored Tim's rudeness and soon became so invaluable he couldn't do without her. Slowly she had firmly established herself as a valued member of the team. She began to call him on his less than desirable behaviours and the sparks would fly. Sydney, confident, in the standard of her work, felt buoyed by the feedback she received from key people in the firm. So, when Timothy Winthrop demanded,

'I want this file back on my desk before you leave tonight,' without thought for anyone but himself. She would smile sweetly and tell him,

'You do realise there is at least three hours work there Mr Winthrop? It is four thirty now.' The first time she had taken this approach Tim replied rudely,

'Well, I need those papers for the case tomorrow, it's imperative.' She nodded politely then told him, 'and you will have them. However, this case has been scheduled for months and the file has been on your desk for two weeks. Three times I've asked you what else needed doing for this case and you assured me you had it all under control. Now half an hour before I'm due to finish work you remember this file.' She stared at him, her warm brown eyes blazing.

'This kind of inconsideration is unworthy of you.'

Slowly his lips quirked, and his eyes sparked he leaned over his desk smiling contritely at her.

'Thank you for drawing this behaviour to my attention Sydney, it won't happen again, I promise.' Moistening his lips he added, 'and please call me Tim.'

Agreeing, she started on the work, noting the arrogant prat hadn't actually apologised. This heralded the beginning of their unique working relationship. Tim thought of himself as God's gift to women and at thirty-six it seemed true. He could be a handful to deal with although she managed him.

Sydney, so different from her twin brother; he like to dream, she preferred to be pragmatic. Perry an artist, a romantic, loving and totally unrealistic in his aspirations for his sister. His dreams were big hairy audacious goals to become a famous movie director. Already he was well on his way to accomplishing it. He had no idea what had happened years before to change his sister. The bubbly, feisty go-getting girl had gone, replaced by a quiet, sometimes withdrawn woman who worked hard and never went anywhere much.

Months, and sometimes years went by before he saw her. Perry wondered if delayed grief over their parents' sudden death had dulled her sparkle.

The Martins were older parents. The twins had been lucky to be born not as a result of fertility treatment but simply a gift from God. Their mother had been well over forty when they were delivered. Their father older, in his mid-fifties, when the twins arrived, fatherhood had been a huge shock to his system. He organised for some help in the house and spent his time working on the farm, avoiding the twins.

Sydney, the first-born twin, weighed five hundred grams heavier than Perry. Right from the word go, she ruled the roost. Bigger, louder and more independent. Perry, quiet, needy and smaller until about the age of eleven when his preadolescent growth hormones kicked in. By secondary school, he stood six feet tall, desperately thin. His huge shoulders looked like he would never grow into them. By the time he had he noted his twin appeared shorter than her peers and curvy everywhere. What she lacked in stature she made up for in personality, hers as big as all outdoors until just before Finn arrived.

MIDNIGHT MARCH TWENTY-five, 2020

Sydney came back into the large farmhouse kitchen.

'Sorry about my son. Finn has been off school sick, there's not a lot wrong with him. He had a sniffle on the weekend. The school's a bit paranoid about colds at present. He went to bed early and woke up about ten thirty wanting a warm drink. Then you...' she rambled, embarrassed to be sharing her house with a stranger.

'I'm fine thank you; your spaghetti bolognaise tasted great.' Fletch watched as his host quickly tidied the kitchen. She could not be accused of being dumpy, but neither was she svelte. Her clothes did her no favours, he decided.

'I've made up the bed in the spare room,' she announced, not looking at him. 'Tomorrow we'll try and get hold of Perry. Finn has hidden my phone and lost it, the second one doesn't work. I emailed my neighbour to phone me, so I can locate it, but God knows when he will look at his emails. He's a farmer and his parents are both technophobes,' shrugging, she yawned.

'I can ring your number again but ...' he held up his phone and she grinned.

'Mobiles don't work here. Unless you find a spot somewhere on the tops of the hills there is no signal. Didn't Perry give you the landline number? He knows what the reception is like' This time Fletch gave her a strange look. Hadn't she just told him she lost her landline phone somewhere? Too tired to think anymore, he wanted his bed.

Next morning shrieks and giggles woke him. Picking up his phone from the bedside table he noted the time now read ten minutes past eleven. Geez he'd slept for twelve hours. Emerging from the bathroom dripping wet, he could smell coffee. The delicious aroma called him, and he dressed hurriedly to taste it. Real coffee sent his senses into the stratosphere.

'Hi ya, I'm Finn, what's your name?' the small boy asked from beneath a tent made up of a bedspread draped over two dining chairs in the family room.

'I'm Fletch. How old are you, Finn?' he wanted to know as he looked over towards Sydney in the open plan kitchen. Today she

11

looked different, but he couldn't quite work out why, dressed in jeans and a tee shirt tucked into her pants, he noted the little muffin top roll at her waist. Then Fletch noticed her generous bosoms not wanting to focus on them he turned back to Finn who now stood beside him as he sat at the table.

'I'm six. I had my birthday party in February. How old are you?' Sydney chided him about rudeness and they both turned back to her. Her hair, he saw it now. She wore it differently, straight and long a classic bob below her shoulders. Well below her shoulders cascading thick and straight halfway down her back. She smiled a tad stiltedly.

'Coffee?' As she handed him the mug she pointed to the milk and sugar on the table, he thanked her then turned back to Finn.

'I'm forty.' he said.

Finn whooped telling him, 'you're old.' Then he added as Sydney joined them at the table,

'Mummy's thirty-one.' His mother shook her head there were no secrets where Finn came from. Fletch checked his phone out of habit. No signal! Frustrated he put it down on the table.

'No devices at the table,' Finn parroted. Irritated, Fletch narrowed his eyes at the child. He would need to set the rules of engagement if they were going to be sharing this house for any length of time.

'Fletch,' he looked across the table at her and sipped his coffee. For about half a minute he sat drinking her in. Warm eyes, like melted brown sugar, framed by well-defined dark brows. When she stopped worrying her bottom lip with her teeth her full mouth looked pretty. What he read in her face made him squirm. Vulnerability and something else. He'd seen it before surely, she is not afraid of him. 'Fletch,' she said again a little more assertive this time.

'We need to attend to some housekeeping matters; you know set some ground rules.' Gee, she read his mind. Grabbing a pen and paper she wrote a list. 'Email Perry urgently, go over to the neighbours and get them to phone me, housework roster.' She recited the list aloud and hearing the housework roster he balked.

'Housework? I don't do house wor... er happy families,' he growled.

'Well, I have to work and mind a child so if you're living here, we share the domestic chores.' Fire blazed in her eyes, he scowled, she's right. God, he knew it; he just couldn't deal with the six-year old's continual inquisition. 'Bacon and eggs okay for lunch?' she asked pushing the daily paper across the table. 'I'll get lunch, the Prime Minister will be on the box at one with an update.' What the hell does she mean, he wondered.

Setting the food down in front of him he could see they wouldn't starve but he couldn't afford to get spare tyres around his waist either. He pushed the eggs off the toast and simply ate his bacon and eggs. Sydney watched him; the man had a certain attitude and what about the no carbs thing, she wondered hoeing into her toast. A wicked grin came over her face and she wrote something down on the list, then something else and something again. Soon the smirky grin became a full-blown smile. He wanted to ask what she had written but had the feeling he'd find out soon enough. Her smile lit up her whole face, making it striking.

After lunch she quickly loaded the dishwasher and handed Finn an I Pad.

'You can watch a movie on this. Mummy needs to listen to the Prime Minister.' Fletch watched amused as the digital native, barely able to read, navigated his way around the I Pad.

'Disney movies,' Finn advised. They took up their positions in front of the TV, ah 'the box' Fletch realised. The worldwide news sounded grim, and the Prime Minister and the Director General of Health were severe in their dire warnings. They gave a blow-by-blow description of the path of Covid 19 around the globe. An eerie calm pervaded the room as they watched.

The Prime Minister insisted for New Zealand to be safe the 'team of five million' as she referred to the population, would need to pull together and follow the Director General of Health's instructions, she finished up 'be kind to one another. We will go early and go hard with lockdown. All the borders will be closed only emergency and medical supplies will land in the country during this time' the she advised.

On the couch at right angles to Sydney, he watched her write like fury. When the broadcast finished, she asked quite seriously.

'What skill sets do you have?' His expression became quizzical. 'I'm serious, I need to know what you're capable of.'

This bossy woman amused him but at the same time he thought, 'whoa,' I bet she can get mad. 'I'm a trained killer?' he smirked.

'Very useful if we need meat,' her voice sarcastic. 'Too bad we already have one of those.'

I bet you she didn't train where I did, he thought.

'It's a pity you're not a ratter like Mercury because he needs help in the barn. I can't lay poison.' she pointed to Finn and Merkee as he called his dog. 'Here's the list of chores. Choose your half.' Tossing the list and pen at him, she stood up and put the remote on a high shelf on the bookcase, out of reach. Finn seemed an obvious handful. 'We're going for a walk, Want to come? Put your sneakers on Finn,' she ordered him. Looking down at Fletch's Gucci loafers she sniffed.

'Hang on I'll just get my trainers.' Good idea Mr Hollywood movie mogul.

'Trained killer, my arse,' she muttered under her breath as he went to his bedroom.

They headed outside in the clear March weather, the ground hard and dry even cracked in places. It needed rain desperately.

Fletch couldn't see any livestock he asked why as he watched Finn and Mercury run on ahead.

'The farm is leased out to the neighbour except for the house and twenty acres. I sold our stock when the feed started getting low and the prices were still reasonable. I have a few killers in the gully, for meat' she explained.

'Killers?' he asked quizzically.

'Yes, sheep bred to be killed for the freezer.'

Fletch noted Sydney needed two steps to every one of his long easy strides but being quite fit she easily managed.

The beauty of the property struck him. Gently undulating hill country dotted with old specimen shade trees and small stands of natives. In the distance he could see a purple haze covering the mountain range.

'See those clouds covering the top of the ranges, they indicate the wind will whip up this afternoon. It's sparse today so it will probably die down at sunset.' Finn threw sticks and Mercury chased them sometimes coming back to him with the them. Poultry ranged free near the barn but as he got nearer, he could see they were fenced off and netted. He commented on it.

'How would I find the eggs and how would I know how old they are?' She sounded reasonable to him. An Army brat brought up in army housing under martial law on various bases around America and Hawaii, he had no clue about farming.

'Do you ride? Finn and I have a horse each, I'm teaching him.' She saw him look at the horses. Fletch thought they might belong to the neighbour at first. They walked for about forty minutes and passed through several gates. He felt sure it didn't take forty minutes to walk around twenty acres but once again said nothing. The three of them sat on the nub of a hill and looked down at a winding river. He took out his cell phone and not getting more than half a bar he shoved it back in his pocket and asked,

'Where does your water come from?'

'It comes from a spring in the hills and is gravity fed into the tanks. Then it's pumped to troughs and the house. We treat it like gold at this time of the year, it's precious.' On the walk back to the house, Sydney pulled two macramé string bags from her pockets and walked over to a couple of old walnut trees and began scooping up the nuts from the ground.

'The crop's not good this year. we had a one last year. Some years it's not good and I have to beat the rats and possums. As soon as they're properly dry, I freeze them. The rodents can't open the freezer yet,' she grinned. Quickly she filled the bags and he offered to carry them for her. Within sight of the house, she pointed to the entrance of the chicken coop. Finn ran to retrieve a container from the top of the fence post. Scrambling up the fence he climbed over the top, carefully ensuring Mercury didn't get inside the yard.

'He's done that before,' Fletch commented.

Sydney grabbed the old aluminium sieve full of eggs, so Finn could climb back over the fence. As they passed an old shed attached to the barn Fletch asked, 'what's inside here?' She shrugged and let him poke around in the old tools and other treasures. An old wooden telephone box with a circular dial and large numbers on it hung on the wall. Studying it carefully he took it down then hung it back up again.

'Finn wouldn't be able to lose this huge landline,' he mused.

'No, but it doesn't work, more's the pity.'

Back at the house Fletch got out his laptop and started working on it at the kitchen table. He took little notice of Finn or Sydney, who busied herself making a batch of scones. The tasty smell stimulated his appetite. He noticed she was helping Finn to make playdough, bright pink playdough. The child sat quietly. Apart from giggles and whispers the pair were silent. When he looked up from his laptop again the table was now set for afternoon tea. Once again, his hunger piqued. This time the cheesy smell and the sight of huge home cooked scones, fresh whipped cream and strawberry jam had him suppressing thoughts of muffin top rolls and spare tyres.

He handed back the list of chores his chosen ones marked with circles around them, he accepted a coffee and a scone as she drank tea, they all tucked into the delicious scones.

'Have you ever done any of these chores before?' she asked, amused. 'Chop the wood, hang out the washing, bring in the washing and fold it up. Tidy the shed, fix the loose floorboards on the back porch. Mend the bunks in the back room. Cook every second day, weed the vegetable garden, he suspected the list had been created for his benefit. He would never let it be said he didn't pull his weight.

'Some, well none, apart from the cooking. I mainly constructed dishes from packets. We eat out mostly in America or get takeout.'

Right on cue he heard the honk of a horn and the rural delivery bloke yelled out he would put the groceries on the front veranda. Finn and Sydney waved at him from metres away.

'Don't you dare touch those boxes' she called as Fletch bent to pick up the groceries. 'There is a procedure, follow me.' Sydney pointed to a trestle table. 'Please lift it on to the veranda and set it up.' She followed with child and dog in tow. She produced latex gloves, disinfectant and hand sanitiser. After watching while she wiped down everything. He did as instructed and carried the items inside in a large plastic laundry basket.

'What a bloody job and a half,' he complained.

'The groceries and you are the only weak link here. No offence, but I know where we have been for the last couple of weeks but not the groceries or you.'

Geez, she really took this shit seriously. Considering this place is down under and at the back of nowhere, why the panic?

'Well, all I can say is, I hope you're on my team when the zombie apocalypse strikes,' he drawled. She gave a half eye roll. Finn helped his mother put the groceries away in the old-fashioned walk-in pantry and kept asking her 'what is this funny stuff,' as he looked at the small packets and jars of food. He was not used to seeing store bought items like soup in plastic packs, dried pasta, sachets of porridge, a few vegetables and salt-reduced crackers. His eyes lighted on a box of chocolates and several bottles of wine.

'You ordered my favourite wine, thank you.' Sydney said, turning to Fletch, He smirked having asked the shopkeeper for Sydney's favourite wine. Perry had said she and the shopkeeper were on first name terms with everyone in town, he exaggerated of course... Lindauer, the grocer replied in his email.

'Yeah, someone said you liked it,' he frowned. 'Next time I'll get your input on the food before I order,' his voice apologetic.

'It's the thought that counts and as you can see, we will never starve around here,' she tried to reassure him. When Finn and Merkee went out to bounce on the trampoline Sydney put the meat on for dinner then sat down at her laptop to answer her emails. Fletch disappeared into his room or so she thought.

Chapter Three:

An hour or so later Fletch came inside with the old wooden box telephone which he proceeded to plug into the phone jack point.

'Let's see if this will work, I think I've fixed it,' although, he sounded less than confident until he let out a whoop. 'I got a dial tone! Can I attach this old beauty to the wall? I reckon you could get a few bucks for this old phone online. I don't recommend you sell it.' After tapping to find the studs he proceeded to screw two holes through the brass brackets at the back of the phone and into the wall. Less than a minute after he'd finished the phone rang and he lifted the receiver as if to check his handiwork functioned properly.

'Sydney Martin's phone. what do you mean who the hell are you?' he said aloud for her benefit. 'I could ask you the same question.' Sydney reached for the receiver and Fletch stood up straight holding it well out of her reach, intrigued by the man's tone. 'Oh, you're Jamie Dalton, the neighbour, Sydney asked you to phone her. How, with smoke signals? The phone's been down. Did she say, 'save me Ted Bundy's moved in?' By now Fletch burst out laughing and Sydney became furious. 'She's right here mate, I'm Fletch Carter, Perry Martin's business partner. I'm just getting a rise out of your girl here, Jamie.' He handed the phone to Sydney.

The look she gave him he recognised to be the same 'piss off look' her twin brother used but he usually accompanied his with the words.

'Yeah, I know Jamie, Perry never mentioned he had a Sherman tank for a partner either but here he is in lockdown with me.' Sydney went on in this vein with her neighbour for a bit and then hung up.

'Well, the phone works. I suppose I should thank you.' her eyes narrowed on him, 'but why the hell do you have to wind everyone up, now Jamie thinks we're an item.' A huffing sound came from her mouth as she sat down at the table, lips pursed and ticked off. Sitting back down at the table he went back to his computer working out the time zone in various countries he needed to call.

Looking up from the screen he stretched, noting Sydney studying him. He felt proud of his great physique and worked at it. Rubbing his dark stubbly jaw with his index finger, thick dark brows furrowed together, from his lofty position he stared down at Sydney wondering if he could ever penetrate her prickly armour and find out what made her tick. Perry, her twin brother shone. A man full of brilliant ideas. Always thinking about his next big production, and a laugh a minute along with it. Perry, a man so focused he managed to get seventy million dollars plus, out of some investment bankers. They could become equity partners in his wild but artistically creative madcap plan, to film their next big production Downunder. However, Perry, always focused on the big picture, he forgot the small detail he had promised such as 'I'll phone my twin sister Sydney and let her know you'll be staying at the farm till this Covid thing is over. You'll be able to work from there. I've had some of my best ideas on the farm.'

However, he forgot to mention Sydney's domestic situation. Sydney seemed different, bossy, a prickly girl. Actually, there were other things Perry forgot, he didn't tell Fletch his twin sister was a single mom with a kid, Perry could have emailed them both.

As they sat at the kitchen table, each working on their laptops, it hit them both at the same time. Each eyed the other recognising the same embarrassed expression, wondering why Perry would throw them together. Sydney knew her twin always tried to marry her off, first with Ryan Murphy and then with Jamie Dalton. All three were still single and Sydney hated how Perry continually tried to matchmake. It had been the only thing they had ever argued about. Pointing out to her twin his single status made little difference. In fact, Perry's reply felt so cutting neither of them had ever mentioned it again.

Perry had said 'I don't have a young son who needs a father. I wouldn't worry if his father actually appeared in the boy's life. You won't even discuss him and it's not like he arrived via an immaculate conception for God's sake. You're going to have to talk about the man sometime Sydney. If you don't, you'll never be able to move on and Finn will suffer.'

Tears stung at the back of her eyes. She felt even more embarrassed now and turned away. Fletch felt like a heel, a complete heel because, if his good friend Perry has thrown him together with his twin sister with expectations of a relationship, he was way off the mark. Not his type. Not remotely his type. He wondered what his type looked like.

Well not her for sure, she had dark brown hair not blonde, for a start and she looked short and dumpy. With a few workouts she could be voluptuous, and he did like voluptuous although he'd never dated any voluptuous women figuring they were too high maintenance. Then she had a kid, not for him. Kids were a commitment and he'd spent years avoiding commitment, when he did relent, he ended up badly hurt. Never again. Shaking thoughts from his mind he stood, went to the phone and dialled a number.

'Skype me in ten minutes,' he said before hanging up. Then bundling up his laptop he moved to his bedroom and shut the door. Perry Martin what have you got me into? he set the laptop up on the small table by the window and thanked God that at least they had wireless internet. Suddenly, he realised he'd not thought this through. What good could be gained by berating Perry, better to let him think they might work.

The two men sat staring at each other on the screen.

'You can see I'm holed up in the guest room at your farm. Finn and Sydney made me welcome,' not true but they were warming. 'How's it going with you buddy?'

'I'll be finished shooting by the end of this week and then we'll go into postproduction. I can send you some stuff to work on, but we'll need to liaise daily. How about you skype me after breakfast every morning?' Perry insisted, Fletch thought he's bloody checking up on me.

'You mean next week when you've finished shooting? Nah man, too rigid, what about every Tuesday and Thursday, from next week New Zealand time. Remember you're five hours ahead on the previous day.' Counting the hours allowed Fletch to keep track of things.

'Just a minute I'll get Sydney, so you can say Hi,' he scooted down the hall and called to Sydney, not noticing Finn already standing in front of the screen shyly waving to his uncle. Fletch grabbed her hand and almost dragged her up the hallway.

'Act natural don't give your brother the satisfaction ...' he hissed as his voice trailed off, realising, she really didn't like him.

'Hi Perry, you did it again, you dropped me in it.' He knew what she meant. 'How's California? Covid-wise I mean.' She watched horrified as he shook his head, his expression grave.

'The authorities are busy turning the Los Angeles Convention Centre into a huge field hospital. I wish they were doing what you're doing over there in New Zealand. Take care Sis.' The sad and serious look on Perry's face told Sydney he was scared. Their mother, a nurse had spoken of pandemics to them, but children don't really listen to doom and gloom stuff, although they had absorbed something, the fear. Fletch began to understand what Perry had done, he wondered at the unspoken plea? Take care of my family.

'Chrissakes, the Los Angeles Convention Centre you say. I've been following developments online, but I know the news is pretty watered down. I thought the papers may be exaggerating too. The authorities don't want to cause panic,' Fletch drawled, frowning. 'Don't worry your sister is taking good care of me,' he joked as she elbowed him in the ribs Sydney caught a waft of his after shave, he did smell divine.

'Mummy's cooking a hogget for dinner.' Finn pushed his way forward so he could get a better view of Perry.

'A whole hogget?' Perry grinned. 'Gee I wish I could be there for dinner. You'll have to explain to my mate Fletch here what a hogget is.'

They were all smiling at the small boy who announced,

'A hogget is a big lamb.' Fletch didn't appear much wiser.

'Is it some kind of sheep?' he asked.

'Only the very best kind of sheep,' Finn informed him.

'Well for dinner anyway,' Sydney said quietly while Perry studied her face.

'I miss you sis,' his voice quiet. A doorbell could be heard behind him. 'My takeout has arrived. Ironic isn't it, the farm boy from Hinakura eating takeout, while the Yank from Fort Bragg is dining out on the best home-grown New Zealand hogget and cooked by one of the country's finest home cooks.' He gave a rueful smile. 'Talk next week Fletch, bye Finn, love ya buddy, love ya too sis.' Perry and Finn gave each other a high five against the screen.

Chapter Four:

After the best feed he'd had since Thanksgiving 2018 at the home of an old army buddy, Fletch loaded the dishwasher. Sydney put Finn to bed. Tomorrow he'd have to go for a run otherwise he'd soon run to fat, he told himself. A heavy-set muscular man he could go either way.

The phone rang. Quickly Fletch picked it up not wanting it to wake Finn.

'Sydney Martin's phone.' The caller hesitated at the other end of the line.

'Good evening, it's Ben Howarth calling. Is Sydney available please?'

'Can I have her call you back, she's just settling Finn for the night.' A pregnant pause stretched out between them.

'I'm sorry I didn't realise Sydney lived with someone. Oops none of my business, except she's been with our Law firm for years and I thought she would have said if she was having company during lockdown.' As Fletch listened he let out a long breath. Hr thought, she never mention you either.

'I'm Fletch Carter, her twin brother's ... er good friend.'

'Look I'll email her; I didn't want her to worry ...about anything. Sydney's my right hand. I needed her to feel secure in her employment and our case load, er just tell her I'll email tomorrow.' They hung up and Fletch put on the coffee machine. Minutes later Sydney appeared, she looked like she had fallen asleep her hair all messed up.

'Can I make you a pot of tea?' he asked, knowing it to be her beverage of choice. Thanking him for clearing away after dinner she busied herself tidying the room.

'I'm worried about Perry. America, Britain even Italy, none of those countries appear to be taking this thing seriously enough. In fact, I thank God I'm living on an island at the bottom of the world with a caring woman, who's also a mother, as Prime Minister.' She collapsed on to the sectional lounger sighing. 'I'm tired can we call a truce tonight and talk.'

'Sure, so long as you don't put me through the third degree. Just name rank and serial number. Okay?' She nodded. He set down her tea on the coffee table.

'Better still, what say I tell you what I have observed, and you can add or correct things. Then it will be your turn.' He smirked nodding agreement.

'If you and Perry are partners you must be driven, creative and have skills he doesn't. I think you're ex-army; you don't mention any family, significant other or children, so I'm guessing you're like Perry, single too.' Sipping her tea, she watched his amused face and continued. 'From the grocery shopping you purchased, you live in an urban environment, and you are also image conscious, those Gucci loafers and your relationship with food.' She grinned. 'Although you ate well tonight thank you. I enjoy cooking. Am I right so far?'

'So, what is your question apart, from am I right so far?'

'You don't particularly like me, why?'

He scratched his short dark hair.

'Let's take this back a step. You were correct in all your assumptions.' he sounded surprised. 'As for why I don't like you, well not true. I don't know you. You are covered in prickles designed to keep people out, people like me I guess, me and Ryan Murphy and Jamie Dalton. I'm picking it's only men,' he said, about to elaborate and ask his two questions, but he'd struck a nerve and she shut him down.

'Do you play board games?' she wondered. He shook his head 'Okay what do you do at home when you're not working?' Annoyed now she wanted to slap him.

'Drink beer watch the game on the box as you call it, or at the Hollywood bowl, go to the gym.' Chase skirt, he grinned, knowing he irritated her.

'You left a few things off your list...but I don't want to know about them. I can imagine.'

He looked at his watch, a military tactical time piece, completely out of place with the Gucci loafers. 'Let's watch the late news.'

'Yeah, we can see if your Zombie apocalypse has arrived yet,' she mocked as he sat beside her on the sectional settee. They both watched in disbelief and apprehension. Fletch agonised as he watched his investments going down the drain. Sydney worried about her twin catching Covid 19 and dying alone. Then she thought of her little boy and worried more.

Chapter Five:

Alone in her bed a pang of guilt gripped her. Finn had a right to know about his father. But not yet, at only six; besides the thought frightened her. These thoughts were not new over the years she'd been plagued by thoughts of Finn's father. Fortunately, she had learned much from Timothy Winthrop. Drifting off to sleep she remembered with fondness the first time she watched him at work in court.

Eight years earlier, in Wellington City 2012.

Sydney had accompanied Timothy Winthrop to Court and sat in her own special place reserved for legal staff while the case proceeded. Tim had been magnificent; his cross examination a performance of its own. On occasions Mr Winthrop senior would sit beside her and scribble notes, sometimes pushing them in front of her with statements like,

'I did not see that coming. Or where's he going with this?'

As the years went on both Winthrops came to depend heavily on Sydney. One night after a particularly gruelling trial she drove Tim home as while not drunk he would never have passed a breathalyser test. Dropping him off at his old villa in Thorndon she refused the offer of joining him for takeaways and a post-mortem on the case. Instead, she drove the few kilometres on to her own little rented villa. While retrieving her coat and handbag from the back seat she noticed he had left his mobile and some papers there.

This time when she arrived back at his house in Thorndon she relented and agreed to stay for pizza and a celebratory drink. He opened a bottle of bubbly specially for her, his mood buoyant and full of largess having another 'not guilty' verdict to add to his now significant collection of success stories.

'I'm surprised you didn't stay for the office bash, being the man of the hour and all.' Accepting a second glass of bubbly she hoped the pizza would arrive soon.

'As I said to Dad, I'm not tired now I've got my second wind. I'll enjoy a quiet drink with you mother mouse.' He went to top up her glass and she covered it with her hand. 'I'll get you a taxi if necessary but please don't be a bore, not tonight, mother mouse,' he pleaded. Mother mouse, the slightly derogatory name he called her while flirting or sucking up, as she thought of it.

If he thinks of me as a mother and a mouse, then he's definitely not attracted to me, she rationalised. Besides the man had a bevy of leggie beauties. He had never been short of a date. However, his had always been most particular about Tim's liaisons. Winthrop senior ensured all the young female staff, no matter who they were or what they did were off limits to Tim. In fact, after Sydney had been at Winthrop and partners a year or so Mr Winthrop senior as the staff referred to him, had commented to her he had had reservations when she first came to the office, but no longer and he even obliquely referred to the revolving door of his son's relationships.

'They don't know how to handle him. Thank God his work life is stable thanks to you.'

What would Tim's father think if he knew the kind of things his son continually said to her, full of inuendo and sometimes quite overt suggestions. Any employment lawyer worth their salt would have a field day. Sydney would give him a taste of his own medicine. She had a quick wit. When Tim said, 'I'd love to run my hand over your round mousey bottom,' Sydney had shot him a reproving look and told him in no uncertain terms, 'down rover, you couldn't handle me. My bottom's so far from mousey you wouldn't know what to do first.'

The doorbell rang. Tim returned with the pizzas.

'Two pizzas, you planned this, you rat.' he had, and he grinned. Feeling lightheaded she hoed into the pizza. 'It's been such a long week I think I'll sleep till noon tomorrow,' she mused thinking aloud.

He sat opposite her, wondering aloud, 'how many years have we been together now?'

'Almost four' she answered without thought.

'A damn sight longer than I imagined, for sure.' He sighed.

'Yes, imagine my claim to fame, I'm the woman other than your mother with whom you've had the longest relationship.' She licked pizza sauce from her lips.

'At least my mother let me suck her tits.' He sounded almost wistful.

'You're disgusting.' She picked up a cushion from the settee and threw it at him.

Tim laughed, 'breastfeeding is a perfectly normal act, my little mouse. Nothing disgusting about it.' His face held a self-satisfied expression.

Sipping her drink, she gave him a sneer and commented, 'I bet your mother found it impossible to wean you, too. A mummy's boy, I bet.' He held up the wine bottle, was it the first or the second.

'Don't worry I will definitely get you a cab, but you're welcome to stay over,' he smirked.

'Bugger off. You never let up do you?'

He simply smiled and changing the subject suggested,

'A very observant comment of yours, noting that smart arse police detective Wilson didn't like me. What did you say he thought of me?' he asked amused and knowing the answer.

'Milksop, the guy thinks of you as a foppish milksop. But those limp wristed affectations while questioning him were a bit over the top. Still, he showed his gender bias and so you scored points with the jury,' she told him, thinking about how he had managed the crown's witness.

'So, but how did you know? You have never spoken to him, have you?' She shook her head. 'Well then how did you know?' He wanted her to spell it out for him.

'I watched him and his expressions when he related to different people. The guy is a redneck who thinks you were born with a silver spoon in your mouth, and he has a short fuse,' she grinned, knowing the silver spoon bit to be correct.

'Do you know what I love about you my little rodent, you see things other people do not?'

'Yeah, and I can see right through you too.'

He cleared the pizza boxes away and came back sitting beside her.

'I've put the jug on just for you,' he said, looking to score brownie points. Sydney smiled and set her glass down on the coffee table. He leaned over her and quickly took the pins out of her hair, then messed it up.

'I have wanted to unpin that school ma'am hairdo of yours for years,' he sighed. She could smell his glorious aftershave his hands still in her hair. Taking her face in his hands his lips touched hers, lightly at first then hungrily as though he wanted to consume her. Sydney parted her lips. She wanted this despite all their silly banter she wanted him, even though all the warning bells went off in her head. Shutting her eyes tightly she blocked out those thoughts and lived in the moment; glorious, exciting. Alive with wanting him. Tim deepened the kiss, he too had wanted this for so long, he told her. It hardly seemed real now as his hand crept under her silk blouse and navigated her bra, with urgency thinking expecting Sydney to reject him. The rejection never came. Instead, she loosened his shirt as he undid her skirt. Quickly he shed his shirt. And She ran her hands over his glorious chest covered in soft down, sending her wild. Both topless now, he luxuriated in the feel of her generous bosoms.

She groaned in pleasure as he lifted her off the settee. A big man, and not comfortable on the settee, he moved to his bedroom, releasing her on the king-sized bed before he dropped his trousers. The hall light glowed warmly behind him.

'Sydney darling, please let me make love to you.' before she could answer he covered her lips with his again and started kissing her slowly, every inch of her until she lay desperate for him to enter her.

Daylight peeked through the curtains. Lying in his huge bed, Tim relived the events of the night remembering how many times they had made love and how it felt. On reaching his hand out to touch her he realised she had gone. Now awake with the surprise of it he quickly pulled on some clothes and scrambled to find her; she had definitely gone. He phoned her; she didn't answer. Annoyed he showered and dressed they didn't usually work on Saturdays. Still, he drove the short distance to her house and banged on her door.

Sheepishly Sydney opened it. Tim pushed in and wrapped his arms around her and covering her mouth with his. He pushed her back against the door, his kiss punishing. A little whimper escaped her mouth. he stopped to look at her and she pushed him back.

'No Tim, we've screwed the pooch,' she said, and he smirked at her turn of phrase.

'A pooch I loved screwing, Sydney darling,' he breathed into her hair. 'Let's sit and talk about this, I mean talk about us.' Following her into the little kitchenette she offered him coffee at the tiny café table. Tim sat, adamant they should give themselves three months before they take their new situation to his father. Using his silver tongue and smooth arguments he persuaded Sydney, this, whatever they had between them, felt too special to ignore. They needed time to nurture it. Every time the warning bells rang in her head, she shut them down. They both knew he had been her first and heavens above he didn't want to give her up. Their sex had been so good, so spontaneous and urgent, he could only imagine what it would be like after he had taught her a few things.

'We simply need to keep work separate; do you think you can?' Assuring him she could he soon had her back in bed, this time in her cosy queen bed and beautiful smooth satin cotton sheets. They practically spent the entire weekend there.

For the next couple of months all went well at work and both were idyllically happy. Then Sydney began to notice some little differences between their relationship and Tim's previous ones. Apart from the odd breakfast or brunch he never took her out to restaurants. They never went out on 'dates'. They did use the company's season tickets at the Wellington 'cake tin' stadium for the big rugby games. Sometimes they even took clients.

However, there were never any the really deep and meaningful occasions one might expect if they were practically living together. Sydney dismissed it, believing Tim was intentionally keeping a low profile until he and his father had the conversation. Usually careful about contraception, Tim suggested she go on the pill. They had been together in the biblical sense for three months. Believing Tim was geared up to tell his father, she went off to the family planning clinic with the idea of going on the pill.

Sydney made the appointment where they checked her thoroughly. She barely had time to produce a urine sample and sit back down in the consulting room when the doctor advised her.

'You are pregnant Ms Martin, it's very early days, but the test is positive no mistake.' The older woman spoke kindly, and Sydney felt ill.

'This is not what we planned; I'll have to tell Tim.'

'How will he take it your young man? You do have options you know.' As the doctor spelled out the options Sydney burst into a flood of hormonal tears.

'Well, I'll pass on your details to your GP but feel free to get back to us at any time.'

Just as well that Tim and his father were both away at a Law Society conference. Tim had phoned her a couple of times saying they were busy most evenings and he couldn't wait to get back to see her. However, the phone did not feel like the right way to have this particular conversation, so Sydney put her worries in her pocket and got on with business. By the time they were due back Sydney had received a call from the clinic advising her she needed to make an appointment immediately, one of her tests had come back positive for chlamydia. Horrified, Sydney made the appointment and as she sat in front of the doctor this time a man in his middle years she felt as though her whole world had come crashing down. The doctor comforted her sympathetic to her situation, because from where he sat this young woman seemed naive and vulnerable.

'How old is your young man?' he asked in a detailed history taking telling her 'chlamydia is an STD and they come under the notifiable diseases category.'

'Tim's thirty-six' she said feeling completely out of her depth and aware of Tim's high profile in the town. The doctor said nothing for a moment before commenting, 'so, he's eleven years older than you?' Sydney merely breathed in deeply. Tim would turn thirty-seven in a month. She could tell the doctor had an opinion about their age difference. Suddenly she felt stupid, and small. 'So, what does Tim think about your pregnancy?' he asked in a paternal tone. Sydney didn't answer, instead she burst into tears. Adding 'used' to the growing list of negative emotions surrounding her. Sucking in a breath she regained her composure.

'He doesn't know, he's been away on business. We have not had time to discuss it, he won't be home until the weekend. I'm more concerned about how this chlamydia may affect my baby,' she blurted. The doctor went on to explain in detail the treatment.

'A course of antibiotics should fix it, but we will monitor the situation carefully. No sex until you are cleared, a week or ten days should do it. All your other tests were fine.' Returning to his notes he wrote something down then asked,

'this Tim is he the only man you have had sex with?' As soon as the question had been spoken aloud Tim's sexual history flashed before her eyes. She burst into tears. The foolishness of her behaviour struck her. Did Tim love anyone other than himself? He had been the only man she had ever loved or had sex with but now she felt vulnerable. Still in her mind Tim was a good man who defended some of society's most defenceless people. Besides he did love her, he had told her, so she must trust him to do the right thing. By the time Tim planned to be back in the office her antibiotic treatment had been well underway, and she knew she must tell him about both the pregnancy and also about the STD. Regrettably Sydney never had the chance.

A police officer arrived at her home early in the evening to deliver her the awful news. Still the vivid memory plagued her thoughts. When the doorbell rang, she scurried to welcome Tim only to see a very white and drawn Ryan Murphy standing there in his shiny new police uniform. A recent graduate from the Police College tonight, a Sergeant accompanied him. As soon as Sydney saw his face, she burst into tears knowing something dreadful must have happened. Her heightened hormonal state exacerbated her tears.

The Sergeant a large man almost filled the tiny living room as he delivered her the news no one ever wants to hear.

'I'm sorry to inform you Miss Martin, both your parents were killed in a freak boating accident on Lake Tekapo this morning.' Sydney almost threw herself at Ryan, she had known him since her first day at primary school. Ryan had been like another brother as she grew up. The Murphy family also farmed in the district; their parents were good friends. He had only ever wanted to be a Police Officer. Tonight, he stood at the very front line of policing as Sydney sobbed uncontrollably in his arms. The Sergeant made them a pot of tea. Ryan told her he had been granted leave.

'Perry knows, he's flying in from Auckland in a couple of hours. We can all drive home together,' he advised as they drank their tea.'

Sydney tried to contact Tim, but he had switched off his phone. She called Mr Winthrop senior instead, who sounded most understanding. He told her to take all the time she needed, adding not to worry about Tim, he would speak to him. Ryan and the Sergeant waited while Sydney packed a bag, then Sergeant drove them to Ryan's flat and they waited while he too, packed a bag. Later they met Perry at the airport and drove over the Remutaka Pass to the Wairarapa. They then on to the little township of Martinborough and from there out to the rural district of Hinakura.

The three of them arrived at Boar Gully, the family property well after nine at night. The weather became diabolical, cold, wet and windy. Ryan's mother had insisted they stay with her, but when Sydney refused, she sent her husband ahead of them to light the wood burner to heat the house. Ryan stayed with Perry and Sydney to help with the funeral arrangements.

The next day the phone rang off the hook with condolence calls as the news got around the district. Sydney felt distraught, needing to talk to Tim urgently and in private, at a time when privacy seemed in short supply. He called her first thing in the morning, Perry had taken the call, as Sydney, overcome with grief, couldn't handle any calls according to her twin. Little did he know she woke being violently ill due to morning sickness and stress. Their parent's bodies were flown back to Wellington and the funeral took place on a bleak June day in Martinborough.

Tim arrived in good time and had arranged to speak with Sydney ahead of the funeral. The three Musketeers as the Murphy's called

Perry Sydney and Ryan were lunching at a café before going on to the service, when Sydney got a call from Tim. He agreed to pick her up in his vehicle and drive somewhere private. Tim opened the car door.

'Sydney, I'm so sorry darling, let's go somewhere private so I can hold you.' His words set her off sobbing again. Tim drove off into a quiet suburban street and parked. Then sensing all was not well, he simply took her hand.

'Something else has upset you mother mouse. tell me what it is?' he whispered.

'I'm pregnant,' she burst out, 'I know it's not what we planned...but...'

'But nothing Sydney, bloody hell how did it happen? How far along are you?' he demanded, his tone intimidating.

'Ten weeks.'

'Ten weeks! how come you didn't know till now? What about your monthly? Surely no bloody period sent some fucking warning bells.' His nostrils flared, and she shed more tears. 'Well, we better get busy. Thank God you're off work, we've got a two-week window. I know a doctor who can organize the termination.' Sydney shocked to silence, narrowed her eyes, and fixed him with a steely gaze through her wet lashes.

'You want me to kill our baby?' She watched his expression change to fury.

'We did not plan this, Sydney. Since when have you been bloody religious about this sort of thing? We've only been sleeping together for three months, for pity's sake.' He had a nasty hard edge to his tone and in an instant, she saw him for what he was, an arrogant entitled shit.

A long cold silence stretched out between them before Sydney spoke.

'There is something else you have chlamydia. You know I haven't been with anyone else; you were my first, my only, I can't say the same for you.'

'Bloody hell Sydney. Is there anything else I need to know?' his lip curled in disgust.

'Yes, a course of antibiotics will fix it, but left untreated there can be dire consequences. You didn't deny it, I'm guessing you're not surprised, even though there are often no symptoms.' He said nothing. 'I will not be aborting this baby; you can go to hell for all I care Timothy Winthrop. Now take me to my parents' funeral.' Her voice cracked. He decided now was not the time for further debate on the future of this child.

A couple of days later Perry and Sydney had an appointment with Ben Howarth, the family lawyer. The farm had been in a family trust and now the only surviving members were Perry and Sydney, who had equal shares.

'When probate has been passed on your parents' estate there will still be a clause prohibiting the sale of the property until you turn thirty-one.' Ben gave them the blank stare he had perfected.

'The over thirty clause had been one my father recommended because as he used to say God is not making any more land and unless you are at least thirty, you're too young to dispose of generations of your families' hard work, because you choose a different path.' The twins were aware how the trust worked. Their father, a man of eighty had leased out the family farm to the Daltons for the last five years. The Daltons, their neighbours, were aware they had security of tenure.

'I want to live there, if I can get a job in the district,' Sydney announced confidently. Her brother frowned.

'Really?' Ben Howarth looked surprised. 'My current PA is talking about retiring, maybe we can work something out. But

Sydney, the Winthrops will not want to lose you.' Ben seemed pleasantly surprised by the idea.

'The truth is I want to come back to the district, I'm over the big city. I'm serious Mr Howarth I hope you are too.' Sydney's heart skipped a beat. This could be the answer to her prayers.

On the journey home Perry now felt quietly pleased. He never wanted the burden of the farm, he wanted to make movies, not crutch sheep. Also, he knew both Jamie Dalton and Ryan Murphy had tickets on his twin sister. As far as he could see, the problem of the farm would be Sydney's. The income from the lease arrangement would be a huge bonus, his sister could take care of the legal requirements, law being her field.

The formalities agreed, Sydney resigned from Winthrop and Associates, citing her desire to return to her family home. Perry went back to his film and documentary making and Sydney packed up her little house in Wellington. One night as she packed, a knock at the door alerted her to Tim. Opening the door to him, Sydney stood surprised, to see a very contrite looking man standing in front of her.

'I'm just about to make tea would you like some?' she chirped, imagining they needed to at least be on speaking terms with a child on the way. Tim took off his coat and flung it over a chair in the living room.

'Thank you, you were right, I've had the treatment. I'm clean again. Thank god.' Typical Tim, it's all about him, no hello darling you look positively glowing, well, she felt positively glowing. Her morning sickness gone, and she looked healthy and rested.

'I'm pleased for you,' she said. Tim launched into a diatribe about her avoiding him by not returning to the office. Taking a tea tray, she set it down on the coffee table. He leaned over and grabbed a big fat Afghan biscuit with a generous dollop of chocolate on the top and a walnut.

'God, I miss your baking.' Noticing her disdainful expression, he corrected 'we all miss your baking.' Demolishing the biscuit in short order he looked around at her little house.

'So, it's true then mother mouse, you really are going back to your rustic idyll.' Taking another biscuit, he sat back comfortably with his tea.

'To what do I owe this visit?' she asked coldly.

'I thought I had better see where things stood between us, as you have obviously not had the termination.' He sipped his tea and smiled at her. 'You are going to be the size of a house; how many weeks are you? tell me again?' he asked smugly.

'Fourteen weeks and thank you for the sympathy flowers. Well, I sent a thank you note to the office as they were signed from everyone.' Sitting in a chair opposite Tim she did not feel entirely comfortable with him after his last outburst in the car the day of her parent's funeral. His voice had reverberated around the vehicle as if the sound might smash the windows out. Sydney put her mobile phone down on the coffee table.

'Tell me something mother mouse, do you get half the farm?'

'What business is it of yours?' she said furious. 'What difference does it make to you?'

'I'm just wanting a picture of your assets if you expect me to part with some of mine because you refused to have an abortion.' His tone haughty, how dare she expect him to pay for his child. She could hardly believe what she heard. How could she have been so wrong about Tim.

'I won't starve if you're concerned about me. You can keep your money. I can take care of myself and my baby.' Something made her stand up, although he looked taller than her even with him sitting down.

'Good, because frankly I'm not interested in coparenting or any other of those trendy situations. You knew when you worked for me, that I don't get emotionally engaged.' Tim pursed his lips in determination.

'Oh yeah, I knew. I just didn't understand why.' Sydney mirrored his body language on purpose, folding her arms and pursing her lips. 'But now I know the why.' He sat up straight, his face indignant as he listened to what she said. 'You have commitment phobia; emotional engagement only comes when you are emotionally invested in a relationship. and you are scared of being vulnerable. Apart from being a classic self-absorbed egotist whose only able to donate sperm, you could never be a father, so I get it. I want nothing from you.'

Nobody had ever spoken to Timothy Winthrop like Sydney did. He lashed out.

'You know your trouble Sydney Martin, you're a short, plain dumpy little creature who will end up all bitter and twisted and looking frumpy and mumsy with nothing to offer a real man.' He stood up leaning down close to her face he looked threatening. 'You are a manipulative bitch, and I must have been very drunk the night I had sex with you.'

'Yeah, and the hangover lasted a good three months,' she spat out, not letting him bully her.

'Get out of my house and my life.'

'Don't expect anything from me because I'll drag it out in Court and make you look like a promiscuous tart and stupid to boot,' he called back over his shoulder as he slammed the door.

Chapter Six:

Day three of lockdown in New Zealand. Saturday March twenty-eight, 2020

Giggles could be heard from the living room and a low rumbling sound. Sydney stirred, realising Finn and Fletch were both up. She could smell coffee too. A quick glance at her bedside clock told her she'd slept in, it read eight thirty.

When she finally emerged from the shower, dressed and smelling 'pretty' according to Finn Sydney could see the pair had been playing cards.

'I taught Fletch last card, I've beaten him just about every game.' He sounded so happy about. it the child glowed.

'You haven't been cheating, have you?' his mother asked.

'No,' his expression crestfallen.

'No, he hasn't but every game I've learned a new rule I didn't know before I started losing.' Fletch's eyes twinkled, and Sydney gave him a half eye roll. Mercury slept on his cushion under the coffee table.

'What do you fancy for breakfast, it's Saturday?' she asked.

'Fletch is cooking pancakes.' Finn tossed his hand of cards on the table.

'How very American, I have blueberries in the freezer if you want.' Noting the paper on the table she asked, 'Have you been down to the road Finn?' He shook his head.

'No, I went,' Fletch said, 'he told me he needed permission to go down the driveway to the road.' Sydney agreed, she didn't want a six-year-old down on a lonely country road on his own. There had been a few incidents causing concern.

'Do you fancy some pancakes too?' when she hesitated, he added, 'we can go for a big walk after lunch if you'd like.' Before she answered Sydney thought for a moment, not wanting to be churlish.

'Yes, please on both counts,' she said and grinned at him.

As the days in lockdown at level four rolled on, a relationship of sorts developed between Fletch and Finn. The boy made an impression on him with his cute giggle and his closeness to his mother. The bond between mother and son was strong and loving. They had fun together.

Sydney's silly child appropriate jokes set Finn off in peals of laughter and Finn often repeated the jokes to Fletch in fits of giggles, like yesterday's effort.

'What did one toilet say to the other?' he asked Fletch who shrugged saying,

'you tell me.'

'You look a bit flushed!' Finn advised before dissolving in a fit of laughter. Toilet humour a favourite with him.

'It's a six-year-old boy thing,' his mother explained. Fletch had one or two jokes of his own and even though they both spoke English; language definitely presented a barrier.

'Why did the superhero flush the toilet?' he asked Finn.

'I dunno.' The child's face delighted.

'Because he did this doody' Finn didn't get it, Fletch looked at Sydney to explain. She shrugged, not wanting things to deteriorate. Most of the time Finn and Fletch bonded on a serious and creative level. Fletch made a cardboard camera using a simple square of card and a felt tip pen. He made one slit in the top and another in the bottom of the square where the lens would be. Taking an A4 sheet of paper, he cut it into three strips. Joining the strips into one long strip he marked the paper into frames. Then he quickly drew cartoon characters with three slightly different versions of the same picture.

He pulled the paper through the card at speed to display the cartoon characters in movement.

'This is how we make animated cartoons,' he explained. Fletch created the beginning of Finn's interest in movies. Soon he made video clips on Fletch's phone of Merkee in action fetching a stick or chasing a bird. From there, it went to the more serious performances with him as a superhero star or interviewing Fletch, like on the news.

One morning sitting on the sunny back veranda catching the morning sun and enjoying a cup of tea, Sydney stood up complaining she felt like the princess and the pea, something felt lumpy under the squab cushion on her cane chair. Lifting it, she saw not a toy truck or some Leggo creation, but the missing walkabout landline phone.

'I'll have to charge it, then I'll get you to check it for me.' She looked at Fletch in amazement. Little wonder they had not heard it ring, the back veranda caught the morning sun but sat away from the kitchen and living area. They truly were in their isolated bubble.

Easter approached and the Prime Minister had declared the Tooth Fairy and the Easter Bunny to be essential services so they would work during lockdown. Delighted, Sydney read the news item to Finn. Immediately he needed to confirm with Fletch.

'Yes, true buddy, but she did say he may have trouble getting through to everyone.' Finn paused while he thought about it.

'So, the Easter Bunny's a boy then?' pause again 'right,' Finn sounded full of business. 'Do you have his number?' Fletch covered his tracks saying even if they went online and found it, chances are it would be out of range.

'Don't worry, we'll email him.'

The night before Easter Sunday Sydney painted hardboiled and fresh eggs in bright colours and added glitter and diamantes. Then she added them to a small basket of foil covered marshmallow eggs and put the basket out of sight on a high shelf in the pantry.

'Tomorrow morning I'll distract Finn with breakfast, and you can slip out and hide the eggs in the garden. Then we'll let him out to find them.' Sydney busied herself. Fletch could not remember doing this as a child. Next day when Finn began the search for hidden eggs Fletch photographed him and the delight on his face. It fascinated him; Sydney had spent hours decorating the eggs but the hunt to find them lasted less than twenty minutes. Mercury helped.

One afternoon Fletch answered the phone while he worked at the kitchen table.

'Sydney Martin's phone,' he had his greeting off pat.

'Jamie Dalton, I've been leaving her some milk on the kitchen porch every couple of days. Do you need anything?' Perry had told Fletch about their neighbour Jamie Dalton, saying the guy had been divorced for years. Seven years ago, when newly married he came back to the house unexpectedly one day to find his wife of three months in bed with the stock agent. Jamie needed someone to confide in. Sydney became a good friend to him. At the time she had her own issues, being pregnant and unmarried. They supported each other with their friendship. Jamie had wanted more from the friendship over the years but like everyone else in Sydney's life, she kept him at arm's length. Now Fletch thought Jamie sounded like a good guy.

'Why don't you come to the fence near the barn at four and I'll tell Sydney.' Silence descended for a moment.

'I will but I must keep to the rules because my parents are over seventy. They live on the property here in a cottage, they're in my bubble. My father's not been well and he's immunocompromised. Tell her to bring Finn.'

Later, observing the social distancing rules, which seemed ridiculous and an oxymoron in such an isolated place Sydney and Finn invited Fletch to meet Jamie.

Sydney leaned over the fence and set down a shopping bag containing a couple of two litre ice cream punnets filled with her baking.

'I thought about leaving it on the porch, but this is better. Thanks for the milk and cream.' The fence line conversation started out a little stilted, but Fletch made the best of it and Jamie acknowledged he loved her baking raising his eyebrows up and down at Finn and asking,

'Did mummy make me some of her famous Afghan's do you think?'

Finn wanted to know when they'd be able to go for a ride.

'Jamie's horse is called Houdini because he's an escape artist,' he told Fletch.

'He's a stallion' Sydney explained.

Fletch frowned and Jamie elaborated saying,

'Brandy, Sydney's mount is a mare, and he likes to visit her.' A knowing smirk crossed both men's faces. Sydney protested,

'Don't you dare read anything into it.' Both men grinned agreeing they wouldn't dare. James asked if she wanted him to kill a couple of her sheep for the freezer and she thanked him.

'I'll do it tomorrow, then let them hang for a couple of days before I butcher them. The usual cuts, okay?' he asked.

'Thanks Jamie.' The two men studied each other, each wondering at the other's relationship with Finn and Sydney.

Every evening they recorded the news and watched it after Finn went to bed. He already asked questions and had absorbed some things by listening to the adults talking. Sydney sensed the child's growing anxiety about the state of the world. Although technically on school holidays, Sydney had no plans to home school Finn him at present. At six he absorbed so much every day without the structure of a classroom.

One night, while the child slept, and the adults were enjoying a glass of wine Fletch voiced the question on his mind since he had first met this pair.

'Does Finn have much to do with his father?' He watched as the shutters went up and Sydney's expression became closed.

'No, he was a sperm donor.' Fletch thought he knew this woman and he saw her differently now. For a start he did not believe her for one moment. Sydney, now thirty-one, had been only twenty-five when she had Finn. Women of twenty-five do not normally look for sperm donors to conceive. What was she hiding, he wondered? Not wanting to alienate her, he didn't push it.

Life went on in their happy little bubble. Fletch felt so comfortable with it he now took old pieces of furniture out of the shed and repaired them before refurbishing the character-filled pieces.

'Gee where did you learn how to work like a craftsman?' Sydney wanted to know, expressing her surprise at the superb skill he displayed, having removed all the watermark stains from an old walnut burr afternoon tea table.

'My grandfather spent his life as a cabinet maker. and he used to do repairs for a couple of antique shops in town. He taught me some tricks of the trade.' Fletch beamed with pride.

Chapter Seven:

One day Fletch let slip to Finn he had a birthday coming up and Finn delighted in telling his mother they should bake Fletch a birthday cake. Finn's favourite, always chocolate; he loved licking the bowl and the frosting dish a treat for him. They decided to keep it a surprise. It would not be difficult as Fletch often took Zoom meetings in his bedroom or spent time in the shed attached to the barn, where he had found a veritable treasure trove of things to restore. Now he even turned his talents to odd jobs around the property having completed the list Sydney first gave him.

On the afternoon of his birthday Finn called him inside for afternoon tea.

'Mummy's made a treat for your birthday,' the child exclaimed excitedly. Fletch washed up in the laundry and entered the open plan kitchen dining area where he could see the table set for an afternoon tea and a gift-wrapped box and parcels sat at his place at the table. Sydney carried out the cake and lit the candles.

'We couldn't get a fire permit for forty-one candles because it's so dry, but you get the idea,' she grinned. Finn started singing Happy Birthday and Sydney joined him.

'Blow out your candles and make a wish Fletch,' Finn instructed.

'Can I ask your Mummy for a favour instead? it's kind of a wish.' Sydney frowned and Finn pleaded he be allowed to ask.

'Can we have a date please?' She gave a bit of an eyeroll.

'We're in lockdown, how will it work?' Embarrassed and apprehensive she looked to Finn, who agreed.

'You're not allowed out; how will it work Fletch?' the six-year-old asked.

'Well, we can dress up and I'll cook dinner for your mother and me. I'd invite you too champ, but you don't like liver and bacon and I'm cooking liver.' He grinned at Sydney who grimaced, thinking neither do I, until he winked at her.

'Okay, thank you. Now who's for birthday cake? You can open your gifts too.' Fletch opened the cards, both homemade and covered in stickers and glitter. Then he opened the scroll to find it a drawing of their bubble with Fletch, Sydney, Finn, and Mercury surrounded by dark ominous Covid19 virus cells. He actually felt a bit choked up when he thanked Finn, calling them his bubble family. Sydney's gift, a woollen scarf from her gift box. She always knitted gifts and stored them away for these kinds of events.

'Thank you, Finn tells me it gets very cold here in winter,' he said knowing she had done this to please her son.

Finn and Fletch reminded her she had to dress up for the date night dinner. She made the effort of getting out of her jeans and putting on some smart black drapey slacks and a pink merino scooped neck jersey. Even going to the trouble of high heels and a little make up. Then she put her long dark hair in an elegant updo. When she came out to the living room Finn told her she looked beautiful, and as Fletch studied her he realized the boy was right. Sydney Martin looked hot. Huskily he acknowledged the fact.

'You're beautiful,' her face flushed, and he wanted to kiss her glossy lips, but he wouldn't.

Finn went off to bed without fuss and when Sydney returned to the living room, Fletch had changed. He too wore black slacks and fine black merino jersey. Each muscle of his big frame seemed defined, and he smelt divine.

Pouring her a glass of bubbly he asked her about her work with Ben Howarth, watching her face light up.

She explained, 'I really like working with Ben, they are more family lawyers than criminal. Ben is such a good man. He married a widow with two children and now they have a daughter of their own. Mary Howarth, his wife, is a qualified horticulturalist and has helped me with my garden. I've been with the firm since before Finn was born. Ben persuaded me to get my law degree. I started doing it part time. I had a Bachelor of Business and my legal executive qualifications when I started at Winthrops. Some subjects I could cross credit. I managed to get maternity leave as Ben's previous PA came out of retirement for me and then between us, we shared the work for a few years. It suited us both. Ben has mentored and encouraged me. I think he was so understanding because his wife had been a single mother. He taught me about estate planning, divorce, and family trusts. Our local vet's wife, Emma Jacobson, works there part time. She's a lawyer too and she has kids. I did enjoy being a paralegal, there's a lot of mopping up after lawyers you know. Things changed after I took the bar exams just before Finn started school. Ben runs a family friendly firm. I'm blessed.'

Fletch sat down beside her to watch the news before they ate the vegetarian lasagne he prepared, belying all his protests about cooking. They watched in horror as the world fell apart around them, seeing trucks loaded with dead Covid victims being driven slowly in convoy to their open graves, a sombre affair.

'What sort of world am I leaving for my child to inherit?' she whispered.

'We'll be all right, I'm sure we will. But until there is a vaccine this will be bad.' The events unfolded so fast they decided not to watch too much on the pandemic. Instead, choosing to watch something different after dinner. They binged watching a few episodes of the British series "The Bodyguard" on Netflix. Fletch watched as she squirmed while the sex scenes played out in front of them. Sydney got up to make coffee. They were living in strange times.

As she sat down beside him to pour the coffee, he covered her hand with his and she froze. Warm, kind and loving Sydney froze at his touch. Undeterred, he took her face in his hands. Instead of kissing her he undid her hair.

'I want to touch your hair, it's beautiful.' All the pins now gone, he buried his fingers deep into her thick soft dark hair and leaning over her drank in the fragrance of her shampoo.

Tilting her face to his, he watched in horror as the tears silently streamed down her cheeks. Instinctively he hugged her and held her firm, but it seemed too much for Sydney, her body convulsed with silent sobs. Alarmed, he whispered her name.

'Sydney, hush honey, what's wrong?' Looking up at him she bit her lip between her teeth as though unable to speak. He held her for a bit longer. She pushed him back.

Finally, she spoke, 'thank you for the date and being patient with me. Good night.' She stood up and left the room. Fletch had no idea what he had done to distress her but unpinning her hair and running his fingers through it was exactly what Tim had done the first time he touched her. Tonight, in those few short moments she had relived it all over again, scared of what her future held and what this man wanted from her.

Bewildered, Fletch instinctively felt something from her past must be holding her back. The same thing making her prickly with strangers had kept men at arm's length.

For the next few days, she seemed a little awkward with him. Yet when she spoke to Ben Howarth, she sounded confident and business like and Fletch could tell she managed several critical situations and did it remotely. One involved the death of a client whose family were overseas. With no likelihood of a funeral under Covid lockdown that required a great deal of paperwork and diplomacy. Ryan Murphy, the police officer, had been involved also and spoke to Sydney from the driveway telling her to stay on the veranda. He then said he would deal with one of the man's children overseas as Sydney and Ben Howarth were unable to contact them. Between Ryan and Sydney, they organised for a neighbour to check on the man's livestock. Fletch didn't exactly eavesdrop, but Ryan had a loud voice and Fletch heard him call out above the engine of the patrol car,

'You look a bit-tired Sydney, is everything okay? I mean with the Yank; Perry sprang him on you, didn't he? He has always been a bit thoughtless your twin. Call me if you need anything, anything at all.' Then he drove off.

LIFE IN THE BUBBLE at Boar Gully for Fletch Carter felt surreal, like life in another time, slower and more gentle. He had begun to view Sydney quite differently. Now he enjoyed her company. he loved her sense of fun; she didn't take herself too seriously. Her inner strength impressed him. He could even see what Perry, Ryan and Jamie saw, a beautiful woman of substance, not some long, tall drink of water. She had so much more to offer.

Finn, who had started out as an irritation getting under his skin, still did, but now in a good way. The little boy stirred something inside him he had never felt before, a need to care for someone other than himself. Fletch's own father had been a military man, a Vietnam veteran and a career soldier. The man had expectations of his son and Fletch had joined the Army and graduated military college as expected.

After twenty years active service on the Army, Fletch chose to follow his dream of making movies. While working on a movie in Canada he met Perry and the two hit it off immediately. Their skill sets complemented each other. Although Perry was a good ten years younger than Fletch, had ten years more experience in the film industry. Now they had completed two movies together and just when they signed a contract to shoot a third in New Zealand, the pandemic hit the world. Fletch found himself prepared to accept the fact the movie would happen, but it wouldn't happen overnight. Even if New Zealand came out of lockdown soon, the borders would be closed and quarantine still in place. he resigned himself to being at Boar Gully for the long haul. Perry would stay in Hollywood. It suited them to have someone over there and Fletch liaised electronically with a screen writer on the script. Meanwhile he had enough to occupy himself.

He discussed his stay at Boar Gully with Perry. Both men could see it would be easier for him to stay put and work from there for the foreseeable future. The only problem occurred because Fletch had an Entrepreneur Visa which allowed for three years in New Zealand. However, the holder is required to work for one year and then apply again for the next two years. Now, only nine months into his first year a huge doubt hung over the timing of the project.

Perry who had a green card in the United States sold his place in the greater Hollywood area. He now lived in Fletch's apartment. This meant they kept their expenses down, Fletch felt reassured Perry kept his home in safe hands and in turn his presence at Boar Gully reassured Perry his twin and his nephew were also in good hands.

'Uncertain times,' Fletch had commented on one of their many Skype conversations. 'Worse than war, because not only is the enemy unseen but the economy's gone down the toilet.'

Chapter Eight:

New Zealand was now at Level Three.

For the past few weeks Fletch had insisted he do the family shopping online and pay for it.

Sydney suggested he shop for New Zealand made goods.

'The shortages will be for imported goods,' she advised. He took her list and added a couple of surprises for Finn then drove the farm truck into town to collect their order. They didn't need much but Sydney figured lockdown made him stir crazy and driving into town to get the groceries was his only escape.

Today, Sydney needed to go to town to collect a prescription for Finn's eczema. It only flared up when he became anxious. Missing his school friends made him fretful. It would be another couple of weeks at least before the schools could reopen. Being schooled virtually with a programme the kids called 'Seesaw' gave his learning another dimension. He enjoyed it but missed his friends. The parent's input was vital to the programme for scanning and uploading work. In Finn's case his little video movies needed to be shared with his teacher, so Fletch helped him there. In reality, about two hours a day of schooling turned out to be all he had, and Sydney divided the time into two one-hour blocks which Fletch gladly shared with her when she worked from home.

Today Sydney also had some files she needed couriered to Masterton. Unable to get a courier to come out to Boar Gully she used plan B. Normally any number of her neighbours would have obliged but these were not normal times she reminded herself. So today Sydney would do the grocery shopping and get some wine, at the same time as running her other errands.

Sydney's girlfriend Sara joked, 'Level Three is just Level Four with takeaways. We can't even get together for a coffee or lunch.' Sydney smiled; Sara always had the ability to make her see the lighter side of life. The pair had been friends since ante natal classes. In the beginning they had little in common except their babies. Now Sara owned a gift shop in town, and she sold some of Sydney's handmade scarves and hats, especially if they were alpaca or possum mixed with wool. They were the most popular with the tourists. Sydney knitted as a hobby; she had her career at Howarth and Howarth, and Finn. So, she had very little free time. She simply did it to fill in the long winter evenings alone at the farmhouse.

Although she had good friends nobody knew the details of Finn's paternity. Sydney always refused to discuss Finn's father.

Sara, divorced with a small daughter the same age as Finn, understood. The children were good friends. Their mothers organised a skype date for them to enjoy while in lockdown. Sara's ex-husband had moved to Auckland with his new partner. However, after a while, his daughter Olive stopped talking about him and folks never pressed her on the matter. It had been the same for Finn. As he grew so did the speculation. A tall boy for his age, with mesmerising blue eyes he had lovely blond hair. So different to his dark-haired mother with sugar brown eyes. Sydney had long since given up seeing anything of Tim in the child. Now all she saw was a handsome dear little boy. She relished the joy he gave her, and she loved him deeply.

Today Fletch cared for Finn. The pair were busy playing Monopoly the New Zealand version when Sydney drove off to town. Fletch noted she'd dressed in navy slacks, her red merino jersey, a sleeveless puffer vest with her long bob in a high ponytail. He liked what he saw.

It must have only been ten minutes after she left when the phone rang. Distracted Fletch allowed Finn to answer the phone.

'Boar Gully farm,' he answered. Fletch looked up at him he sounded very articulate. However, the expression on Finns face Fletch recognised as bewilderment, his big blue eyes widened, and he said 'Finn' then silence. 'I'm six, I had a party,' the boy said. As if by instinct Fletch almost propelled himself to Finn. Grabbing the receiver from the child he said,

'Hello,' then turning to Finn he said forcefully 'You can watch a movie on your I pad, son.' The caller heard his command.

'No, I think you'll find Finn is *my* son,' a strong male voice told him. As he walked down the hallway to his bedroom to have this conversation in private, he hissed down the phone,

'well, where have you been for the last six years?' Furious, Fletch desperately wanted to shield the child from the fallout from this, which he knew would be toxic.

'Sydney knows exactly where I have been.' The voice had attitude and Fletch didn't like it.

'Tell Sydney to call me. She knows my number.'

'Don't tell me what to do if you're not prepared to identify yourself,' Fletch snarled. The voice sounded arrogant and Fletch would not be intimidated.

'If you don't do as I say, I'll see you in court,' the voice persisted, sounding high handed.

'Bring it on.' Fletch told him as he hung up and sat down on his bed. He hoped against hope, he wouldn't regret what he'd done. It was none of his business, but he had made it so, because he realised, he cared for both Finn and Sydney. Now what would he tell her about the call when she returned? Could he risk not telling her? Thinking about it he remembered what Ryan Murphy had said to Sydney, 'the country's gone to hell in a handcart. All the nutters in Christendom have found some hobby horse to whip while they have been in lockdown with time on their hands.' Perhaps this was a case in point?

Fletch walked down to the living area and replaced the phone in its cradle then he went over to Finn who sat playing on the floor. He sat down on the sectional settee near him.

'Finn, come and sit here, I want to ask you a question.' The boy sensed something amiss and did as Fletch suggested. 'Did you know the man on the telephone?' Finn shrugged. 'Tell me exactly what he said,' Fletch said, his voice kindly, aware of the enormity of the situation.

'He said what's your name? and he said how old are you?' Finn frowned and pulled a coy face.

'Do you want me to make you a hot chocolate? Mummy left us some pikelets for afternoon tea, with jam and cream.' The boy's face lit up and Fletch launched into one of his corny knock-knock jokes to take Finn's mind off the call.

By the time Sydney arrived home with all sorts of treats and new craft supplies, the phone call had been long forgotten. Fletch thought he'd choose his moment to tell her, especially as she looked so happy and buoyant after 'escaping to town' for the afternoon.

They enjoyed a glass of Pinot Gris with their homemade burgers, and for dessert they made ice cream sundaes, with different toppings. Fletch read Finn a bedtime story while Sydney cleared away the dishes. A great storyteller he put on various voices for the different animals in the book and when the child's eyelids began to droop, he whispered to Sydney, he would carry him to bed and beckoned her to follow him. It warmed her heart these two had bonded so well.

Later, while the pair watched the news Fletch commented,

'You're very happy this evening, it's good to see.' He put his arm along the back of the settee. Her face beamed and her eyes twinkled.

'I've enjoyed having you here at Boar Gully.' She looked up at him through her dark lashes. Grinning, Fletch asked, 'Are you trying to get rid of me now we're at level three?' Immediately she frowned, and he rested his hand on her shoulder.

'I thought you were staying until this thing is over and the borders are open again,' she looked bereft it made him smile, and he leaned down and kissed her giving her no warning of his intentions. As soon as his lips covered hers, she opened her mouth slightly to welcome his tongue, they both drifted off to another level. Frissons of pleasure coursed through her. Fletch's hands were solely on her face. He didn't want to spook her tonight. Then remembering the phone call, he pulled back.

'I must tell you, a man called today. I'm sorry I forgot to mention it.'

'Who? Did he leave a number?'

Fletch shook his head. Inhaling deeply, he added, 'he said he was Finn's father, and you were to call him. When I asked for the number, he insisted you knew how to reach him.' Fletch stared in dismay as Sydney's expression changed.

'Hang on a minute here, tell me again exactly what he said. His exact words,' her voice was firm yet apprehensive at the same time.

'The thing is Sydney; I didn't take the call originally.' He watched her eyes widen and saw her hand shake as she moved a strand of hair away from her face. 'Finn answered and he sounded quite articulate for a six-year-old. He said, 'Boar Gully farm' then he said 'Finn' then when I heard him say 'I'm six I had a party;' I grabbed the phone from him and told him to watch a movie on the I pad. I took the call in my bedroom.' Sydney's mouth dropped open, and she covered it. Fletch went on to say, 'the guy on the phone said something about Finn being his son and he said, get Sydney to call me.' Covering her face with both hands now, Sydney visibly shook. It had arrived. The day she had been dreading since Tim stormed out of her house in Wellington and slammed the door, all those years ago. But why now? She had absolutely no intention of calling him. Taking in a deep hitching breath she let it out on a sigh.

'Oh God, the day I've been dreading. I don't want to deal with him.'

'The sperm donor?' Fletch asked, knowing there must be more. Sydney nodded, looking deflated and anxious.

'The same,' biting her lip she stood up and rummaged in the fridge for the half empty bottle of wine. 'Fancy one?' she filled two glasses and he smiled at her.

'One or two or the whole bottle, I'm sorry, I should have been on my game. The thing is, whoever he is, he thinks we're together. I hope it doesn't make matters worse for you.' Tucking an uncooperative strand of hair behind her ear he admitted, 'I feel for the past month we have become a little family, of sorts.' Sipping his wine he asked earnestly, 'Did I do wrong?'

'No, he might think twice about bullying me. I will need to get advice from Ben. But half of me says stuff him, let him stew.' Some of her sparkle reappeared; she giggled, a cute giggle just like Finn's.

'I won't let anyone bully you.' He leaned in and kissed her again. Being locked up with him did strange things to her equilibrium. After Tim, she determined if she ever met someone who made her feel like Fletch made her feel she would have 'the conversation' with him before the liaison progressed. Only, this proved more difficult than she ever imagined, and now Tim might be hovering in the background.

'Thank you Fletch, but I need to go to bed...' oh, it sounded wrong, 'alone.' She gave him a weak grin. He felt as though he had made some progress with the prickly one.

Next morning Sydney and Finn were out riding their horses. When Fletch arrived in the kitchen, she had left a note for him on the bench. After pouring his coffee he went out on the sunny back veranda to enjoy it and wait for them. The peace and quiet of this place had been eerie at first, now he loved it. The late April morning hinted at another month until official 'winter, the Indian summer as kiwis called it, felt wonderful. However good the weather, the best part of this equation had gone out riding on 'the range' as he thought of the place. Mercury joined him on the veranda and sat at his feet. As he bent to scratch the dog, he could hear unique birdsong he didn't recognise, he must ask Sydney to identify the birds. His mind drifted off until he heard voices. Sure enough, he could see them in the distance moving sedately along the driveway. Finn looked bigger on his horse his riding helmet made him appear taller. The pair rode on to the stables and Fletch stood up and walked towards them. Fascinated, he watched unseen as Sydney dismounted, her backside in lycra jodhpurs made him swallow hard he wanted to touch it. Instead, he told himself to be a patient man. Ever since the 'voice' phoned, Fletch acknowledged to himself he had invested emotionally in this family, and he wanted more from this woman.

Greeting them, he stood in the doorway of the stables watching Sydney rub down Finn's pony before letting it loose in the paddock.

'Hiya Fletch,' Finn smiled, then pulled a face, 'phew Pickle just farted.' Looking towards Pickle he commented amused, 'he always poos after a long ride.' Sydney shook her head smiling, trust Finn to comment on it, she recognised the boy's toilet humour again. The three of them walked back toward the house.

'He's growing up,' Fletch acknowledged when Finn moved out of earshot.

'He's a typical six-year-old,' Sydney replied. She walked slightly ahead of Fletch who slowed to admire her bottom again then shaking those thoughts from his head, he put his arm around her shoulder.

'I've lost all sense of time. I worked on a scene for the new movie script until two this morning, totally lost in the work. I had no idea of the time. Do you ever get totally immersed?' he asked. Squinting up at him as though he were from a strange other world, she grinned thinking him odd.

'You're mad, completely mad, no one with a small child ever willingly gets totally lost in work till two in the morning.' She pushed him playfully and he pushed her back. Before long it had escalated, and they were horsing about gently pushing and shoving each other.

Finn, who had been watching from a short distance away, called out, 'stop it you two, otherwise it will all end in tears.'

Suddenly, looking from one to the other, the pair stopped and burst into laughter. Finn had become the parent.

'Mrs Lomas, my teacher always says, it will end in tears when we fight or play rough at school,' the child advised, grinning.

After lunch while Sydney stood busy baking, Finn went outside to play with his dog and Sydney suggested he fill a couple of bags with walnuts to give him something to do.

A couple of hours passed before she started to wonder why he had not yet returned, then dismissed the thought. Fletch was busy working in the shed sanding down an old dresser. Sydney thought Finn must be with him, so she continued cleaning up after her baking.

Chapter Nine:

Satisfied with her afternoon's work she decided to walk over to the shed and see if the boys wanted some afternoon tea, although it seemed closer to Finn's dinner time now, at four thirty.

'Wow, you're doing a great job. To think for the last thirty plus years Gran's old dresser has been used to store tools.' Fletch looked up from his work, his face serious, his hair covered in a fine dust from sanding down the old Welsh dresser by hand so as not to disturb the carved elements of the fine piece.

'It's a beautiful specimen,' he whispered his voice husky from silence and his dark hair grey from dust. He gently fingered the wood.

Then it occurred to Sydney.

'I thought Finn might be here with you, he went off after lunch to get some bags of walnuts and it's four thirty now, have you seen him?' she sounded worried.

'No, I've not seen him, but Mercury is with him, isn't he?' Fletched wiped his hands on an old cloth. 'The dog will look after him, they'll be home soon looking for food, I'm sure.' He gave a half smile as if to reassure her.

'But the wind's up and it's getting cold. I need to find him,' she said anxious now. 'I'll get him a jacket from the house.' Sydney hurried off. The weather had changed quite severely in the last hour.

Fletch called to her, 'wait, I'm coming with you.' The back of the house housed the laundry, a spare shower room and toilet and utility room where they housed all the old raincoats, boots, and cold weather gear. Finding a big jacket for Fletch she offered it.

'Here this one's Perry's, it will fit you. Then grabbing her binoculars and a jacket for Finn, she quickly shrugged herself into her own jacket and they hurried back towards the stands of walnut trees.

Fletch used his booming voice to call out to Finn, with no results.

Scanning the countryside for any sign of the boy or his dog, without success, Sydney handed the binoculars to Fletch.

'Finn never wanders off alone, there are too many hazardous things on a farm like this for an unsupervised six-year-old.' Her voice cracked. 'It will be dark in an hour, and it looks like it might rain, typical,' her voice rose a few decibels. 'The bloody drought decides to break just when my little boy is lost.' They could smell the rain coming now but still they saw no sign of it.

'Sydney, you go back to the house, turn all the lights on and get some torches. Phone Jamie Dalton while you're at it and maybe Ryan Murphy, rather than wait until it's dark. Then saddle up your horse, and Finn's too. I can ride Brandy; you can take Pickle. I'll keep looking around here.' Running as fast as she could back to the house, Sydney realised Fletch had taken charge. She felt grateful for his clear thinking.

It took another twenty minutes before Sydney arrived back at the walnut trees. Dark now, she had the foresight to turn on all the shed lights while she saddled up the horses.

'Have you ever ridden a horse?' she asked.

'Not for twenty years, let's hope it's like riding a bicycle, never forgotten. Hey, look over there someone's coming.' They could see a rider with a lantern.

'Here comes Jamie, thank heavens. He knows the tracks down the gully, and he knows the property like the back of his hand.'

Houdini, Jamie's stallion reached them in a gallop and Jamie circled them slowly.

'Go back to the homestead Sydney in case Finn returns. Someone needs to be there for him. Also, Ryan called me, he's on his way. I've saddled up Trigger for him and left the gelding tethered to the fence near the stable. We will find Finn; the dog might be injured, and the boy might not want to leave him.' he shot a stern look at Fletch who agreed, noticing two rifles in canvas scabbards either side of his horse.

'Do as Jamie says please Sydney.' Fletch leaned over and held her arm firmly in reassurance.

'You can busy yourself getting us some food, Finn will be starving.'

'And so will I.' Jamie insisted.

'But you're not in our bubble.' As soon as she had said it, Sydney thought it sounded pathetic.

'Buggar your bubble,' Jamie cursed, urging her to move.

'He's in our bubble now,' Fletch called as she turned her horse and rode off. Then he turned back towards Jamie,

'what's with the guns?' Fletch asked as he started to move forward Jamie and his huge lantern slightly ahead of him.

'It's not called Boar Gully farm for nothing,' he called over his shoulder.

'I reckon I know what's happened. The dog has gone off down the gully after a rabbit or something and the boy's followed. It's steep and maybe one of them got injured and the other has stayed with the injured one.' Jamie, a skilled horseman, led the way Fletch followed carefully.

'We go through the gate and down the track to the right of it. We may need to dismount and walk for a bit.' He held the gate open for Fletch,

'Have you ever fired a gun before?' Jamie asked him seriously.

'Once or twice. I never hunted boars though' he said earnestly.

'Don't worry we don't need to hunt them. Here they hunt us, or they used to, until our families, the Daltons and the Martins began a systematic cull. We only get the odd one these days, but it would only take one ...' his voice trailed off and then he added, 'I never tell Sydney when I see one, don't want to worry her. I simply hunt it down,' Jamie said as a matter of fact.

'When did you last see a wild boar in this gully?' Fletch asked as his horse shied. He pulled it up and dismounted.

'Exactly what I'm worried about,' he sighed, 'only last week.' Fletch let out an expletive. Jamie also dismounted as the path narrowed.

'Cripes a wild boar is all we need.' The heavens opened up as thunder reverberated around the hills. The temperature seemed to drop as though on cue. The two men froze a loud growling could be heard in the distance, twigs snapping and loud snuffling. Jamie handed Fletch a rifle, he checked it quickly like a pro.

'Where's the ammunition?' Jamie handed him a box which Fletch opened and loaded the weapon without looking at it. Jamie watched by the light of his lamp.

'Once or twice my arse, where did you learn how to handle a weapon?'

'The army,' he cocked the weapon, pointed it to the sky ready to fire off a round when Jamie called 'Hold your fire, if that's a boar I want it.'

'Finn,' his booming voice bellowed around the hills echoing in the gully. They listened in silence for several minutes, no reply.

Then a horse came thundering across the paddock above them. The rider called out.

'Jamie it's Ryan wait for me, where are you?' Jamie directed his headlamp at Ryan called back.

'I see you, hold on.' By the time Ryan joined them he sounded breathless.

'I've got back up checking the road and the culverts. A big black four-wheel drive has been seen around here, even since lockdown. If I didn't know better, I'd say Sydney has a stalker.'

The police officer wore a rifle slung over his shoulder allowing him to ride his horse and be armed.

'Is that for the stalker or the boar?' Fletch asked glibly, Ryan and Jamie exchanged glances. 'I've just remembered something; a man called the house yesterday. Sydney had gone to town and Finn answered.' Fletch told the Ryan the story.

'We have both wondered when Finn's biological father would appear on the scene. Sydney doesn't talk about him and when she first came back to live here, she was a mess,' Ryan explained to Fletch.

'At first we put it down to her parent's sudden death,' Jamie expanded. 'I always knew it had to be more. But why would the man not come forward? Unless he didn't know, we thought. But obviously she told him otherwise he would not be calling her?' Jamie questioned as he remounted and carefully descended the track down the gully.

'I've talked to her about the boy's father, and I believe he hurt her badly. Do you think this vehicle has something to do with him? How come nobody's bothered to get the registration number? Does Sydney know about the vehicle?' Fletch had all the questions but neither of them had any answers.

'Look it's all very new, something Jamie drew my attention to about the second week in lockdown,' Ryan told him.

'Shoosh, I thought I heard something,' Jamie called. Then they all heard it. Mercury barking, it sounded weak and tired. They could only hear it now they had changed position.

Fletch dismounted and with his rifle slung over his shoulder he ignored the cold and wet, pushing his way through the bush and scrub towards the sound of the dog's bark. Ryan kept close behind him.

'Masterton are sending the dog handler but by the sound of things we won't need him,' he whispered. They homed in on Mercury's voice.

'Tell me what the law is in respect of Finn's biological father?' Fletch's breathing sounded calmer, he was fitter than Ryan.

'He has rights, but Sydney will know better than most, it's her field, family law.' Fletch let out a low groan and called out to Mercury.

'Mercury, hang in there buddy.'

'You think the dog understands what you're saying?' Ryan questioned.

'Yes, he understands the tone, not the words, the tone. *Mercury*' he called again.

In the distant hills behind them they heard a single shot ring out. Stopping dead in their tracks they heard a voice, a child crying. 'Finn,' Fletch yelled, shining his torch in the direction of the sound they saw Mercury dragging his back leg and limping towards them on three legs, his tail wagging weakly. Scrambling around in the bush in darkness Ryan held up his torch. They couldn't see Finn. The crying had faded to a whimper.

'Poor bastard, the dog's broken his leg and he's bleeding.' Ryan checked him out while Fletch looked for Finn. He saw him lying down in the foetal position whimpering. Wet and cold he lay curled up in the scrub. Fletch took off his jacket and quickly checked the child.

'No broken bones... I can see, but whoa, he's got a huge egg on his head.' Picking the boy up he cuddled him up under his warm jersey and called to Ryan to give him a hand with his jacket which once into it he managed to pull the sides together and zip up. You couldn't call it snug tight would be a better description. Ryan rode behind him, Fletch took the large lantern so Ryan could lift the dog in a sling. Mercury yelped in pain. Fletch moved quickly up the track towards where he believed Jamie held the horses. In the distance Jamie shone his headlight down on the track and both men saw it, sprawled out dead across the track. A huge black boar.

'Gees, what a grizzly mean mother. How old is he?' Fletch exclaimed as they approached and walked around the beast whose huge tusks were evident.

When they reached Jamie, and the horses Finn became more animated. Undoing his jacket Fletch wrapped Finn in his own warm dry jacket and sat him in the saddle on Brandy.

'Hang on till we get to the top of the gully then you can ride with me.'

'But we haven't any helmets,' Finn argued.

'I know, but I'm too tired to walk, so don't tell your mother. Besides it's an emergency isn't it, Ryan.' Fletch smirked knowing Sydney had strict rules about helmets.

'See you back at the house,' Ryan called as Jamie handed him the dog. 'What are you going to do with the boar? he asked as he pressed his heels into Trigger's sides and the horse moved off.

'Buggered if I know, might leave him till the morning. I'm too bloody old for this caper.'

Chapter Ten:

L evel three lockdown New Zealand May 2020
      A grand old villa in Thorndon was home to Mr. and Mrs Timothy Winthrop.

It had been seven years since Tim had spoken to Sydney. A lot of water had passed under the bridge since then. The first four of those years, he had a string of unsuccessful personal assistants. None had been a legal executive of the calibre of Sydney Martin. As both Grant Winthrop the senior partner, and his entitled arrogant son Tim, agreed. One of the very few things on which they did agree.

In the end Grant persuaded his own PA to work for his son. Mr Winthrop senior even suggested she could name her price and report back to him anything she felt may be untoward. Ms Monica Hegarty, a woman similar in age to the senior Mr Winthrop had been with the firm long enough to know about Tim.

The remit Winthrop senior gave her provided the ammunition she needed to rein Tim in. After a while and a few frosty screaming matches he did toe the line and now they rubbed along satisfactorily.

Tim, now established as a formidable criminal barrister had become the 'go to man' in Wellington for those convoluted and expensive cases, where the defendant had run out of options and needed defending in a trial by jury, while claiming his innocence.

In Tim's personal life unfortunately, he had not been so successful. His long-suffering parents decided to bring some pressure to bear as he approached forty. Still a highly active member of the 'playboys' club, Tim enjoyed a revolving door of women friends, until he had a nasty affair with a married woman. Neither the woman nor her husband would disappear quietly when Tim decided the affair must end. For the first time in his life, he seemed a little scared; the husband a bankrupt ex-football player with all the looks and no money lived on the fringes of society and his friends were thugs. Rumour had it, when the husband learned of the affair, he saw an opportunity to milk it for money. When Tim refused to be forthcoming, he got 'roughed up.'

This had the sobering effect of having Tim look for a legally permanent arrangement with someone more suitable. The last three years Tim had been married to the long leggy blonde Amanda. Tim had chosen someone for the position rather than fallen in love. Amanda was a beauty, who held she thought of as a great job at the bank. Great for Tim because it would never overshadow his position. Amanda, like Tim came across as demanding and self-centred. They deserved one another.

The first year of marriage proved wonderful and Amanda completely refurbished the old villa in Thorndon, giving it her own personal stamp; very minimalistic and sleek. Anything resembling clutter, like his prize collection of first edition classics were given the heave ho. Their ideas on what represented comfort in furniture were completely different and so the sleek black leather and chrome look presided. When she softened it to accommodate his complaining it now resembled a hair dressing salon more than a home. All chrome and mirrors. But they were working it out and the only real stumbling block to their happiness came when they wanted a family. Having tried hard for a year, normally no sacrifice for Tim, but with no results, they visited a fertility specialist. Amanda, the doctor confirmed appeared in perfect working order. Tim on the other hand had read the small print on the posters at the sexually transmitted diseases clinic all those years ago. Chlamydia, if left untreated can cause infertility.

'The DNA of the sperm becomes unstable, basically it's code gets scrambled,' the doctor had told Tim. Fortunately he had the good sense to anticipate a poor outcome and had taken the doctor at the fertility clinic aside and had a discreet word with him.

'I understand Amanda must be told it is me who is infertile, but please could we spare her the unpleasant details.'

Amanda wanted her own baby. Tim completely understood, so when sperm donors were mooted, he needed time to consider 'their' options. All the time he was haunted by the fact at one time he had been fertile, and he had a child. A child another man was bringing up as his own. It hurt Tim to think about it. He knew it had been his own stupidity and for the first time in his life he felt shame. If he and Sydney were anything to go by, the child would be bright, funny, good looking and so much more. This began to occupy his conscious mind and had set up shop in his dreams. He began to think of little else. This child he did not want a bar of wormed its way into his mind. During lockdown he often shut himself away in his home office and tried to glean what he could about Sydney's child, or his child as he now thought of the little person.

He trawled social media. Sydney had no profile, no Facebook, damn her, why couldn't she be like other women her age.

Twice during lockdown, he had ventured over the Remutaka Pass road to the Wairarapa on the pretext of attending to some urgent legal matter. Fortunately for him, he had never been stopped on the way over. Once the police stopped him on the way back and reprimanded him for breaching the rules. Due to Covid movement restrictions, Tim hired a private detective to take some photos of the child and send them to him. Poor Amanda had no idea what he got up to, nor did she know about the child. He planned to bide his time, then claim he knew nothing of the child whose mother had kept Tim from having any part in his child's life and deprived him and his parents of enjoying their grandchild's formative years.

One day the private investigator emailed photographs of the child, a boy, out walking on a country road with his mother and a man. They looked like a family. The pictures were taken with a telephoto lens. The investigator had done an excellent job. Besides the family photo there were several others where he had zoomed in on the faces individually. One had struck Tim like a knife to his heart. Looking into the face of his son he could see himself as a young boy, he didn't need the DNA test he intended to demand. The shape of his face, the vivid blue eyes and fair hair, the child looked like a mini me. It seemed surreal and eerie.

Tim began to resent the tall man who walked swinging the child between him and Sydney. Then he saw Sydney, no longer did she have the plumpness of youth yet she ... he couldn't define it, her figure looked voluptuous, her face fresh and healthy but most of all she looked happy. He could see something between the tall man and her something he felt defied words. He envied them. Sydney's long dark hair billowed around her in the autumn breeze, her mouth open and smiling as she looked up at the man. She was no 'mother mouse.'

At alert level three there had been no opportunity to introduce this new perspective of his life to his wife and parents. Tim would need to plan it carefully. Always a strategic thinker he anticipated Sydney's reaction. Only she no longer appeared the naïve young woman she had been, now a lioness protecting her cub and he would do well not to underestimate her.

Chapter Eleven:

Fletch arrived back at the homestead with Finn in his arms. Sydney heard them coming and went running out to greet the pair.

'I think he's got a concussion, there's a nasty lump on his head.' Setting the small boy down on the couch he said, 'Ryan has taken Mercury to the vet. He's broken his leg.' Fletch pulled a face indicating pain. He failed to mention the dog also had a nasty gash on his body as the result of an altercation with a wild boar. Hugging Finn, Sydney wiped tears away from her face.

'Ooh what a nasty lump. He needs to see a doctor, possibly get an X-ray.' Fletch gently rubbed her arm in support.

'I thought you would say he needed a doctor. I'll drive.' Neither seemed to notice, the man looked a sight, his face filthy from wood sanding dust, rain and dirt. Nor did they worry about dinner, Sydney simply switched off the oven.

On arrival at the hospital, they could see quite a performance to get inside the building let alone be seen by a doctor. A long queue of people waited at two metres apart. As soon as Fletch saw the queue and medical team wearing full personal protective equipment and looking like something out of the movie *Pandemic* he instructed Sydney, 'Leave this to me.' Fortunately, Ryan had phoned ahead telling the medical team a child with a head injury is being driven in from Hinakura and gave Finn's name.

At the start the medical team permitted Sydney to be with Finn, then as it became clear the boy, although coherent, had suffered a concussion, and needed an X-ray, Fletch and Sydney were left outside in the dark under the porch light. Someone gave them to fill in the required paperwork while a nurse took Finn to X-ray. They were cold so when the forms were completed and collected, they returned to the warmth of their vehicle. During this time Fletch regaled her with the story of the boar. Pete Jacobson, the vet, telephoned to say he would keep Mercury in overnight after having pinned his leg and sutured the wound.

A nurse came out to their vehicle and asked them to come to the door of A and E. A doctor arrived with Finn in her arms saying she would be keeping him in overnight for monitoring. Fortunately, he hadn't broken any bones, but his legs were covered in cuts and scratches and his pupils were showing a slightly different response, one definitely larger than the other. They needed to conduct regular checks. Finn seemed happy enough and called out to his mother.

'See ya in the morning, I'm getting ice cream and jelly.' Feeling redundant Sydney and Fletch drove home. During journey Sydney rang Jamie and thanked him.

'You owe me a dinner remember. I left one of my horses and a saddle for Fletch. Take him with you when you go riding. He's a good guy Syd.' She smiled, high praise indeed coming from Jamie. Fletch caught sight of her secretive little smirk and wanted to know what Jamie said.

'Whatever you did, or said you made an impression on Jamie,' she allowed.

'Yeah, we owe him dinner,' Fletch added, using the royal *we*. 'Do you eat the wild boar meat?'

Sydney turned up her nose, 'I'd rather not. It's probably full of worms and you have to be very careful about the cooking process, you can get trichinosis, a nasty disease with a raft of side effects. Pork's a cheap meat to purchase, why risk it?' Such a pragmatic woman.

Ryan phoned to check on Finn and Sydney thanked him for his help and updated him.

'You're welcome, but tomorrow I'll stop by I need to talk with you.' Sydney shrugged, wondering what about.

After they had showered and were enjoying dinner she mentioned, 'Ryan wants to come over tomorrow he needs to talk for some reason.'

Fletch nodded and standing up said, 'I think I know what it's about.'

Raising her eyebrows Sydney asked him. 'what do you think exactly?'

'Both Jamie and Cameron St. Clair have seen a strange vehicle in the neighbourhood.'

'I have too, I thought I'd mentioned it to you,' she reminded.

'I don't remember, well regardless, I told them about the phone call from the voice claiming to be Finn's father.' Sydney's expression changed; her eyes narrowed; she did not look happy.

'I know they are watching out for me, but really I wish they would mind their own business.' Fletch noticed she didn't include him in her statement.

'You're a pragmatic woman, I wouldn't be surprised if you had a plan of action ready for this day. After my two second conversation with the voice, I've given it a bit of thought.' Sitting down next to her he put two big mugs of tea on the coffee table.

'Why do I feel now I'm going to get the benefit of your observations, whether I want them or not?' Putting her feet up on the pouf she folded her arms, as if to shut him out.

'Because I care for you, both of you. Do you know this is the longest time in my entire adult life I've spent in the company of a mother and her child, I had often thought about it especially when I was married.' He sighed 'sadly it never happened.'

'You never mentioned you were married.' She frowned realising she didn't really know this man. He never spoke of his past much.

'There is a great deal about you I don't know, apart from how I feel,' he admitted.

'I never told anyone about Tim, I was young and scared and so ashamed.' She sipped her mug of tea.

'I thought of myself as ten foot tall and bomb proof,' he said. 'Only my wife wasn't, and I couldn't take the sympathy. I couldn't deal with people wanting to talk about it. I wanted to wallow in my private grief. I know now it would not be what Emily wanted.' Holding his hand, she asked softly, 'please tell me what happened.' Watching him she noticed his Adam's apple move up and down. He turned his face from her and sucked air in through his clenched teeth then he squeezed her hand.

'Only if you tell me about Finn's father,' his soft blue eyes locked on her. 'Please,' his voice barely a whisper. 'I'll go first.' Nodding and unable to say a word, as she bit her lips between her teeth, she breathed deeply to avoid her emotions getting the better of her.

'I had just turned twenty-nine when Emily and I married at Fort Bragg, Massachusetts. I had been tasked with running Special Operations training courses. By then I'd been in the Army eleven years if you count Military college. I'm an army brat; my dad had been a soldier too. I had this honest belief that if I worked hard and kept my shit together, I would be untouchable.

Emily taught grade school, we met at a charity function. I felt drawn to her, the all-American beauty, tall blond, slim and sporty. I thought I was driven but compared with Emily, I was a slacker. A funny thing though, her drive focused on everything except her career. Never once did she worry about me being posted somewhere and her not teaching. She had this image thing driving her. The need to be fit and beautiful. I never fully understood it until too late. At the beginning of each year, she trained daily for the Boston Marathon which is held in April. The training programme seemed easy, but the rigid dietary regimen drove me bonkers.

On April 15, 2013, two homemade pressure cooker bombs were detonated near the finish line of the race. Some ISIS cell apparently. Three were killed and hundreds were injured. Emily had been badly wounded, and she later died.'

'Oh my God, how awful, the poor woman, imagine surviving something so awful, only to die of complications. How painful it must have been for you. First you think, thank God she's alive and then you go through it all again only to lose her.'

'It's not what you think!' His booming voice bellowed at her. She pulled away from him shocked by his outburst. Her hurt look shook him to the core.

'Emily topped herself,' he finally said. Sydney sat embarrassed. She stroked his face gently in consolation; he took her hand and kissed her upturned palm.

'Do you know why she did it?' he asked quietly.

'Quite clearly her mind must have been disturbed,' she whispered. He shook his head slowly.

'No there had been no hint of poor mental health. Never once did she display any signs of depression. In her mind she no longer looked perfect and according to her journal, she refused to accept anything less than perfection. After her death I began to notice so many things I had chosen to ignore previously. We wanted to start a family and Emily led me to believe she wanted it too. I had no clue until after her death when I found out she still took the pill. I found a current prescription, even though she told me she had gone off it three years earlier.'

'But she may have gone back on it after the accident, you know, till she became well again.' Sydney made excuses for the woman.

'I thought so at first, but her doctor let it slip by accident, saying just as well we chose not to have children. I asked him if the contraceptive pill could have had depressive side effects. He doubted it as she had been on her particular brand for more than six years with no problems. The doctor mentioned Emily had always been fastidious about contraception since we had chosen not to have a family.' He sounded exasperated.

'I couldn't believe she had lied about something so important to me. Especially when I looked back and remembered all the times, I had talked about having a family and even consoled her when it didn't happen. She promised me before the last Boston marathon, as soon as the race was over, she would schedule an appointment with a fertility specialist. I knew I had no issues because my doctor checked me out and did a sperm count,' he sighed.

'After her funeral I had been going through her things and I found evidence of a long-time affair with her personal trainer.' It hurt him to tell Sydney about his past, it made him feel a failure as both a husband and a lover.

She put her arms around him gently rubbing his back, 'I can see how this has affected you. I'm sorry for your pain,' she told him on a faltering breath as she wondered about Emily.

'Tell me your story Sydney,' his voice, now recovered and firm. Leaning back on the settee Sydney began her saga. When she finished the story, she added, 'so, you see, I was just a silly naïve girl and getting an STD became the last straw. I felt so embarrassed and scared. I have never been with a man since then. Just scared, of getting pregnant and going through the same drama and scared of getting an STD. I learned some nasty facts of life from Timothy Winthrop.' She sniffed, 'I'm a lot more street wise now, but mostly I learned I belong here.'

Fletch sat listening to her story. He had met Tim's type of man before, but not in the military. Not in his circle of friends at least, they were men of honour, and the services didn't tolerate promiscuous behaviour. As a result, many of them married way too young. Besides, when you've seen action like he had and worse still you've bagged and tagged the bodies of your friends, or your men, your life's priorities become more sharply focused. Looking at her now he could see Sydney's resolve had been strengthened by recent events.

'I could just imagine the kind of thing Tim would say about me. I have a plan to balance the truth and the fact he is Finn's father. Fletch took her face in his hands and kissed her slowly and with tenderness. Sydney responded and Fletch could feel her trembling as he kissed her. They had been honest with each other and told their stories, warts and all. He had flown into her life under her personal radar; he had grown on her and she trusted him. Seriously attracted to him her feelings for Fletch ran deep and Sydney felt they were reciprocated. Especially when he whispered, 'I want to make love to you tonight.'

Sighing she breathed, 'me too, but too bad. I don't have any condoms.' Her fingers were in his hair.

'I do,' he smiled, continuing to kiss her.

After a few moments she gazed at him wickedly.

'Then what are we waiting for?' she giggled.

He scooped her up and carried her down the hall to his bedroom.

Turning on his bedside lamp he shed his clothes down to his underpants. When she started to follow suit, he stopped her.

'Let me' slowly he undressed her studying every inch of her and kissing her as he went. 'I'm in no hurry we have all night.' He ran his hands over her backside as he rolled her on top of him, groaning pleasurably as he kneaded the shapely bottom. She wriggled her bare breasts pressed up against his hard muscly chest. Rolling her over again he scooped both breasts into his hands as he ran his thumbs over her hardened nipples. Emitting a little mewing sound, she writhed in pleasure. 'Where's the contraceptive thingy?' she wanted to know. He opened the drawer and held up the packet then whispered.

'Not yet too soon, we're in no rush. Let's enjoy this.'

Next morning, he woke to a light filled room. Feeling her naked body against his he smiled, remembering the previous evening.

'What time is it?' Sydney wanted to know. 'Doctors" rounds are nine, they will only discharge Finn after the doctor sees him.' He ran his hands over her soft feminine shape. 'It's only seven, do we have time?' He felt her lips smile against his chest.

'Silly question.'

By eight forty-five they arrived at the hospital with clean clothes for Finn. Who pleased to see them waved eager to be going home. The duty doctor said his pupils had normalised and his vital signs were good. Providing he took it quietly he could go home. The doctors didn't want to keep anyone in hospital unnecessarily, given the pandemic.

'Did you get breakfast Champ?' Fletch wanted to know as he strapped him in his car seat.

'Yeah, but it tasted yucky ooh porridge,' he grimaced. 'I'm hungry.'

'Well buddy, what about Mackers?' Fletch drawled.

'McDonalds? Yes please.'

Chapter Twelve:

New Zealand announces Alert Level Two will commence Wednesday thirteenth May at 11.59pm

Sitting in the comfortable home office of his grand villa in Thorndon, Timothy Winthrop mulled over the events of the past few weeks. Amanda had excitedly told him about her pregnancy. Tim sat stunned; he had not told her about his infertility.

When their specialist had confirmed Tim's infertility with him, they had agreed to tell his wife he had a low sperm count with poor motility. The specialist and Tim had a connection from their University days. It had been easy for Tim to convince the doctor that rather than have the over-anxious Amanda become fixated on the situation, they would couch it in a different way.

'It's not a lie, simply a kind omission,' he told the doctor.

An omission he found now changed his life. Amanda had been unfaithful, and recently. Thinking about, it he started to piece together in his mind a picture he found hard to accept. This last year she'd had a complete change of heart about his working late when he had a big case to prepare. She'd phone calls and texts she secreted away from him with excuses he had dismissed from his mind as stupid. A year ago, she had changed jobs, same bank, different role.

He remembered how she eulogised about how wonderful she thought her new boss. He knew the guy was married with a couple of kids. Tim met him once, more Amanda's age, a good-looking guy. The more he thought about it the more he joined the dots. However, he said nothing, instead he garnered as much evidence as he could about the man. Amanda had been behaving oddly during lockdown and the tension between them had stretched into a yawning gulf.

Now over a month since she announced her pregnancy and quit her job, their relationship had gone from bad to worse. Money had never been a problem. Amanda's timing made Tim suspicious, also the fact she loved the job. Over the past six months Amanda had not been so hung up on the fertility issues plaguing them previously. He had the evidence, bank statements, hotel receipts for non-existent conferences, and her phone records. He had dismissed the countless times their friends and colleagues had seen them together. 'They work together,' he would say, feeling a tad uncomfortable.

Tim decided to tell Amanda about his child, the child he had always thought of in a detached way as Sydney's child. He outlined the story as honestly as someone like him could, telling her now he wanted to acknowledge his paternity. He wanted to know this child. This huge bombshell sent Amanda over the edge; furious she threw a complete wing ding, hurling plates, and stamping her feet no tears, Tim noted unless they were the crocodile variety as she screamed at him. Finally, pushed beyond his limit, Tim launched into a tirade about her affair. All hell broke loose. Tonight, alone in the house, regret his only companion, he threw himself into his work determined to salvage what he could of his life. His marriage now beyond repair, he had no idea where Amanda might be tonight. Sadly, he remembered his father's lecture about fidelity prior to his marriage to Amanda. Tim had taken on board his father's words knowing if he failed to keep the vows he made, his life would be meaningless. Looking back, he accepted full responsibility for his situation.

Chapter Thirteen:

At Boar Gully farm Sydney phoned Tim's father.

'Mr Winthrop, Sydney Martin, I'm sorry to trouble you...'

'Sydney, how nice to hear from you,' Grant Winthrop realised it was not a social call. 'What can I do for you?' he asked, sounding tired.

'I need to talk to you. It is a private matter, just for you and I and it is urgent,' she felt her voice quaver.

'I see, when would you like to meet?' He knew Sydney would never dramatize a situation.

'As soon as possible, but not in or near your office,' her voice was firmer now.

'Would you like me to drive over the pass to you?' Now he became concerned, what did she want to talk to him about? All kinds of horror stories filled his head.

'No thank you, it won't be necessary. What say we meet at the café at the bottom of the hill?' as she referred to the Remutaka Pass. 'If we made it noon then you're less likely to draw attention to the meeting.' He assured her in his authoritative tone, what he did is nobody's business but his own, and he would be there.

OPENING HIS EMAILS, Fletch read one marked urgent, from Perry.

Fletch,

Our equity partners, Goldstein and Lewis, have just gone into voluntary administration. I can't get hold of anyone from their office to speak to me. It seems they have taken a huge financial hit and our contract with them isn't worth a tin of fish, according to our lawyers. The stock markets have crashed again, worse than last week. I didn't know rock bottom had a basement. We have lost our funding. I'm frantically working on some ideas. It's the bloody Covid thing. Pray really pray.

Perry

Fletch felt ill. Of course, he had read the papers online and he knew things were bad. But they had a contract and the equity party had provided seeding finance, now spent. They were supposed to get the first of their three-part payments of more than twenty million dollars each so they could start on the film. Thank God they were still in dialogue with the actors telling them they couldn't sign them till they had the money in the bank. But they had signed heads of agreement on the big picture. This was his worst nightmare. He could not discuss it with Sydney or anyone, until he spoke with Perry.

'I THINK WINTHROP SENIOR suspects something because he agreed to the meeting with no fuss.' Sydney sounded surprised as she passed the toast rack to Fletch. The three of them sat down to hot leek and potato soup for lunch.

'Do you want me to come? I'd like to be there so the man knows you have support,' He raised an eyebrow, waiting for her reply.

'Thank you, I'd like you to, and we can take his nibs,' she indicated Finn with her eyes, 'in case it goes better than I expect.' Fletch understood.

'What say we play cards after lunch? he elbowed Finn softly, 'what do you say Buddy?'

'So long as you don't cheat.' Finn grumbled half peeved.

'Only if you don't either' Fletch told him firmly. Sydney chastised them both, unsure who seemed the bigger kid.

After a great afternoon of cards and board games Finn sat ready for cake and Fletch took the opportunity to ask, 'if I'm a good boy, can I stay here with you and Mummy.'

Great, now he's calling me his mummy, Sydney thought. Fletch ruffled the boy's thick blond hair, wondering if he had his father's colouring, suddenly brought back to the present by Finn's curt question. 'Why?'

'Why what?' Fletch grinned. Standing beside Sydney he bent down and kissed her cheek.

'Oooh you like girls, you're always kissing her.' Finn observed.

'I do like girls, but I like your mother best,' he played along with the six-year-old.

'Are you going to marry her?' Fletch froze. Not because he didn't want to marry Sydney, but because he had learned just earlier in the day, he may no longer be eligible for the Entrepreneurs Visa. Not wanting to worry Sydney he had failed to mention it to her. He simply couldn't tell her the truth; he and Perry had lost the seventy million dollars of funding for their movie. The investor's funds had collapsed. Now his financial picture looked very grim. Sydney covered her face, out of the mouths of babes, 'Finn,' she chastised.

'Do you think I should marry her,' Fletch asked feigning innocence. he had wanted it only last night but today he had nothing to offer her.

'Yes, 'cause then you could be my Daddy.'

'I need some air,' Sydney stood up she had seen the look on Fletch's face. He felt like a heel.

A COLD BREEZE WHIRLED around, whipping all the autumn leaves up in swirling piles along the driveway. Sydney watched as Jamie's truck drove past her. Hardly lifting her head, she didn't acknowledge him. Simply pushing her hands deeper into the pockets of her jacket, she tried to ignore the annoying thoughts, struggling to garner more space in her head. She had seen the desperate look on Fletch's face when her dearly beloved six-year-old man of the house had asked Fletch what his intentions were. For the love of God, it felt so bloody embarrassing. From the expression on Fletch's face he had been caught completely off guard; he had no intentions towards her, apart from bedding her. She didn't notice Jamie double back.

'Sydney,' she jumped as she turned. Jamie drove slowly along beside her. 'Get in, you'll freeze.' He opened the door of his truck and without thinking she hopped in. He immediately pulled over on to the shoulder of the road.

'You look like you've got the worries of the world on your shoulders,' he said, leaning on the steering wheel with both hands.

'Sorry but I feel like I have the world's worries today.' Shrugging, she flicked her thick plait over her shoulder.

'What happened?' he wanted to know, imagining it may have something to do with the strange vehicle seen around the neighbourhood.

'It's nothing really, just something Finn said, I should be used to it by now,' she pushed up her lip and raised an eyebrow.

'Oh, did he ask Fletch to be his daddy?' Jamie chuckled.

'What makes you say that? It's not funny' she said annoyed. Then it dawned on her,

'Oh gees, he's asked you too?' Jamie smirked and Sydney flushed scarlet.

'It's bloody embarrassing,' she moaned.

'What did Fletch say?' Jamie sobered.

'I could see, he looked embarrassed he just said something lame. What did you say when Finn asked you?' she wondered.

'Something lame,' she gave him the side eye, 'well what could I say? Finn was all of about four years old at the time,' they both laughed.

'You've been up to something Jamie Dalton, spill the beans.'

'I asked your friend Sara out. Well, we couldn't go in level four but now...' his eyes sparkled.

'Good on you, she's lovely.' It cheered Sydney's heart to hear. She had introduced them months ago; Sara seem quite keen but Jamie not exactly being a fast mover, had dragged the chain. It took a long while to get his ex-wife out of his system and then it took him a few more years to realise the schoolgirl crush Sydney had on him had ended years ago, soon after she left school. But she still liked him they were good friends.

'I'll drive you home, they will be wondering where you are.' In seconds he arrived on her driveway and pulled up outside her front door. She climbed out.

THE STATE OF AMERICA during the COVID crisis alarmed the world if the evening news could be believed. But then the World Health Organization verified the situation. President Trump decided to pull out of WHO, blaming them for the state of the situation.

'Do you think we can persuade Perry to come home?' Sydney wondered aloud. 'I'm worried about him and none of us knows what's ahead.'

'He's considering it, we had the conversation just this morning,' Fletch told her.

Lifting the mugs off the coffee table she replied, 'I hope so.'
Sliding his hand around her waist he nuzzled her neck, she squirmed,
'I'm tired.' He stepped back, raising his hands away from her.

'Tired of me? or tired, tired?' He watched her turn away biting
her lip, 'you're upset with me, aren't you, because Finn want's me as
his father?' A half honest assessment, she knew.

'No, how could I begrudge him a father?' now she spoke the
truth. 'Good night.'

Fletch kept loading the dishwasher, wondering what Sydney
agonised over. When he had finished, he cleaned his teeth and
stripped off in his own room then climbed into bed alone, rolled
over and went to sleep.

Next morning after breakfast, Sydney attended to a few chores
then picked out a nice trans seasonal dress in a warm red, then she
sorted out something smart for Finn to wear. He grew constantly,
like a weed, so it took effort to keep up with him. She took extra care
over her appearance simply because she wanted Grant Winthrop to
report back in glowing terms. With her hair in an elegant soft bun at
her nape and just the right amount of makeup and pearl studs in her
ears she slipped into her stiletto heels giving her a few more inches.
Then she sent Finn, dressed and ready to go to Fletch's bedroom
which doubled as his office.

'We're ready to go when you are, mummy said.'

'Send mummy in, I want a word before we leave, please Finn.

Sydney stopped in the doorway, 'will you drive please?' she asked
as Finn scooted past her to his Leggo.

'You look lovely. How do you want to introduce me to Grant?'
He stood, dressed all in black, apart from his tan dress boots and tan
leather jacket.

'I'm not lying to him,' she sounded indignant.

'I don't want you to lie, but Sydney, we need to talk.' he held her
arms gently, looking into her warm brown eyes.

'Why? I know you don't love me,' her tone short.

'Are you asking me or telling me?' he devoured her with his soft blue eyes. She wanted him desperately. 'No, don't answer,' he said. Checking his tactical time piece he hurried her along, 'come on there are road works on the Pass.'

'There are always roadworks on that damned hill.'

The trip over the Pass was uneventful apart from the stern glances he shot her every few moments, like he had something eating at him. Had he not been honest and a decent bloke she would assume he was up to something. Who was she kidding, he was definitely up to something. Deciding to play the game, she closed her eyes considering what she would say to Tim's father, how many times over the years had she played this conversation in her mind?

When they arrived at the café Fletch announced,

'Finn and I will go ahead and get a separate table, in the adjoining room,' then looking at Finn he added, 'Mummy will join us when she has finished her meeting.' The pair went on ahead and Sydney waited a few moments before proceeding.

Setting off from the vehicle she heard a voice call her name,

'Sydney, I thought I recognised you. How well you look my dear, what a beautiful woman you have become.' Turning she offered her arms in a hug; she knew the older man didn't mean anything disparaging in his attempt at a compliment. Grant Winthrop saw Sydney through fresh eyes, she looked different to him now and he felt a stab of sadness at her no longer being in his life.

'Are you keeping well Mr. Winthrop?' she asked, as he pulled out a chair for her at a table near the fire. 'Please call me Grant. Thank you I'm well.'

'And Mrs Winthrop, is she well?' after they had passed the pleasantries and ordered coffee. Grant had noted she made no reference to Tim, and he volunteered, 'Tim's married, it's coming up three years soon.' She smiled and then asked.

'Do they have children?' Grant's face saddened and he waited till their drinks were set down on the table before replying,

'No sadly, they've been consulting a fertility specialist but...' he shrugged. Then looking at her hands for a ring he commented, 'Not married?'

She smiled and reassured him. 'I have someone, but what I came to talk to you about is...' He nodded realising her personal life had never been open for discussion. 'When I resigned from Winthrop and Partners, I was pregnant, with Timothy's child.' Immediately his expression changed, his eyes narrowed and his jaw set. 'Tim and I had been seeing each other for about three months.'

Grant interrupted her, 'seeing each other I take it is a euphemism for sleeping together.'

'Yes, exactly and given your policy on fraternising in the office, Tim wanted to be sure of how we felt before he went to you with our changed circumstances.' Grant had his elbow on the table and his hand cupped around his mouth in a closed expression. 'So, after three months I went to the family planning clinic to get the appropriate contraception. Not only did I turn out to be ten weeks pregnant, but I also had chlamydia.' Sydney watched the expression on Grant's face become hostile. 'I'm telling you this because it has a bearing on matters. I took the course of antibiotics and the chlamydia problem disappeared but not the pregnancy. Tim became furious with me; he blamed me for getting pregnant as though he'd had nothing to do with it and demanded I had a termination. I refused and we had a row. In the middle of this debacle my parents were killed on a fishing trip. I decided to move back home and have the baby. Tim yelled furiously telling me because I refused his help in getting a termination, I could go to hell. He wanted nothing to do with me.' She could see the man looked torn his only child had been a big disappointment.

'Why are you telling me this now? Did you not think you could come to me, back then?' he said sadly, on a sigh.

'Oh, I thought about it alright, but I didn't trust Tim. After his almost violent outburst at me I felt I couldn't trust him not to interfere. He steadfastly refused to have anything to do with me or our child. You and I have both watched him manipulate witnesses and show them up in a poor light to get his desired result. I wrote a statement outlining all the details in the event of my death or in the event Tim reappeared on the scene, for whatever reason, along with a recording I made of the last time we spoke. I did it on my phone it's not the best quality, but his voice is distinct, and his intentions and attitude are clear.' Sydney had said her piece and now Grant appeared annoyed.

'Your recording would not be admissible in court.'

'Who needs court? there are other ways to skin a cat in the twenty first century digital world,' She sipped her drink. 'We both know it won't come to that. You asked why now?' Then she went on and told him about the phone call and the strange cars, one of which belonged to a private detective she knew, because Ben Howarth had used him.

Grant sat for a moment fingering the handle of his cup.

'Do you think chlamydia can cause infertility?' he wondered aloud.

'Yes, according to the literature it can, Tim was my first... but we both know about Tim and women. He did get treated as soon as I told him, apparently,' she explained.

Grant sat thinking for a moment. His expression brightened.

'Please can I meet my grandson? his tone now mellowed.

'I hoped you would ask, he's here.'

'What, here in the café?' she nodded and stood up. Fletch caught her eye and she beckoned them. Finn ran over to his mother and Fletch arrived a few short strides behind him.

'Finn, this is your grandfather. What do you want him to call you?' she asked noting Fletch stood behind Finn.

'Grandpa call me grandpa.' He beamed, fascinated with the boy who studied him intently.

'Hi ya,' Finn managed, coyly hiding his face in his mother's bosom.

'Fletch Carter,' Fletch grinned, offering his hand which the older man took, noting the accent.

'You're American,' then still holding Fletch's hand he noted a large fraternity ring with West Point 2001 on it.

'You're a West Point graduate,' the older man's face full of admiration.

'Yes sir, I am.' Grant let go of Fletch's hand and they both sat down.

'I've never met a West Point graduate before, where did you two meet?' he asked, curious.

'Sydney's brother and I are close friends,' he said. 'Would you like to join us for lunch? Fletch added, then he turned to Finn.

'Tell me what you'd like for lunch, son,' Fletch said in a calculated statement of ownership.

'A burger and fries please.' Grant sat intrigued by Finn. he looked the image of Tim at the same age. A wave of emotion washed over him, remembering a delightful child.

'Catherine would love to meet this little man,' his voice faltered.

'Has Sydney told you about my son? Grant asked Fletch.

'Yes, sir she has.' Fletch looked directly at Sydney for her reaction.

'I hoped you could act as intermediary between Tim and us,' she swept her hand around including Fletch and Finn. The luncheon conversation stayed general with small talk. Grant seemed interested in Fletch as much as Finn and suddenly, Sydney felt like a schoolgirl taking her date home for the first time. As Grant questioned him about his life and prospects, Fletch answered showing the utmost respect and humility. Sydney listened, seeing a different side of this man, a side seen by the rest of the world. Not the man covered in wood dust and workshop grease who fed the chooks and played ball with Finn.

On the journey home she sat quiet and a little frightened. Why would this flash decorated soldier want to stay at Boar Gully Farm when the movie making world had become his oyster? Fletch had never talked about his adventures in the army. When Grant Winthrop asked questions, she saw the man in a whole new light. The contacts he had made around the world in Government and showbusiness never came up before and she had never asked the questions Grant did. The more she thought about this public side of his life, the more convinced she became Fletch Carter could never include her in his life. The boring little homebody, what could she have to offer him?

Chapter Fourteen:

Grant Winthrop had half expected Sydney to report an embarrassing tale of a staff member complaining in retrospect about Tim forcing his unwanted attentions on her. A 'Me Too' case.

Never in a million years did he expect Sydney to have given him a long-awaited grandchild. If Tim had come to him seven years ago, well he would have huffed and puffed, but Sydney, he always liked and respected her. He would have moved heaven and earth to make it work. She must have loved Tim. Why couldn't Tim have told him? Well, this time at least, he felt pleased with the result. Finn behaved like a delightful child. Polite and articulate, not to mention the living image of his father at the same age.

Arriving at his impressive home on Oriental Parade overlooking the harbour, he felt surprised to see Tim's car parked in the visitor's space allocated to his apartment. Tim and his father had been working from their homes as required and apart from no client contact it had been a very workable arrangement.

Entering the light filled living room with its panoramic view of Wellington, he glanced around the room. Catherine his wife of forty-five years, looked anxious and drawn. Tim's wife Amanda sat, lips pursed, jaw set ready to brook no challenges.

'Amanda has some alarming news' Catherine said, voice agitated.

'Oh yes,' Grant said questioningly, almost sure he knew what the woman would say. As Catherine twisted a tissue in her fingers, her face tear stained, turned to him.

'I could hardly believe it. How could Sydney do this to us, after everything we did for her over the years, treated her like family.' Her voice cracked and she sniffed. 'You tell him Amanda, I -I can't' her voice faltered, on the verge of tears.

'Tim never told you at the time, he had an affair with Sydney when she worked as his PA. Well, hardly an affair, both were single, and he wanted to come clean and tell you because he claimed he loved her. Sydney begged him to say nothing, because of the office politics and the rules. When her parents were drowned in the horrible boating accident Tim knew something had happened. She'd met someone else, some cop. He noticed something between them at the funeral.' Amanda feigned hurt, biting her lips and covering her face with her hands.

'Poor Tim, Sydney doesn't deserve his child. Anyway, you know the rest, remember how devastated Tim became when she resigned and told you she wanted to use her annual leave and her family bereavement to avoid coming back to the office. He even went to her house; she told him to get out, she didn't want to see him again and claimed he was the one being unfaithful.'

'Where's all this leading Amanda?' Grant didn't understand his daughter-in -law's charade.

'Tim's got a son Sydney's been keeping from us all these years, depriving us of our own flesh and blood.' Now Catherine cried almost hysterical.

'How do you know? Grant asked plainly.

'I heard a rumour, someone said she had a six-year-old son, so I did the math and Tim hired a private detective. Look at these pics,' Amanda pulled out her phone.

'How could she deny him his child, he's always wanted children. I won't let the witch deprive him of his son, possibly the only son he'll ever have.' By now Grant Winthrop had had enough.

'Why are you telling us this Amanda? Does Tim even know you're here? I know about Sydney's child.' He had tired of Amanda's games.

'Do you know why Tim's infertile?' she accused, her voice at screaming pitch. 'I bet you Sydney never discussed her STD history with you.' Amanda stood agitated and pacing the room. Grant wondered if she taken something, or had she been drinking? She enjoyed alcohol.

'Stop moving around. Sit still Amanda, tell me honestly what's troubling you? Have you been drinking?' Suddenly furious she mumbled something to the effect she wouldn't stay to be insulted and maligned by a man who had obviously made up his mind about her. Slamming the door, she left. Grant sat flabbergasted.

'I always wondered what the hell Tim saw in Amanda, she's such a lightweight. Scatty as a two-bob watch, as my father used to say. Get Tim over here, I'll stop her from driving.' Handing Catherine his mobile phone he hurried towards the door to stop Amanda driving.

'Don't worry Grant, she left her keys here,' Catherine pointed to the coffee table. Then she scrolled through Grant's photos. She saw the three pics, Finn and Sydney, the family of three and Finn by himself. 'Oh Grant, what a lovely family, I always liked Sydney,' she enthused.

'Rubbish, that's not what you said ten minutes ago,' Grant countered as Catherine sniffed.

'Well, I'm just so confused. I don't know who to believe.' She blew her nose on the tissue.

'Believe Sydney, she never kept Finn from us.' Grant had known Tim had been aware all along where Sydney lived and where she worked. 'The woman knows the law; Tim is entitled to see his child. He chose not to until now and what motivated him now? The fact he and Amanda are having fertility issues or did Amanda have another agenda? Sydney could sue Tim for back maintenance.' Grant Winthrop didn't think money motivated her. What motivated Sydney had always been her child and she had plenty of time to plan how she would deal with Tim. Grant stood up and pored himself a stiff whisky.

'Catherine, the child I saw today behaved like a happy well-adjusted little boy and Sydney is relaxed about you meeting your grandson.' Sitting in his leather wingback chair he sipped his whisky, and wondered how this new family dynamic would play out, as he watched out of his window at Amanda getting into a taxi on the Parade.

WHEN SYDNEY AND THE boys, as she referred to them arrived home to Boar Gully, they all changed back into farm clothes. Finn, a little worn out by the excitement of going out to lunch, settled in his room playing with his Leggo as the bitterly cold day only grew colder. Mercury snored a little in front of the fire complete with plastered leg and lampshade collar. The pooch hardly moved when Sydney backed up the log burner. She then set about doing some office work. Jobs had been drying up and she worked around the edges of her life, doing anything Ben Howarth needed as soon as it came to hand. Fletch had gone outside to cut wood. She could tell something painful ate at him and decided to let him stew. Sydney recognised, much as she wanted him, she had no real expectations of him. Still, he seemed to need to somehow justify his relationship with her, not the other way around. And why discuss it with Finn? The boy had been confused enough. It annoyed her Fletch had asked him questions like whether he should marry her or not. Sydney thought Fletch meant it to be funny, but she saw no humour in it. Also, she thought it strange Finn had asked no questions about his 'new' grandfather.

Fletch had been gone an hour. Feeling sorry for him out in the cold Sydney made him a mug of coffee. Thinking he would be working in the shed she took the steaming brew out to him. There he stood, legs apart, stripped to his waist in the freezing cold swinging an axe like he had something to prove. Never before had she seen his strong torso in action like this. Muscles moving in a rhythmic mechanical fashion, sweat glistening on his skin in the crisp air. He had chopped wood enough for a month or more. With every punishing blow of the axe, he let out a little grunt. Oh, he looked mad about something.

'Fletch,' she called because he hadn't noticed her or if he had, he ignored her.

'You'll catch your death of cold,' she called, holding up the mug no longer steaming but tepid warm. How long had she been standing there watching him? Thanking her, he took the mug in both hands and gulped it down in several large swigs. Then he wiped his mouth with the back of his hand. Giving her back the mug he grabbed her and delivered a punishing coffee flavoured kiss. There felt nothing gentle about it. With her hands still gripping the mug she couldn't move until he released her. He stopped, realising she strained against him.

'I'm sorry I didn't mean to...' His eyes locked on hers and, in an instant, she understood he was not angry with her, something else troubled him. Sydney dropped the mug and put her arms around his neck, standing on tip toes she kissed him back.

'Come inside and get a warm shower,' she whispered as a lazy smile broke out across his face.

'Alone?' he asked.

'Afraid so soldier,' her eyes sparkled, 'but maybe when school returns...'

...

The kitchen, come family living space, felt warm and cosy. The smell of something tasty cooking filled the room. Fletch sat at his computer while Finn watched Peppa Pig on his I pad. Someone knocked on the front door. Getting up from her knitting, Sydney answered it. Now the rain pelted the roof and so did hail stones. Surprised to see Ryan in uniform, looking sombre, she invited him in.

'Is Fletch in?'

'Where else would he be?' Sydney flashed him a weak smile.

'Yeah, I suppose it's not like he's got a lot of options.' Ryan had been thinking about it.

'Look can I speak to him alone in the front room?'

'But there is no fire on in there, it's freezing,' she protested. 'I can offer you some hot stoup after if you have time.' she watched his eyebrow go up.

'Stoop?' he queried.

'Yeah, real thick beef and vegetable soup, almost a stew,' Sydney told him. It sounded better than what he had planned.

'Thanks, sounds good, I'll wait for Fletch in the formal lounge.' Something made Sydney tap Fletch on the shoulder and point to the door with her head, finger on her lips so as not to alert Finn. He would have been all over Ryan with boyish enthusiasm.

Frowning Fletch stood up. he had heard the door and Sydney greeting someone, but he hadn't listened, although he had a fair idea who called. When he stepped into the hallway, he could see Ryan standing in the formal lounge. Apprehensively, Fletch closed the door behind him and the two men sat down.

'I did as you asked me on the phone yesterday.' Ryan looked worried. I rang your apartment and then when I got no answer, I called the local police. To say they're a bit overwhelmed is to severely understate the situation. Covid is stretching their resources, but I managed to get an officer, a female to go to his apartment, I think it's actually your apartment. The Super let her in. It appears Perry has not been at the apartment for days, possibly a week.' Ryan took out his notebook.

'You said Perry had missed two scheduled skype calls,' he read from his notes. 'Tuesday and yesterday, am I right?'

Fletched sighed. 'Yes, Perry told me the funding for our next project has evaporated because our equity partner has gone into voluntary administration.' He shrugged, 'economically the world is in chaos. We both know Perry is mentally stable but.... he did sound upset,' Fletch trailed off and Ryan spoke.

'He's vague, thoughtless and definitely not as strong as his twin. Sydney's resilient and single minded. Perry's a dreamer and without his sister he wouldn't be making movies and following his dream.' Fletch could see which twin Ryan favoured.

'So, you think I should tell her Perry's missing. She'll have me checking all the hospital admissions in the state,' he wryly conceded.

'Already being done, and nothing so far.' Ryan sighed. 'How does the loss of your main investor affect your income? he wanted to know, looking at Fletch who shrugged and frowned, looking flat.

'There's another thing, Perry did not touch our funds and our last project is finished but everything's on hold over there. No promotion money is being spent until the movie theatres are open again. If I leave the country, I might not be able to get back in here. My visa situation has changed, and soon I will need to reapply. The Government here appreciates the situation and Perry, and I were busy working on the logistics, so, I can continue on the same visa. He planned on coming back here to cast New Zealanders and some Australians but without funding we can't proceed.' Fletch's brows furrowed, and his jaw muscles twitched.

'What are you living on?'

'I do have some capital and my Army pension, it's not huge and I don't pay rent here. Perry and I had an agreement, he lives rent free in my apartment and I live here. But I won't be able to stay. Unless I can get the visa sorted.' Ryan admired the man's honesty.

'Have you told Sydney?' he asked. Fletch shook his head.

'I needed to talk to Perry first. I will talk with her, but it's complicated.'

'Don't tell me you're sleeping with her.' Suddenly he had a different picture.

'I wouldn't tell you even if I were, it's not your bloody business. If you must know I promised her twin,' Fletch stopped short realising the full implications of his promise. 'I promised Perry I'd look out for her and Finn if anything happened to him.'

RYAN CALLED THE STATION on the landline, then washed his hands and sat down at the table.

'I told them I'm taking my dinner break here so for the next little while I'll be off the air.' Having served four bowls of her famous 'stoup' Sydney set down a large cobb loaf on the table. It had been hollowed out and filled with a delicious creamy mixture of tasty cheese and finely chopped onion with bacon bits cooked in thick cream with herbs and spices. 'I haven't had this for years, your mother used to make it, gee it's good. Just the ticket for a cold night.' Ryan dripped the creamy mixture on his chin, while Fletch cut a small section for Finn who said he didn't feel very hungry.

'I had a big lunch with grandpa,' the child admitted.

'Who?' Ryan didn't think he'd heard correctly. 'Your grandfather?' he asked as Fletch covered Sydney's hand with his under the table.

'Grandpa is what I call him,' Finn announced. Ryan refused to let it go, this little gem came out of left field. He needed it clarified.

'Where does grandpa live?' Ryan looked directly at Sydney who sat absolutely mute.

'Over the hill. Tomorrow Mercury is going back to the vet, to get his stitches out.' Fletch changed the subject, Sydney found her voice.

'Yes, thank you Ryan, the dog's doing well, thanks to you.'

Ryan wanted to know more about Finn's grandfather, and he wouldn't drop it easily.

'Is he nice grandpa? Did you go to his house for lunch?'

'He's okay and he made me a paper aeroplane with my serviette, but he liked Fletch's ring best.'

Funny? Sydney thought. Grant Winthrop did seem very interested in Fletch. Ryan studied Fletch's hands no ring.

'I took it off to shower,' he said, seeing Ryan looking at his hands, 'Truth is, I got a blister chopping the wood' he said embarrassed.

'I'm not surprised, he split at least two months of logs in about an hour.' Sydney took his hand and turned it over, he had a blister alright, a big one.

'I'll fix it later,' she suggested quietly.

Finn, with lids drooping looked on the cusp of falling asleep so his mother took him to get changed into his pyjamas. Fletch promised to read him a story, and Ryan helped him clear the table.

'I'll wait here until we have discussed Perry, then I must go,' he told Fletch. 'He's not booked on any incoming flights from the states, I've had those checked too. I'm worried about him.'

'Do you have any ideas about what may have happened to him?' Fletch asked.

Just then Sydney returned with a book "The BFG by Roald Dahl."

'Just read one Chapter tonight the book's over two hundred pages. This will keep him interested in quite a few days.' Sydney handed Fletch the book. 'He's waiting for you.'

As soon as Fletch left the room Ryan started with the questions.

'Since when has Finn had anything to do with his father's family?' Ryan didn't mean for it to sound quite like he blamed anyone, and Sydney didn't need him to know anything yet.

'Since Fletch,' she said then added 'don't Ryan, it's all pretty new. Don't ask, not yet.' Turning her attention to the dog, a neutral topic, and the boar, they chatted while she made a fresh pot of coffee.

Chapter Fifteen:

When Fletch re-joined them he yawned, then he sat next to Sydney on the settee and took her hand. 'I asked Ryan to do something for me. You know how I skype Perry at least twice a week? Well, he's missed two of the scheduled work skypes. I phoned him on his mobile and landline, no reply.' Sydney sat concerned but not panicking until Fletch went on, 'the last time we spoke, Perry told me our equity partners in Devil's Moon had gone into voluntary administration and our funding had evaporated.'

'What do you mean evaporated, you had a contract,' she said indignantly.

'Yes, but we have not received any money yet,' his voice sounded sadly resigned.

'They were due to settle on it, one third in July 2020 and one third each year till 2022 when we would get the final third. They have lost their money so they cannot invest. There is nothing we can do. We're unlikely to get another backer till the world gets back on its axis. It's Perry I'm worried about.' Fletch told her quietly.

'Don't worry about him, I can just imagine he's running around like a headless chook looking for another backer,' she said logically. 'He will be scoping out his big plan, he's not like us, he'll be telling Bill Gates or someone with his sort of money why they should be investing in Devil's Moon. He's very convincing, and he's passionate about it too.' Looking at the two serious faces she began to feel a little concerned.

'Why are you both looking at me like there is something you are not telling me, you don't think I'm right, do you?'

103

'We're both worried he hasn't been in his apartment for a week. What say he's in a hospital sick somewhere Sydney? We need to cover all the bases.' Ryan had a point, she could see.

'Look Hunny, I don't want to alarm you but the pandemic in the States is tracking too fast for accurate records. It has spread rapidly across California. Experts say the true number of people infected is unknown and much higher than official tallies. The population of Hollywood is similar to Wellington and already California have over 200,000 cases confirmed. Sure, the deaths are mainly in the older population but there are young people too.' Pulling her close with his arm around her, he gave her a reassuring squeeze.

'Do you think he might be sick somewhere?' the awful possibility struck her. Ryan watched them together and realised the pair had become close and knew he might have to be the one to pick up the pieces if Sydney's world imploded. Fletch appeared to be stuck between a rock and a hard place.

After Ryan left to go back to his work Sydney, seemed to discount any unfavourable outcome. How could Fletch tell her his problems?

At eight pm the land line rang, and she answered it.

'Hello Sydney, do you know who this is?' the voice asked.

'Timothy Winthrop,' she answered her hands shaking. Fletch looked up from his book when he heard the name. He watched as she took a deep breath and steeled herself.

'What can I do for you?' she asked, knowing what he wanted.

'I want to see my son,' his tone was clipped.

'Oh, he's your son now, is he?' She couldn't help getting lippy with Fletch there.

'Don't take that attitude Sydney, it won't change anything. When can I see him?' Nothing had changed, Tim still as bossy as ever, but at least he asked.

'It can't happen until the weekend after next as school returns on Monday, and besides, I'm working at the office next week.' Pleased with her confidence she sighed; silence descended at the other end.

'What about this weekend? Be reasonable Sydney, I have a case starting Monday and I'll be busy all through the following weekend.' Thinking about it, she didn't want to give him any ammunition if the situation became litigious. Tim wanted litigious, because he could afford to drag it out in Court. and she hadn't spoken to her legal colleagues Emma Jacobson or Ben Howarth, about the situation yet.

'The weekend... let me see' she pretended to be considering it but knew she had no option.

'Look can you come over the *hill*?' Thinking on her feet she didn't want him to come to the farm.

'We could meet you in Martinborough, but we'll have to book somewhere for lunch, they need bookings these days.' Not looking forward to it at all she added, 'will your wife be coming?'

'No, I'll be alone' he cleared his throat 'we're having a few issues at present and this child is important to me.'

'Too bad you didn't think so seven years ago.' I had a lucky escape, or we would both be scarred, she thought. 'Right Saturday twelve thirty at Medici, see you' she hung up. Fletch put his book down and patted the settee.

'Saturday, so soon huh?' He watched as she covered her face and sniffed back tears.

'He's such a bossy shit, it seemed too easy. I don't feel comfortable.' Complaining she picked up her knitting. Immediately Fletch took it from her and set it down again.

'It's been a long hard day, let's sit and talk.' Putting his arm around her, he wanted to spell out the worst-case scenario for Perry, and also with his visa situation but as he studied her face, he could see she couldn't deal with it tonight. Not now with Tim on the scene again, after seven years, the man who had hurt her so badly, and left her pregnant at the same time she grieved the loss of her parents. Fletch thought the man's behaviour unconscionable and he wanted to sort him out and rearrange his facial features. Experience told him there were better ways to deal with the Timothy Winthrops of this world and still support Sydney and Finn. More than anything he wanted to make them his family, but with Covid19 raging like wildfires in the United States and with no movie, no income and his visa running out and unlikely to be renewed, he had nothing to offer her. Knowing he needed to be honest with her he pulled her closer. His dark blue eyes looked into her warm expressive face. His heart wrenched, and taking her face in his hands he kissed her long and lovingly. No way he could tell her tonight. Also, no way he could make love to her when he couldn't offer her a future. It went against everything good in him. After a few more kisses and before his aching crotch could no longer be ignored, he stood up and huskily said 'goodnight.'

TRYING DESPERATELY to understand why Fletch didn't seem to want to be in her bed anymore, Sydney reasoned it had to be worrying about Perry. Well, he might be her twin, but she didn't worry as much as Fletch appeared to. Perry, always famous for having a flash of brilliance and coming up with some wild new idea where he needed to traipse halfway across the world to act upon it. Only now the world looked a scary place and even her secure job at Howarth and Partners took a hit. Ben said he needed to reduce everyone's hours; the whole executive team were taking a twenty percent pay cut. The Government had offered some sort of wage subsidy, but Ben needed to work through it. The way they would action the cuts would be first, they would take their annual leave, well at least a week of it. Sydney planned to take one day a week for five weeks.

Ben, always honest with them, said the executive team knew the billing hours they were charging for and the cases they were dealing with. Business activity had dried up. Everyone hoped it would be a short-term thing as Emma Jacobson had suggested when they discussed it on the phone that afternoon.

Not wanting to mention it to Fletch she planned to talk to Jamie Dalton, because he had a good business head and the Dalton's were only waiting until Perry returned. Then they either resigned for the lease on the farm or they would purchase it, as per their original agreement, now the twins had turned thirty-one.

Tossing and turning in her bed she couldn't sleep. Sidney tipped toed down the hall to the kitchen to make a warm drink. The house felt chilly as she stood in her nightie, putting more logs into the wood burner. Feeling stupid as she waited for the logs to catch, Sydney wrapped the settee throw around her shoulders then boiled the jug, not even bothering to turn on the light. When you live in a place all your life you can do so much without light. Standing up from the fire she turned as a hand covered her mouth, she would have screamed and woken Finn. It gave her a huge fright and although she realised Fletch stood behind her, her heart pounded. Holding her firm, he whispered an apology for scaring her. The warmth from his strong arms surrounded her. She turned looking into his concerned face she felt his warm bare chest against her.

'What are you trying to do?' he berated her. 'It's the middle of the night. I thought you were an intruder.' Snuggling into him she could smell his maleness and his soap. Drinking it in she wondered how she would ever survive without him. Fletch's rugged face and flinty dark, midnight blue eyes glinted in the flickering light of the log burner. This man looked tough, yet he had shown her his gentle side and he and Finn had become close. Ah Finn, she wondered what kind of characteristics his birth father had given him. The handsome physical ones were already obvious, the less attractive ones not yet evident. Breathing in the essence of Fletch she wished Timothy Winthrop had not reappeared on the scene. The germ of an idea formed in her mind. Instead of thinking it through she burst out with it.

'Fletch, marry me? He flinched as surely as if she had stuck the cold steel blade of a knife into his gut.

'Sydney' he groaned sounding pained.

'I know you don't love me, but I think you're at least attracted to me,' her voice light, upbeat.

'This way you could get permanent residency and Finn loves you. You would make such a good father.' Once again, he said her name pushing her gently and gripping her shoulders.

'Sydney, I can't, I simply can't. It's a noble gesture but it's wrong. I have nothing to offer you, and those kinds of alliances don't stand the test of time.'

'Bollocks. Well, forget it then if it's too hard for you,' she sniffed. 'Frankly, you're a lot like Perry the more I think about it. Both dreamers, dreams are fine but there are more ways to skin a cat. Have you thought about changing visa categories by applying under two sections, both the entrepreneurial visa and the skilled migrant category? Think about all those fancy 3D computer animated programs you use, especially Maya. We have a burgeoning film industry in this country, but you might need to sideline the trip to your dream.' Pulling away from him, she went to the jug, 'want a hot chocolate?'

'Mm thanks' he said. Seeing a basket of clean clothes on a chair he rummaged through it found a tee shirt and pulled it on. 'To be honest I hadn't thought of changing categories,' he sounded surprised. 'As for the marriage proposal, thanks Sydney but as I said, no thanks, all my assets are in the States, if the country implodes any more, I might have nothing. I don't even have a decent suit here.' Handing him the hot chocolate she gave him a wry look.

'Oh, for God's sake, when will you realise, you're talking about *stuff* not people, families, or relationships. At least I have my priorities right.' Her mocking tone quietened. 'When will you understand we have so many options here. You have a myopic view of things,' Sydney's voice trailed off.

Thinking about what Fletch had said about his dreams she understood what losing his dream would mean to her twin, but she couldn't truly understand it because she felt blessed. These last few days Fletch Carter struggled with reconciling his change of status from take "charge entrepreneur with money and ideas," to a jobless foreigner in a tiny country at the bottom of the world. Now here, with the cuddly firebrand offering him love and a life with her and the young boy who wanted him to be his daddy, he felt humbled and sad because he wanted this life more than anything. Life with a woman who loved him and a family. Feeling disenfranchised and sorry for himself would never be an option. He could accept anything. Pain, sickness, struggling even crawling on his belly towards his goals but giving up had never been an option. Ranger school had ingrained in him never to give up, no matter how bad the options.

'Is the chocolate good?' her mischievous smile touched him.

'Yeah, and the big slosh of brandy helps.' She snuggled into him on the settee as he spoke.

'Are you having really vivid dreams? I am. they're so strange not scary exactly, but not normal either. I've heard lockdown and the strange times are doing this,' she prattled on.

'What on earth brought this on?' he asked interested.

'I simply wanted you to know, I think I understand, and I want to help. We've come a long way, you and I. We didn't really like each other to begin with.' He found her honesty endearing. 'I saw the way you viewed me as though I looked like some sloppy hayseed and Finn, an annoying brat.'

'I did not,' he protested but only weakly because he saw truth in it.

'Bullshit,' she re-joined, 'well I can tell you I thought you were from the body image police, and I didn't cut the mustard.' He closed his eyes, had he been so transparent?

'I got the distinct impression you disapproved of me, and I couldn't understand why Perry had thrown us together...until I got to know you.' Biting her lip in her familiar way she asked, 'Perry, he will be alright, won't he? Truth be told I'm scared stiff.' Her voice cracked, and she pulled the blanket around herself fighting back tears. Fletch enveloped her in his arms and it felt so good, so reassuring. 'Let's get to bed.' he said. Oh gees, *bed* what a Freudian slip.

'Yes, please, I need you to hold me,' taking his hand she pulled him up from the settee. He wanted her with a passion and yet he felt torn he should swallow his pride and accept her offer, even if it seemed wrong. Dropping the throw, she climbed into his bed as he stripped off the tee shirt. When they were together at last, and his inhibitions departed with a slight pang of conscience. 'Sydney hunny,' he whispered 'you deserve more than this. The truth is I have feelings for you...'

Before he could finish, she groaned and added, 'I can feel a *but* coming and before you deliver it let me say this, I know the timing is a bitch. It's like war, this maybe all the time we have, let's make the most of it. Let me help you accomplish your dream. You will get another backer for Devil's Moon but *when* is another question. In the meantime, why don't you buy a few antiques, restore them, then sell them online. You could advertise you do restorations too.'

Hearing her chatter he mused, 'shush, you're making me tired.' He could never make his hobby a career, he didn't have sufficient passion for it. She had gone quiet. He hugged her, within minutes he saw she had fallen asleep. Fletch didn't know what hurt more. Not to admit he loved her or find he had been relegated to the friend's zone. Anyway, he might soon have to return to the States and leave his little family behind.

Chapter Sixteen:

At breakfast, much to Fletch's surprise Jamie Dalton arrived at the kitchen door.

'Here's your milk Sydney, I'll take Finn back with me to save you taking him to Mum's cottage.' He sounded like he'd been up for hours.

'Great thanks, you fancy a coffee?' she grinned at him as he pulled out a chair at the table.

'Thanks, will you be away all day or what?' he wanted to know.

'No. Tell your mother I'll pick him up at four.' She handed him his coffee.

'Have I missed something here?' Fletch poured himself a second coffee. 'Am I not looking after Finn.' Sydney shook her head then noticing a fleeting look of hurt, she bent to kiss him. Immediately Fletch's gaze turned to Jamie, and he watched Jamie smirk.

'Sorry, I thought I'd mentioned it, Nana Dalton is minding him today as preparation for school next week. Mrs Dalton's a teacher, she taught Jamie and Perry and me and Ryan, in fact everyone over twenty-one and under fifty around here she taught before she retired. Besides, it will give you a free day to do what you like. Jamie and Sara are coming to dinner tonight and Olive is having a sleepover with Finn so Sara will be free.' she smirked at Jamie.

'You've thought of everything.' Jamie breathed quietly then he bent down and pulled his socks up so she wouldn't see the smile on his face.

'I certainly hope so' she muttered, knowing Sara and Jamie could be alone together tonight.

Half an hour later, dressed in a navy trouser suit cream silk blouse, with her hair up and her laptop under one arm and high heels in her hand she commented, 'Mercury doesn't look very happy. Let him stay inside if you go out, he looks a bit peaky.'

'And you look quite stunning.' He bent to kiss her; she fingered the scar through his lip.

'Did I tell you how handsome this scar makes you look?' Fixing him with a naughty look she said, 'I'm looking forward to tonight, for all sorts of reasons.'

BY THE TIME FINN AND Sydney burst through the door it had passed four o'clock. Each were armed with bags of goodies and shopping which they dumped on the kitchen counter. Mercury hobbled over to greet Finn and Sydney commented, 'he looks happier than he did this morning.' Fletch looking up from his book he appeared happy and relaxed.

'Welcome home sweetheart.' His lazy American drawl sounded so sexy.

'You look good, how was your day? I can see you've been busy. Thanks for mowing the grass. did you have fun on the ride-on-mower?' she enthused, watching him greet Finn with a hug.

'Oh, look, you even put fresh flowers on the table' bubbling away she smiled.

'Thank you, and the wood box is full and the laundry's all folded. You're a keeper.'

He bent and covered her lips the only way to silence her.

'I've had a good day and I've had a call from Perry, he went to stay with Carl Thalburg at Temple Lake, apparently, they had internet issues. He said he needed to get away from the city to think and Carl had some worthwhile ideas about Devil's Moon. They're working through them. The internet at Temple Lake is fine now some construction workers accidently cut the lines. Carl's family have a lake house it's isolated and they have supplies enough for months he said. They plan on hunkering down. They feel safe there. I would have called you, but we just got off the phone.' Looking down at her he could feel her relief and she could see his, written all over his face.

'Sara and Jamie will be here shortly. I need to change into something comfortable.' She called from the hallway as she ran off excited, 'I feel like life is getting back to normal.' He could hear the smile in her voice. Finn sat patting his old pooch. Mercury, although only eight years old, in dog years he clocked around fifty-six. he had been Sydney's mother's dog.

Fletch felt so good about his conversation with Perry he followed Sydney to her room. He watched as she began to strip off, not seeing him as she turned her back away. Hearing the click of the privacy lock she turned around. Seeing the look on his face she knew he wanted her. He moved towards her, she stood in her bra and knickers, she stood silently drinking him in for about a minute. The man dressed to impress in his clean jeans and smart boots, his dark fine wool top tight over his muscly chest.

'Fletch, we have visitors due in less than an hour.' She watched as he raised an eyebrow. He hadn't even laid a finger on her, yet her heart beat a tattoo, pounding her chest. The heat he radiated grew intense. Closing her eyes to escape his penetrating gaze, she felt his arms around her, holding her gently. At the feel of his breath on her lips she tilted her face towards him. Overcome by his sensual aftershave her lips parted ever so slightly as he covered her mouth. The kiss tasted intoxicating, slow and gentle, then grew in urgency along with his need.

'Let's shower' he whispered', his voice a low rumble as he too started stripping off.

'Mum, where are you?' Finn called from outside her door. For a split second they froze,

'I'm getting a shower Finn, go and play... I won't be long...' her voice trailed off and now in a frenzy they stripped, closed the en suite door and with urgency continued where they left off.

Warm steam filled the en suite and muted their ragged breathing as an ecstatic little cry escaped her. In minutes, panting and spent he groaned, 'protection.'

'Don't panic, I went on the pill a month ago.' Relieved, Fletch sank back against the tiled wall as the water beat down on them. 'Thank heavens.'

They emerged from her bedroom, clean and dressed, faces still flushed.

'Will you sleep with me tonight in my bed?' she asked.

'Sleep, no,' he grinned. Sydney knew what he meant. The pent-up tension of the past week vanished with their sexual energy but they both wanted to go there again, however a small child, a woofing dog and dinner guests meant they needed to hold it together.

A cold wind whipped around the hills rattling the windows of the old villa. Fletch went off and lit the second log burner in the room they called the 'good room.' it helped to keep the old homestead warm, as it lacked insulation in the walls. Meanwhile, Sidney prepared some paua fritters. Fletch called them abalone. When Jamie went fishing, he always gave a few paua to Sydney she had frozen the minced meat of the mollusc to make her entrée. She simply added a little finely chopped parsley, an onion, half a cup of self-raising flour an egg and some milk. Scooping spoonful's of the mixture into a little heated oil she cooked the fritters then drained them on a paper towel and placed them in a warm oven to keep hot.

Looking into the fridge she saw with surprise a lump of dough and several small dishes of chopped up toppings. Fletch had remembered she usually had easy dinner on Friday nights, often home cooked pizza. Quickly she whipped some cream then made a chocolate sauce. One cup of sugar, a big nob of butter, slosh of cream and cook like fudge. It thickened too fast she added more cream. Then set it aside.

Finn yelled, 'they're coming up the driveway.'

Finn, Fletch and Sydney all appeared at the door to greet their visitors, Jamie drove Sara's sedan. Sara lifted Olive out of her seat and carried her to the porch. The cold rain made the weather was diabolical, Jamie had his arms full of gear. Finn and Olive hugged like siblings; well, they had been together as friends since their mothers gave birth to them a few days apart. Jamie hugged Sydney and Fletch followed his lead kissing Sara's cheek. Curious about this man, she gave Sydney an interested glance when the women hugged, and excited little voices ran down the hall.

'What is it about these times since lockdown? Sara wondered aloud.

we have all been so starved for hugs.'

'God knows, but I feel blessed. I hope it's behind us now.' Sydney held up the bottles of bubbly Jamie gave her. 'These look ... great,' she gushed. 'Thank you.'

'My pleasure, I'm not a fan, you know me a few beers, an occasional red wine,' he beamed.

Before long Olive and Finn were nibbling on crisps and sipping lemonade, in fits of laughter as they watched a cartoon about a bunch of dogs. The four adults sat on bar stools around the island bench, sipping bubbles and beers having the strangest catch up. All talking about their experiences from lockdown. Sara explained her parents were in Britain and their Prime Minister, Boris Johnson went around the countryside shaking everyone's hand. Sara's father, a semi-retired GP became distressed when Bo Jo as they referred to the Prime Minister, caught the dreaded Coronavirus. No one seemed surprised. The man had been lucky to survive.

116

'This herd immunity thing is never going to work.' she added and talked about the UK's pathetic attempts at eradicating the disease. They shared horror stories of online shopping and Jamie admitted as soon as the regulations allowed, he added Sara and Olive to his bubble.

'How did that work? Sara lives a good half hour's drive from here,' Sydney wanted to know as she moved to top up their glasses. Fletch took the bottle from her, doing the honours.

'It worked' Jamie said amused. Normally he told Sydney everything but since Fletch had moved in he didn't feel the need somehow. Sydney's joy for her friend was obvious. Sara thought Jamie pretty cute and hot even, but it took a global pandemic to get Jamie to acknowledge his true feelings. When Sydney served the nibbles of paua fritters, Fletch offered to construct the pizzas he had prepared. Jamie watched with scepticism.

'I thought you said you couldn't cook,' he accused sardonically.

'No, I said I *don't* cook, it's true. But I've been conscripted so we take turns now.' They all watched interested as he built the pizzas from the assembled ingredients he had prepared.

'Did you make the dough?' Sara wanted to know.

'I watched Sydney,' he said. Remembering a phone message from her work he passed it to her.

'I think you need to deal with this.' She could see the message from Emma Jacobson on a post it note. Excusing herself she phoned her from the scullery with the hands-free landline.

'Em, how did he take it?' Sydney had asked Emma to act for her in relation to Timothy Winthrop's paternity claim.

'He surprised me, he seemed so reasonable. He signed the agreement with only minor changes, he increased the amount of maintenance and asked for your bank account details, Of course I didn't give them, saying he could put the monies into the Howarth and Partners trust account for you.' Emma sounded stunned.

'He wants to see you alone before he meets Finn.'

'Oh, I expected nothing less,' Sydney said pragmatic as ever. 'I have a support person who will bring Finn.' She opened the scullery door to see Fletch putting the pizzas into the oven.

'Thanks Em, gotta go.'

'Don't let him bully you,' she said as her parting shot. But the only words Sydney registered were the last four words 'let him bully you' and she felt nervous. Sara read it in her expression. She knew Sydney had arranged to meet Finn's father after seven years, but she had no idea about the man.

'Don't worry you'll be fine, you're stronger now and Fletch is going with you, isn't he?'

'Yeah, whether she wants me there or not, I'm going,' he drawled.

As they sat around the dining table chatting and joking Jamie made the observation.

'Don't you think it's about time we knew the guy's name?'

Fletch watched Sydney's face. Buoyed by alcohol and the support of her friends she announced.

'It's Timothy Winthrop.'

Sara and Jamie processed the name. Jamie knew she worked for a law firm in Wellington but had completely forgotten who. Sydney had always worked in Carterton since Sara had known her.

Fletch had googled the man when Sydney told him. He read about his illustrious career. Sara and Jamie fell silent. Fletch busied himself getting ice cream and chocolate sauce for the children's dessert. The kids were too busy laughing and chatting to feel the vibe around the table.

Frowning, Jamie found his voice.

Sucking air in through his teeth he said on an expiration, 'Oh Lord.' He wiped his hand across his face as the enormity of the situation struck him. 'I understand your concern, not someone you would want to cross. Brilliant but a bastard.'

Sara elbowed him and he clapped a hand over his mouth.

'Oops, sorry kids.' Now compassion visible on his face.

'He's well heeled, can't you take him to the cleaners?'

Shaking her head Sydney said, 'there's no such thing as a free lunch. I couldn't afford his generosity. It would come at a price.' Fletch served the desserts and bent down and kissed her.

'Why now? Did the black four-wheel drive seen hanging around here have anything to do with it?' Jamie wanted to understand what had motivated the man after all this time.

'In my mind I thought I needed seven years, you know the Jesuit saying, "give me a child till the age of seven and I'll give you the man." So, I guess I should have prayed for eight years.' She set the dessert bowls down on the table. Sara could see how difficult for Sydney this situation appeared, so she asked Fletch to tell her about his movies.

'They're all different the next one could be a series, Devil's Moon also, it's animated.' He grinned at Sydney; he hadn't told her about the change.

'Since when? That's a new slant on it isn't it?' Sydney sounded surprised.

Fletch agreed. 'Yes, Carl Thalburg is a well-known animator and he and I have worked together before. I've been cogitating some ideas about income streams after your comments about the furniture restoration. I need to keep the furniture restoration as a hobby. Jamie if you had an alert on your device warning you when any wild pigs in the gully, would that be helpful? Sydney said the sows can get pretty grumpy when they have piglets.' Jamie agreed.

'I've been thinking about a prototype for a heat seeking drone to find animals in the gully, without risking man or dog.'

Listening, Jamie pulled his chair closer as Fletch elaborated.

'The drone could send a signal to your device, with pictures. Frankly, they don't cost much to make. The device could even take the beast out, although, I don't think it would be legal in this country. Still, I could fit it with a locator beacon so you could get close to it and deal with it.' Jamie liked the idea.

'It's not a new idea' Sydney countered, 'but if you checked out what's on the market and came up with a point of difference and priced them right, maybe.' She poured the coffees.

'Listen to you, Sydney Martin, the hardnosed businesswoman.' Jamie grinned.

'No, I need constructive feedback. I can build and programme any of these gadgets, just show me the problem and I'll find the solution,' Fletch said. Sara suggested next he'd be making a microchip for children so the parents could keep an eye on them. Fletched laughed.

'They are not new either, mine would take their temperatures, do their bloods and other vitals.'

'Oh gee, beam me up Scottie,' Sydney groaned and called, 'pyjamas and teeth cleaned kids. It's almost bedtime.'

Olive called out from the bathroom.

'Finn's got a wiggly tooth, he let me wiggle it, ooh gross' she giggled.

'Can Merkee sleep in our room Aunty Sydney?' Olive asked, keen to know. Thinking on her feet Sydney said, 'he's old and snores and hasn't been well so he needs to be near the log burner.'

By the time Jamie and Sara left for his farmhouse down the road at nine o'clock the kids were finally in bed. It would be another half hour before they were definitely asleep.

Chapter Seventeen:

Driving his new Ford Ranger into town Fletch silently caught little glimpses of Sydney sitting beside him. He noted her designer jeans, tan ankle boots with killer heels, and a bright red snug-fitting top highlighting her assets, he smiled. Sydney's thick dark hair hung smoothly down her back with bangs framing her face. Fletch understood exactly what Sydney planned. She intended Timothy Winthrop to see her as a desirable woman and definitely not the mumsy mother mouse he accused her of being. The faint but sensual fragrance of her perfume and her full glossy lips had him swallowing hard.

The little town buzzed in the crisp sunlit morning. He checked Finn in his car seat in the back. He too, wore new jeans and new leather dress boots. His navy-blue jersey in a fisherman's rib seemed to highlight his freshly trimmed blond hair.

'He's growing up,' Fletch's voice rumbled, jolting Sydney back to reality.

'Yes, he is. When we get there give me half an hour then join us. Like last time,' she said, distracted. He wished he could be there with her all the time. As Sydney helped Finn pull on his puffer jacket, she explained she had a meeting and when it finished Fletch would bring him to her and they would have lunch.

When she arrived at Medici, Tim had already seated himself. The café looked smaller than the last one where she had met with Tim's father. Fletch told the waitress he and Finn were waiting until Sydney and the gentleman had finished their meeting before they all got together for lunch. In the meantime, they would have a warm drink. He positioned himself in a corner with a good view of proceedings.

Fletch could see a big, tall, fair-haired man greet Sydney and take her jacket. The guy looked about his age, maybe older. Definitely not as fit, too well covered Fletch could see. He did have a certain refined presence; born with a silver spoon in his mouth, crossed Fletch's mind. He exuded confidence.

'Sydney, you look well. Let me help you with your jacket,' Tim appraised her, his vivid blue eyes sparkling, meanwhile thinking, she is so much more than I remember, she's quite lovely.

'How are you, Tim?' Oh lord, he has Finn's blue eyes or is it the other way around and the same chin. 'My lawyer told me you signed the agreement.' Suddenly the things she planned to say vanished. 'Why now Tim?' her warm brown eyes looked up at him.

'To be honest, it was not one single thing but a number of things. I guess lockdown started me thinking about my own mortality. Then the Duncan McKenzie case;' the whole country had been riveted to the case, a home invasion in a large arts and crafts style house in the upmarket suburb of Karori. The father had been shot in his own home by a masked man while his wife and children slept upstairs. The man had been seen by a neighbour, but no formal identification could be made. The family knew the man charged with the crime and Tim got him off the homicide charges despite the damning facts which later came to light. After the trial, the police said they were not looking for anyone else in relation to the crime.

'Your father said you and your wife were having fertility issues,' she stirred her coffee and Tim shrugged.

'Honestly, we have many issues and sadly, fertility is only one of them. They won't go away, and we have separated.' Full of natural empathy Sydney expressed sympathy.

'Don't be, the gods of karma,' he said. She frowned watching him finger the rim of his coffee cup thinking. 'When I said fertility problems, I meant to say it had not been one of Amanda's problems, she is expecting another man's child. You can see it's a complicated story.' Sydney thought it karma, definitely karma, she mused.

'What has the McKenzie case got to do with your paternity.'

'Nothing apart from the fact the McKenzie's have two little boys who now have no father. I began to think about them,' he said wistfully.

'But those little boys are entirely a separate matter from your defence of the accused,' she blurted. He smiled taking her hand. 'You always did have a way of making me feel better.' She tried to pull her hand away. 'Don't Sydney, I will always love the mother of my son.' Not knowing quite how to reply she squirmed in her seat, turning to look for Fletch.

'You got room for us?' his drawl comforted her. 'Hi, I'm Fletch Carter and this is Finn.' He turned to Finn 'sit next to the gentleman son.' *Son,* Tim got the message.

'Hi Finn, I think you met my father a couple of weeks ago. Grant Winthrop, you call him grandpa.' The boy looked confused, but he had lots of grandparents; the Daltons and the Murphy's, even Olive's Nana said she would be his Nana too.

'What do I call you?' Finn asked and Tim wanted desperately to get this right.

'You can call me Tim.' Tim flashed his electric blue eyes at Fletch and offered his hand. In fairness to Tim, he made a huge effort to talk to Finn who sensed his mother's unease. Then after a very awkward lunch Tim said he wanted some time with the child alone.

'No, it's too soon, you're a stranger' her eyes welled up. 'Please Tim, he's just a little boy.'

Turning to Fletch Tim insisted, 'would you please give us a few moments.' Fletch stood and took Finn's hand, 'I saw some ducks in the little creek at the end of the street, let's take this spare bread roll and go feed them.' Then he turned back to Sydney and gave her a proprietorial kiss, 'we'll give you ten minutes.'

As soon as they were alone Tim spoke.

'I'm in this boy's life until death do us part. So how do you want to play it?' Before she could say he told her plainly, 'I need to get to know him, and I think his home environment will be the first step, then my place or my parents. You will always be welcome, not sure about your minder.' He flashed her a determined look, 'you two are not married, is he a permanent fixture? what's his status?' he asked her curtly.

'Don't bring him in to this,' she replied.

'Too late he is already in it, but life would be a whole lot less complicated if he weren't. He calls my child son; they have obvious rapport.' Tim sat, his look intimidating.

'Don't do this Tim, it takes a whole village to raise a child and until today you were not around.' Sydney stuck out her chin determined not to be bullied.

'Sydney,' his voice almost saccharine, 'Finn is a delightful child I can see what a great mother you are. Believe me, it took a series of life changing events for me to realise what a terrible mistake I had made. Now I need to put it right. It would be perfect if we could do it together, I know it will take time. I know too, exactly what you believe is the best possible outcome for Finn. A good name, masculine and goes with his looks' he said agreeably.

'Don't let's snipe in his presence or be bitchy about each other in his hearing, I want him to have a happy childhood. I want him to know his father's love, I will earn it. For Finn's sake, please.' Sydney could hardly believe this was the same arrogant Timothy Winthrop who insisted she abort this child. He sounded so reasonable, but then he always did. He waved to the waiter and handed him his bankcard. 'Let's join them down at the creek.' He held out her jacket. 'I underestimated you; I won't make the same mistake again,' he whispered as he helped her into the jacket, and she shivered.

LATER WHILE FINN HELPED Fletch fill the wood basket he asked with a bewildered expression, 'Who is the man called Tim?' Fletch noted an uneasy curiosity on the boy's face.

'Tim, ah he's a relative.' Fletch's voice was low.

'I don't like him,' Finn said.

'Yeah, I know what you mean, but here's the thing. We can choose our friends but not our relations and you don't really know him yet. It will be different when you get to know him.' Fletch watched a wry expression cross the boy's face. Kids and dogs, they know.

A WEEK LATER, ARRIVING back at the farmhouse Fletch helped carry the groceries inside and Finn carried his mother's shoulder bag. He didn't notice Mercury lying beside the log burner had not run to greet them. Fletch did and he scooped the dog up and walked towards the utility room closing it behind him. He could see the dog lay dead and cold. Placing the animal in his sleeping crate, he closed the door.

'Finn, would you check and see if I left my mobile phone in the truck?' Fletch called over his shoulder. The distressed look he shot Sydney told her not to question him. As soon as the boy had gone to check for the phone, Fletch admitted, 'Mercury's dead. I checked him when he didn't move to greet us. I knew we had a situation. He's cold Sydney. Do you want to tell Finn, or do you want me to do it?' The pragmatic farmer's daughter stood for a moment before her face crumpled, then breathing deeply, she recovered herself.

'I thought things were not right with him, especially these last few days. The vet, Emma's husband Pete, he said it had been a nasty gash and without doing an expensive invasive operation he couldn't guarantee there were not internal injuries. But he said he saw no sign of internal bleeding. To be honest I didn't push Pete to do more. The dog has been in scrapes before. Over the years he has cost me a lot of money I didn't have. Like when he escaped on to the road and got himself hit by a car. I paid the ginormous vet bill because the dog's part of the family.' Covering her face, she groaned. 'I guess when Finn ended up admitted to hospital, I didn't take too much time to think of Mercury. Let's make a hot drink and sit down and tell him together.'

Finn's lip quivered and he sat quiet, but he didn't cry. He had inherited his mother's sensible nature so when he suggested they bury him in the garden, Fletch agreed to help Finn. Then very seriously the boy opened his vivid blue eyes curiously.

'Did he get Covid? Will we catch it?' he asked, his voice full of concern.

'No, no dogs can't get the bug. Well, we believe they can't. Besides we are in Level One, and we don't have any Covid in our community at the moment. Mercury never got over his accident because he's fifty-six in human years.'

'Wow fifty-six is really old,' Finn exclaimed, and Sydney agreed for the sake of harmony.

LATER IN THE WEEK DORIS Dalton phoned because Finn had left his box of colouring pencils at her home on Friday, and she had only just found it. Jamie told her about Mercury as Doris knew Mercury had been Sydney's mother's dog. 'Your mother bought Mercury from Claire Blundell, her current dog a distant relative of Mercury, has just had a litter. It'll be another couple of weeks before they're weaned,' she clucked. 'But I know they have a pup going spare.'

Sydney talked to Mrs Blundell and arranged to purchase a pup. In the meantime, she sowed the seed of a new puppy when they could find one. Finn became excited, talking rapidly on the phone to Olive and busy getting ideas for names from his school friends. School had started again although Sydney did not work from the office every day, only when it suited Ben Howarth, which these days meant about two days per week.

Fletch on the other hand, worked from dawn till dusk and still shared the tasks around the homestead. Some days he seemed on a veritable high, full of smiles and enthusiasm. other days he had a face like a thunderclap and kept very quiet. As much as he could he tried to hide the down days from Sydney. His concerns would become her worst nightmare; The lack of funding and the difficulty in converting the movie storyline to an animated production. The amount of time it took to solve each small problem such as making the dragon-like creatures likeable, beautiful or handsome. Also giving them humanoid facial expressions and personalities. He was rewriting the script. All the time he still tried to convince Perry he should return to New Zealand. The Covid stats in California were atrocious, with over three hundred thousand cases and seven thousand deaths reached by July 2020.

Fletch couldn't understand why Perry wouldn't come home, until one day they had a terrible argument and Perry admitted he had a serious girlfriend, and he would not be able to get her into the country. Fletch became concerned about what Perry wasn't telling him. He emailed Carl Thalburg to Skype him privately and they set up a time. When they sat facing each other Carl told him the world had trumpeted the success of the New Zealand Government's ability to combat the dreaded Covid19 and eliminate it. Fletch explained it had not been without issues, 'the economy's biggest earner, tourism has taken a huge hit with the borders all closed and business screaming for them to open as soon as possible. Add an upcoming election and the media with their knives out for any politicians who put their head above the parapet.' He sounded frustrated. 'New Zealanders returning home are forced into compulsory Government quarantine facilities and it's just as well as they had twenty-four live cases found when the returning citizens were tested.' Fletch thought it all very surreal. There seemed to be two or three cases every couple of days. Few, considering the hundreds of returning Kiwis, who could number well over one million or twenty percent of the population if they all wanted to return and then managed to get back. Fletch wondered where they would all live, because of the housing shortage. The country cancelled incoming flights for a few days until they could get more space in the quarantine facilities. The Government had taken over more hotels suitable for the task, but they were fraught with recalcitrant citizens who decided they could break out of quarantine to go shopping for booze or snacks. Two women managed to get a compassionate pass only to abuse the privilege by breaking the rules and being economical with the truth. Some called it lying, saying they became lost (in their own small country), but they managed to run into a dear friend with whom they shared hugs and after one tested positive there were hundreds of people the Government needed to trace and test. The press had a field day. The police and military were called in to manage the quarantine facilities.

Carl had his own list of horror stories and then he dropped a bombshell. Perry did not live with him anymore. He went back to Hollywood because his girlfriend became ill with Covid symptoms. Carl worried because he hadn't heard from him in two days, although he had the girlfriend's details. Passing those details on to Fletch the pair planned to keep daily contact. For Fletch this had become a disaster. He needed to condition Sydney. Today she worked from her office in Carterton, Finn would go to Nana Doris down the road for after school care. Doris Dalton always met the school bus or had her husband Harold do it, even Jamie had been roped in on occasions.

To take his mind off his troubles Fletch prepared the evening meal; a cauliflower and bacon frittata served with a roast vegetable salad. As he cooked the Cauliflower separately to ensure it cooked gently, he chopped a few rashers of bacon, grated some cheese, and whisked three eggs then threw it all together in an ovenproof dish. He then prepared a medley of vegetables to roast. New Zealand farming types ate too much red meat according to him and for a city boy and West Point graduate who liked to keep fit and eat healthy this type of plant-based meal three times a week did the trick. Although not the American norm he told Sydney, as they ate quite a lot of beef. Fletch could never be the norm, he liked to look after himself.

He had hardly finished cleaning up the food preparation when he heard the sound of a vehicle on the gravel drive in front of the house.

A florist's van he watched as a tall dark attractive woman climbed out and called to him, 'Hi I've got some flowers for Ms. Sydney Martin.' the woman pulled a huge arrangement out of the back of the van. 'Is she by any chance related to the original Martins?' she handed the large arrangement to Fletch.

'Original Martins?' he queried.

'Yeah, you know, the Martinborough Martins,' she reiterated.

'I have no idea; you know I never thought to ask her ma'am.' he took the flowers from her.

'Thank you, she'll love these.'

'Hope so, they're a bit over the top but it's what he wanted.' She rolled her eyes, what 'he' wanted? Fletch nodded and the woman drove off.

Setting them down on the kitchen island he noticed the sealed envelope attached. He didn't need X-ray vision to know where they came from. Fletch had watched him, from the moment he first set eyes on her again after seven years. The man still fancied Sydney.

Chapter Eighteen:

At five thirty Doris Dalton arrived at the front door with Finn. Hearing his name called Fletch went to greet the boy.

'Hi ya buddy.' seeing Doris Dalton at the door startled him, and he frowned. 'Where's your mommy?' He beckoned them inside.

'Hello, I'm Doris Dalton, your neighbour. Sydney called she's been held up, Family Court she said, be home around six.' Doris was an attractive grey-haired woman with smiling eyes.

'You must be Fletch, I've heard all about you,' she offered her hand and flicked her head in Finn's direction. 'You've got a fan there,' she smiled and Fletch grinned.

'It's mutual Ma'am, pleased to meet you Mrs. Dalton.'

'I would have come over sooner, but with this nasty bug around we needed to hunker down. My husband just finished cancer treatment before lockdown.'

'Yes, Jamie told me about his father's illness.' Doris looked at her watch and suggested Jamie bring him over sometime then she called goodbye to Finn. 'I've supervised his reading with him and marked his book,' she offered as she opened the front door. Remembering his manners Finn stepped into the hallway, 'Thank you Nana Doris, bye.'

Watching her drive away Fletch wondered about Sydney's visit to the Family Court, surely, she would have mentioned something so serious to him? Waving Doris goodbye, he moved back into the family room and backed up the fire, before suggesting Finn set the table.

At six fifteen Sydney stepped inside the warm house. Finn ran to her with his trademark enthusiasm, and she apologised profusely.

'I needed to go to the Family Court and collect some documents for Ben Howarth, the Court's in Masterton. Covid has caused huge delays in the hearings and ...' she saw the flowers and stopped dead in her tracks, frowning, 'who are these for?' she wanted to know. Fletch gave her a wry smile.

'You have an admirer.' Snatching up the card she opened it. Immediately her face changed although she tried to disguise her feelings and Fletch couldn't quite read her except to note something unsettled her.

'Tim,' she said. 'I should have recognised his style,' now she sounded troubled.

'You've just got time for a drink before dinner,' he suggested, needing to have the chat about his issues with the movie and with her twin brother. Sydney shook her head.

'No thanks, I will need a clear head later when Tim phones.'

So, Tim would phone, and he had a problem. Fletch felt a tad anxious, not for himself, he could handle anything for himself but his emotional attachment to this family made him vulnerable. Not a familiar emotion for him until now. He skirted the issues talking about the technical side of his project and anything else not relevant. Normally Sydney bubbled and fizzed with him but tonight she thanked him for cooking dinner and for all the other things he had done for her during his day. She looked flat and each of them wanted Finn to be in bed so they could talk openly.

While Sydney read to Finn and prepared him for bed, Fletch noted Tim's card open and was surprised there were only three words.

'Thank you. Tim.' Hardly anything to get upset about but for some strange reason his gut clenched and roiled. He didn't trust this man who had waited seven years before claiming his child, the child Fletch had come to love as his own. However, he felt more concerned about the gut-wrenching realisation Tim still showed an overt interest in Sydney. The man's track record said it would pass, he may be interested in her, but he would never love her the way she deserved to be loved. Fletch couldn't bear to see her hurt again by this man. But what did he have to offer her, he could be deported next month; Veteran affairs might stop his pension if he did not return to the States? The movie began to look like a pipe dream. The promise he had made to her twin would be impossible if he could not liquidate some assets he had back in California and get a visa to stay in New Zealand.

When Sydney returned to the living room, Fletch made them a mug of tea.

'What time is Tim calling?' he wanted to know. She told him eight and seeing it was seven fifty he realised they didn't have much time. He sat beside her on the settee wondering why she seemed agitated.

'Tell me what's going on,' he instructed as he put his arm around her.

'Tim wants unsupervised visitation rights with Finn.' Fletch didn't think unsupervised visitation seemed unreasonable, and they would be granted them by the Family Court if the parents couldn't work out a mutually satisfactory arrangement.

'Finn isn't happy about it; I can tell. Tim's not stupid, he suggested a gradual getting to know him type arrangement. First here, then either at his parents' home or at his. But he doesn't want you there.' Fletch wore his poker face, totally impassive, so Tim wants him out of the picture.

'I told him you live here; we live here and so he would have to suck it up.' Fletch's face remained impassive but his eyes flashed gratitude.

'Basically, he's phoning to make a plan. He's already paid me back maintenance via the company trust fund. I don't trust him not to manipulate the situation to his own advantage.' Sydney bit her lip. She had asked Fletch to marry her. He had dismissed the idea, and she would not ask again or beg him. While he obviously loved Finn, he didn't love her. She could see the concept embarrassed him. Except when he made love to her and the whole world disappeared, and they were the only people who mattered. Sydney told herself she was a big girl now, she would enjoy Fletch while she could, and she would deal with Tim. It seemed so unfair. Unfair because she knew if she wanted him, Tim would jump at the chance to be with her again. Who needed hurt and aggravation again? Although if Tim grew up and became the man his father was, he might just make a half decent father, damn him.

'My life will never be the same,' she said wistfully. The phone rang and she put the hands-free phone on speaker.

'Tim, thank you for the flowers, even if good form says you don't say thank you for a thank you gift. They are very... nice' she inhaled deeply, feeling flustered.

'You're welcome, I'm serious you know when I say I will always love the mother of my son.' Fletch and Sydney locked eyes, and his narrowed. She didn't acknowledge Tim's comments.

'I'd like to come to your farm next weekend to see Finn. Which day would suit you?' she looked to Fletch, and he shrugged, palms upturned.

'Sunday would suit me best, but how is this going to work in the future? I need him to have some semblance of order in his life. What are your plans?'

'Oh Sydney,' he groaned as if in pleasure, 'I love the way you cut to the chase,' Tim's voice still as smooth as silk. Listening to him Fletch balled his fists.

'I plan to see him every week, but as you know when I'm preparing for a case, I often need to work weekends. However, I can make up for it in the school holidays, maybe he can come and stay with me.' Sydney gasped, not thinking it through properly. Fletch could see she had been thrown off her stride, he gripped her hand.

'No, that's a bridge too far,' she protested.

'I told you before, you would always be welcome to come with him,' Tim sounded sincere, her eyes shot up to Fletch's gaze. He could see where this would go and made a swashbuckling gracious gesture she understood.

'Thank you, but this is all too much, too soon,' her voice firm yet quiet. Fletch's eyes twinkled. 'Well let's just say, one week I come to you and the next week you come to me.' It did not suit her at all, and she let him know it.

'No, no it will not do, to start with I cannot afford to be traipsing over the hill every second week., Furthermore weekly visitation rights are too much for a parent who has not shown the slightest interest in his child until now, when you get a sudden rush of blood to the head and decide to be a father.' Her tone sounded haughty and school marmish.

'Don't you take that tone with me Sydney, or I may be forced to convince the Family Court judge my intentions are honest and valid, even if a bit late. Look, I'm happy to pay your travel expenses if required, but the judge would agree I have been exceedingly generous so far. I might apply to co-parent if it would make my life easier.'

'You wouldn't dare, Timothy Winthrop. This is not about you. It's about a little boy I love more than...' her voice cracked. 'Children his age might not understand everything, but they are very intuitive, and they absorb things by osmosis. They imagine things, like this strange man who has suddenly come into my life upsets my mother. You don't want to be holding that tiger by the tail.' Rubbing her arm in comfort, Fletch stifled his amusement and Tim laughed heartily.

'Ah, I wondered where she had been hiding, my little firebrand. Don't fret we will work out what is best for our son, together.'

'So long as you stick to the agreement you signed,' she sniffed. 'Twice a month is all I can manage at present.'

'Your agreement contains more holes than a Swiss cheese, trust me I'm a lawyer. We may have to revisit it. Let's say eleven thirty on Sunday, goodnight, Sydney.' He hung up, and she groaned.

'What am I going to do?'

'You are going to play his game, it's the only thing you can do.' Fletch gave her a hug. She recognised he too suffered anxiety.

'Tell me what's on your mind, something is troubling you,' her eyes sparkled concern. Slowly and with considered words he set out the latest drama unfolding in California. When he finished her comments completely flawed him.

'If in a perfect world you faced similar issues,' she touched his hand, 'I mean you lost your funding and your partner's girlfriend became ill, possibly life threatening, how would you handle it?' He paused in thought, then she blurted, 'Finn and I are not in this equation. Fletch sat silent, thinking, he didn't agree with her.

'Only it is not a perfect world, Sydney, and we must work with what we have.' Twisting a long thick length of her hair around his index finger he spoke slowly, thinking about his words.

'The real problem is this global pandemic. Without it, the economy would not have imploded. Travel would not be an issue and my assets would be greater and worth more. But I can only work with what we have.' Looking her in the eye he said, 'moving you and Finn out of the equation but dealing with the rest, there is one possible move, but definitely not my favourite one. I could set up an appointment with the American Ambassador and put my cards on the table. In the army I specialised in digital special ops. In other words, cyber security. As I see it right now, the world is vulnerable to cyber-attack. Countries could easily be crippled by enemies taking out their infrastructure. I've had a lot of time to think while I've been here. Whenever I consider the big picture, I'm forced to think about the what ifs. I'm a strategist and it is impossible for me to look at the big picture without crossing the 'bridges' likely to scuttle plans. I can't say, we'll cross this bridge when we come to it. For me, the bridge is already there so I must have a plan to cross it. Only, I never planned for Covid. I did see it coming in March but by then it was too late.' Squeezing his arm, Sydney interrupted him with a smirk.

'Are you telling me you would re-join the military if they would, have you? You would forget the dream, ditch the movies? I thought you were a creative ideas man; how would it work?' A fiscally prudent woman she had saved for years in case she needed to buy her twin out of the farmhouse and its twenty acres. Now thinking about Fletch and his idea she felt sure he held back, not telling her everything.

'First thing tomorrow morning you need to call the Embassy. I don't know what rank you were but obviously passion has something to do with it because there would be a ginormous pay cut from movie mogul to soldier, presuming, they would even consider it.'

Not wanting to verbalise the list of obvious questions he said, 'I fancy a tea before bed.'

Alone in her bed, she wondered how desperate to stay in New Zealand and make movies Fletch would need to get before he did anything different. Not very, if he considered going back to the military. Perry may be her twin brother but the last ten years he had more or less lived overseas. The germ of an idea formed in her mind, and she grabbed her I pad from the nightstand. Powering it up she emailed Perry.

Perry,

I want to buy you out of the farmhouse and its twenty acres. I don't know when you will return to NZ, and this cannot wait any longer. Finn's father is wanting to co-parent, and I need to prove I'm in a secure financial position. I've had a current valuation done and it is attached. Times are harder in the States than here, I think. You may need the money. Also, you would still get a small income from the leasing arrangement with the Daltons. Please respond soonest.

Love

Sydney

Pressing send, she felt annoyed with her brother. She had always been responsible for the shared property and yet she took no administration fees for doing the job. Plus, she had paid him a peppercorn rental as he wanted, along with his share of the Dalton's lease money. If he mucked her around, she didn't know quite what she would do. Now aged thirty-one they needed to make a decision. Every payday Sydney had put money equivalent to market rent into a bank account so she might one day buy Perry out. Never had she enjoyed the big paydays Perry had. It had been a case of slow and steady.

A sudden thought struck her, what if Perry's girlfriend had Covid. He would have the results of her tests by now. If only he communicated more regularly. An email once a week would be helpful in these uncertain times.

NEXT DAY, SYDNEY TOOK an annual leave day and planned to go shopping while Finn attended school. Loading her I pad into her bag she noted she had an email from Perry,

Sis,

I'm so pleased you offered to buy me out of the house. Amelia and I are living in Fletch's apartment. It's in a top location in the Hollywood Hills area. He could sell it for a very tidy sum should he choose to do so. I have some funds set aside from the sale of my apartment and Amelia is selling hers. We plan to buy a house together. But a house, not this bachelor pad. She tested negative for Covid, the tests came back yesterday. I'm doing some postproduction work on contract for Valentine

Studios. The dream is still very much alive. The boffins have to come up with a vaccine soon, please God.

Love ya Sis,

Perry

When Sydney told Fletch about Perry's email, he expressed surprise.

'I don't get it; Perry never mentioned any relationship. Although Carl alerted me. Until I had a fight with Perry a few days ago he never said a word. I don't think he's telling me everything. So, she has a name, Amelia,' he said thinking. 'I got in touch with Carl, to find out what's going on. So now we know why he won't come home,' his voice, measured.

'You don't think the woman is pregnant, do you?' Sydney asked pensively. 'Perry always wanted to be more of a father to his children than our father. Old farmers, their bodies get a hammering, and they wear out, it's the physical labour thing. He loved us well enough, just didn't have the energy to deal with us.'

'Yeah, old soldiers are the same. it's the reason I changed corps and retired when I could,' Fletch admitted. 'Everyone thought after my wife committed suicide...' he studied Sydney's face.

'People thought her suicide motivated me. But no, when I had done my grieving, I wanted a new life and a family. Then I met Perry and became passionate about movies,' he sounded wistful. 'Now the world has gone mad.' He stopped abruptly not wanting to verbalise his dilemma.

'Are you still going to get in touch with the American Embassy?' She spritzed her perfume then shrugged into her jacket and checked her appearance in the hall mirror.

'To be honest, I'm ambivalent. I'm too bloody old to re-enlist; also, I would have to be stateside. Last time, I managed to get out with all my fingers and toes and most of my marbles. I might just go have a conversation… but who knows.' He stood in front of her now and she had both hands on his chest.

'Well, the offer I made you still stands, although it's not open ended. The clock is ticking.' she smirked, and he kissed her lightly so as not to smudge her lipstick.

'I'll be home at two, so don't worry about Finn,' she called on her way out the door.

SUNDAY AUGUST THE SECOND 2020 Level One, New Zealand Borders still closed.

'There have been no cases of community transmission of Covid 19 for ninety-three days' The radio announcer reported. 'Our borders will remain closed until further notice. Today's new Covid cases total two, both in government managed isolation.'

A beautiful winter day, and the three of them were off for a ride on their horses. Even Fletch had improved according to Finn, who came out with the funniest little phrases.

'You've got a good bottom' he said as Fletch rode. Sydney corrected him saying the expression is 'a good seat,' meaning the rider sat correctly in the saddle.

'You must sit up straight with an independent carriage, it's the way you hold yourself. Like me,' she told Fletch, who looked at her then smirked he just couldn't help himself.

'Yes, ma'am you definitely have a great bottom,' then he laughed, and Finn joined in. Sydney muttered something to the effect, they'd keep. Finn sat tall in his little saddle, his mount Pickle, had benefited from the extra riding too.

Back at the stables as they rubbed down their horses Fletch suggested Finn show his mother how good he had become with his kite.

'We'll get it on the way back to the house. It's in the shed.' While they were walking back to the shed, Finn ran on ahead excited. Fletch bent, about to pat Sydney's bottom and mention her seat when she caught the look in his eye and pushed him. Returning the little gesture, he laughed, and raised his eyebrows at her. Once again, she playfully pushed him, this time he flicked her backside with his hand, and she squealed.

Finn had been watching the exchange and called his usual admonishments, 'I've told you, stop or it will end in tears,' but now he burst into laughter too and joined in pushing Fletch. 'Where's my kite?'

'I hid it. Have you been a good boy?' Fletch took Finn's hand and walking into the shed he took down the bright kite.

'When I lived in Kabul with the army lots of young Afghani boys flew kites like this.' As he took it down from the shelf Sydney watched captivated. He had used an old polyester shower curtain in psychedelic colours, very seventies. Her mother had bought a job lot and used them in the laundry room shower.

'Did you rescue the old shower curtain from the charity bag?'

Fletch admitted he had and proceeded to demonstrate how to get the kite lifted off the ground. There seemed just sufficient breeze and Sydney watched in awe as Fletch and Finn ran around getting lift off. She leaned against a fence post as the kite soared high in the sky. Twenty minutes passed before she remembered with horror Tim would arrive around eleven thirty. She needed to get back to the house.

'I'm going back to the house, things to do,' she called. Fletch acknowledged her comment and went on showing Finn how to hold and tweak the tension on the kite.

Almost running so she could freshen up before he arrived, she got to the house at the same time as Tim's Mercedes swung into the circular driveway in front of the homestead.

141

It left her no time to do anything except greet him. The house had been cleaned and tidied, lunch fully prepared, but Sydney had wanted to look good. Instead, her hair swung over her shoulder in a messy plait, with little wispy bits escaping everywhere. The jodhpurs she wore drove Fletch wild every time she wore them, but she always thought they made her bum look too big. Her boots were covered in horse shit and the jersey had become a tad shrunken in the wash, so it fitted tight under her sleeveless puffer vest.

'Hi, you found us alright then?' They were both well aware of where she lived. He had virtually stalked her Jamie had advised, when he recognized Bill Carter a private detective, parked in a laneway close to her driveway entrance. When Tim got out of the car, she could see he had not dressed for a farm visit, pressed jeans, crisp blue shirt, dress boots and leather jacket. He frowned at her. Completely unaware of just how sexy she looked; Sydney ignored him. Face flushed, hair all mussed up and when she turned saying, 'follow me,' her bottom moving in front of him was more than he could deal with.

At the front door she bent down to scrape the muck off her boots before removing them. A strangled sound escaped him, causing her to turn and face him with a frown.

'I know these boots are bad, I stood in some horse shit. Come through.'

He followed her down the hall drinking in the old homestead with its family photos and huge deer antlers chandelier in the entranceway. A large oil painting of the Monarch of the Glen in an old rimu frame hung on one wall. Turning again, she realised he had been checking everything out. Sydney didn't care. She felt proud of her heritage. They arrived in the cosy open plan kitchen family room.

'Very nice,' he whispered.

'I'll just get rid of these' she held up the offending boots. Coming back with some clean ones she pulled them on. Now, Tim stood in front of the huge bookcase, fascinated by the selection of books on offer.

'Where's Finn? He set down a supermarket bag on the granite countertop. Sydney indicated outside with her head. Before he followed her out to the back porch, he said, 'there are a few treats in there for you all. Put them away before Finn comes in. I don't want him to spoil his appetite.' In the distance he could see Fletch and Finn together working the kite in the crisp winter breeze. It annoyed him Fletch that had such an obvious rapport with the boy. He didn't comment, but Sydney knew better than to aggravate him, so she rang the huge ship's bell hanging on the veranda post. Fletch and Finn looked up at the toll of the bell. She waved to them to come back to the homestead, then turning, she offered Tim a warm drink.

'I'm having tea, Fletch will have coffee and Finn a Milo we'll eat at one.' The inviting smell of the Sunday roast somehow disconcerted Tim.

'I hope you didn't go to any trouble on my account.' he said, feeling like an intruder in their domestic bliss.

'No, I like cooking a roast it's easiest.'

'Ah well, thank you, coffee would be great thanks.'

Before long Finn's animated voice could be heard enthusing about the kite.

'Can we do it again after lunch? It's so cool so much fun, pleeese Fletch?' He almost begged. Fletch's low rumbling voice said something about hand washing and this time instead of singing happy birthday, he counted using the word Mississippi as a spacer for the seconds until twenty-three. Finn giggled, getting tongue tied and then cried foul.

As soon as the boy entered the living room he went up to Tim and greeted him.

'Thank you for coming, sir,' he looked immediately at his mother who seemed surprised, then back at Fletch whom Sydney felt convinced had prompted Finn to say those words because they were not Finn's words. The boy would have shyly said hi ya, nothing more. she had the vibes loud and clear, Finn didn't like Tim. Sydney pushed it from her mind, too difficult to deal with.

'Thank you for having me, son,' Tim smiled. 'Do you remember who I am?'

'Yeah, you're a relation,' he sounded peeved, as though forced to be polite.

'How do you know?' Curious his mother asked setting down the warm drinks.

'Fletch told me.' Fletch looked pleased with himself until Sydney asked,

'What else did Fletch say?' she said nervously wondering what exactly he had told Finn, as she handed out the drinks.

'He said, we couldn't choose our relations.' Finn had been clever enough not to mention being able to choose your friends. Tim smiled, thinking the little fellow shone bright, until he added, 'but Jamie told me relations are like fish, they go rotten after a couple of days.' Tim burst into laughter and Fletch's eyes twinkled with amusement.

'Trust Jamie Dalton to be rude' his mother harrumphed.

'No, no Jamie is quite right,' Tim agreed. 'I promise not to be like a rotten fish. But I'm sure you'll tell me if I go rotten.' Tim looked around, 'show me your dog, you said you had a dog.' As soon as he'd asked, Tim knew something was wrong, he'd made some faux pas.

'He died,' Finn's face looked crestfallen. 'Fletch and I buried him in the garden.'

'He broke his leg, and a boar gored him, poor Mercury,' his mother explained. 'We're looking out for another dog, aren't we? Why don't you show Tim your room and your artwork,' she didn't want to dwell on the melancholy. Tim took Finn's hand and went off to his room. As soon as the pair were out of earshot Sydney looked towards Fletch.

'You told Finn; Tim is a relation?' she hissed.

'Well, he asked who is Tim, so what could I say?' Thinking about it she realised Fletch had said the right thing. But accepting the situation proved hard for her. Sooner or later the boy would know Tim was his father and she would need to deal with it.

A few moments later they returned, and Finn waved the playing cards. 'Let's play Last card.'

'After lunch' Sydney suggested.

After one round of cards, she excused herself to whip some cream for dessert. Finn won one round and Tim another. Tim had always been madly competitive. He desperately tried to win especially if it meant beating Fletch, who worried in case Sunday lunch descended into a sniping match. Soon he'd leave to catch up with Jamie Dalton. Sydney and Finn would be alone with Tim. All three of them went out of their way to be on their best behaviour. Finn, a sensitive little boy seemed to have a wireless connection to his mother's apprehension and fretfully looked from her to Tim and then to Fletch, seeking some sort of reassurance. Fletch read the signs and suggested to young Finn that he take Tim and show him Pickles, his pony, then perhaps they could get the kite going again. Finn agreed, but only after Tim enthused about the whole idea, 'What a great idea I even packed some wellies, but I'd like some apple pie first.'

'What are wellies?' Finn asked.'

'City boys' Red Band gumboots,' his mother grinned, a little more relaxed.

Later the pair went off to check out Pickles and Fletch reassured her, 'The more time they spend together the easier it will be.'

'Then why don't I feel better?' she sniffed, 'I'll tell you why,' she didn't wait for his reply.

'Tim doesn't have a good track record. In three or four months he could well be over Finn who will be left wondering what he did wrong, poor little mite.' She turned her head away, trying to be strong.

'We will be here for him, don't worry,' he tried to placate her.

'Well, I will be, but there are no guarantees where you're concerned.' Seeing the hurt look on Fletch's face Sydney wished she could suck back those words. 'I'm sorry, I know it's wrong of me to lay a guilt trip on you, of all people. I'm grateful for what you've done for him. I understand ...' her voice trailed off, but she didn't understand at all, except to say, she had no right to have expectations of him.

Chapter Nineteen:

The horses were kept in the paddocks, even in winter. They each had a warm and weatherproof cover. Finn called it their coat. Arriving at the stables, with the tack room next door, Finn took a tin from a shelf. The shelf looked like an internal horizontal stud on which stood an old cocoa tin which he handed to Tim.

'We keep sugar lumps in there as treats for the horses, but the tin's too hard for me to open.' Opening it Tim handed a sugar lump to Finn. 'No, I need two more, you can't give one without the other,' he said. Tim studied Finn, fascinated by his child. 'Well mummy says you must be fair,' the child explained.

'Quite right,' Tim offered. Putting the tin back on its narrow shelf he followed Finn to the fence line. The boy scrambled up the wire fence calling to Pickle who came thundering towards him, whinnying loudly on his way. Finn held up the lump of sugar in his open palm and Pickle picked it up using his tongue and lips, no teeth. The dapple-grey gelding had an excellent temperament for a child. At thirteen hands Sydney considered him small. Finn explained all about his mother's horse, Brandy and surprised Tim by casually saying 'Jamie next door might put his stallion, Houdini across her for a good foal.' Then he added 'when I go back to Pony Club, I might need a bigger horse.'

'Has Pony Club been cancelled because of Covid?' Tim asked.

'Yes, but it started again the Saturday we had to meet you in town,' Finn told him. Tim realised his son did have a life before him even at six and a half.

'How do you get your horse to the club?' he wondered, thinking he would talk to Sydney. He had a host of questions.

'I don't take pickles because we don't have a horse float, they cost a lot of money. I use one of the teacher's ponies,' his tone held the same matter of fact tone Sydney used when dealing with reality. It stirred a little stab of guilt in Tim. After giving Brandy and Trigger their lumps of sugar, the pair took the brightly coloured kite down from its hook, and Tim studied it. He had never had a kite. No room in the city for such things, he believed, and his interests lay elsewhere at Finn's age.

'Do you know how to get it to fly?' he asked, handing it to Finn.

'Well, you are taller than me, so you need to run holding the frame with the sharp point into the wind. Once it gets lift, I know what to do,' Finn advised. Tim did as Finn said, but nothing happened except the kite came crashing down.

'No, not like that, hold it with your back to the wind. Hold the kite up by the bridle point and let the line out.' he said, sounding exasperated.

Six, going on sixty, Tim mused to himself.

Seeing Tim do exactly as instructed Finn continued, 'there's enough wind, so hold it properly and the kite will go right up.' The kite took off and Finn called excitedly 'Now give it to me. Don't pull on it, let the kite fly away from you a little.' Before Tim handed the line back to the boy, Finn yelled at him, 'pull in on the line see how the kite points up. Now it will climb.' When Finn thought the soaring kite looked good to go, he called out to his father.

'Please may I have it now, I can show you?' He asked politely. Tim, behaving like a big kid, held the line tightly and out of reach. Busy watching the kite fly, young Finn failed to notice the wind dropping and Tim had let out too much line. It had slackened off. As soon as Finn realised,

he demanded to be allowed to hold the kite line before it collapsed.

'Please let me show you, let me hold it before....' Too late, it came crashing down and landed in the top of a stand of tall gum trees with the line cut. The look Finn gave his father showed the very same mixture of annoyance and hurt his mother showed when she chastised him for his high-handed arrogance. 'You didn't need to hold on to it when I asked you to give it to me. It's your fault it's stuck. Now we can't reach it, even with a ladder.' Finn's crestfallen face held the woes of the world. His lip quivered. 'Fletch made it for me, he gave it to me as my special surprise,' his voice accused.

'I'm sorry,' Tim felt bad for his son, he should not have behaved as though it were a competitive game and he had to be the one to win. Finn was only a little boy and in that instant Tim knew his child did not like him. Watching as Finn turned back towards the house, almost running Tim could see if he did not make an effort to befriend the child, he might never learn the joys of fatherhood. Calling after the boy made no difference, it simply served to accelerate his effort to get away from him.

Back at the homestead, Sydney sat knitting by the fire and seemed surprised to see Tim.

'Where's Finn?' she asked.

'We had an incident.' Tim reported the details to Sydney honestly and felt touched not by how upset she seemed but by her intelligent assessment of the situation and her comments.

'Oh dear, you only have a small window to get this right, Tim. He is a very intuitive little boy and I love him dearly.' He waited for the but... 'Two weeks ago, you told me you would earn his love. Well, it will be the hardest case you have ever undertaken but he is worth the effort.'

'Thank you for understanding.' He had not expected her to be so considerate but thinking about it Sydney had always been a special woman and she only wanted the best for her son.

'Do you have any suggestions?' he asked, earnestly.

'Yes, do what you do best, for his next visit plan a Wellington day to remember,' she urged. 'You know, the zoo, the museum, the cable car. There are a whole heap of things he would enjoy. Don't compete with him and remember your enjoyment will come from his. Come on we better go and find him.' Sydney had a fair idea where Finn might be hiding, but she played his game dragging Tim around his various forts and dens in the garden, calling his name loud enough to be heard inside the house. Then back towards the house which she knew would be the safest bet on a chilly winter day. As she walked nearer the old wash house, come mud room, she called 'coming ready or not, who wants a chocolate covered ice cream on a stick?' they heard a scurry of movement as they entered the room.

'I fancy a chocolate coated ice cream' Tim announced, and Sydney laughed at him,

'I don't know whether or not you have been a good boy' she replied, pointing to the shower curtain and whipping it back.

Finn called 'I want an ice cream please.' He smiled his funk now over. Nevertheless, he added, 'no ice cream for Tim he lost my kite.' Giving Finn a hug she told him to sit at the family room table and she would find the treat. While they were enjoying afternoon tea, Mrs Blundell the woman with the spare puppy phoned, to say one sale had fallen through and she now had two puppies for Finn to choose from. She wanted to know when Finn could come and choose so she might re-advertise the other for sale.

Hearing the conversation between Finn and his mother, Tim insisted he take them.

'Tell her, right away, we can drive over right away.' Straight after their tea they all piled into Tim's Mercedes and drove the back road to Gladstone, thirty minutes away.

The elderly lady made them all welcome. While she spent time regaling Sydney with her memories of her late mother and her dog

Mercury, Finn started playing with the three remaining pups. Then, as though a light bulb had gone on in her head Mrs Blundell asked,

'What did you say your surname was Tim?' She waited for him to confirm what she knew.

'Tim Winthrop,' he replied, vacantly admiring the historic old homestead and its fine décor.

'Ah, right you're the criminal barrister from Wellington,' she said amazed, but too polite to say more. Later she added, 'he is so like you and such a dear little boy.' Tim filled with pride at her comment and Sydney had given up worrying about the whole district knowing who the child's father might be. Now she worried about telling Finn the truth.

A dear little fat bundle of puppy, with a big brown spot around his tail and another covering his eye like a patch, nuzzled into Finn, nudging his hand and demanding his attention.

'I think he's chosen you, Finn,' Tim said delighted, and Finn agreed. Tim insisted on paying for the animal then and there. Sydney protested and Tim turned to Mrs Blundell and gave her the most charming version of himself.

'We are not together but still she is such an independent woman. Sydney, let me do this for my son, please,' he insisted, immediately transferring the money into the woman's account via his phone. Then he suggested. 'since it's really only four days till the pup's nine weeks old. Can we take him now? Finn would be so happy.' Mrs Blundell agreed and produced the dog's health passport and a little cuddly blanket from the puppy bed. Tim thanked her and put his arm around Sydney.

'Come on family, let's get this puppy home.' Loading the boy and pup into his Mercedes he asked. 'What are you going to call him? Patch?'

Immediately Finn latched on to the idea. 'No, I like Spotty better.' He buried his face into the pup's soft round tummy.

When Tim finally left to drive back to Wellington in the late afternoon he felt as though he had redeemed himself in the boy's eyes. Although Sydney thought it lucky timing, she said nothing, allowing him to enjoy the moment and thanked him for his generosity. Buoyed by the events of the day and particularly Sidney's assessment of his situation, Tim resolved to plan the absolutely best and most fun day Wellington had to offer for their next meeting.

Chapter Twenty:

When Fletch arrived at Jamie Dalton's homestead he passed a small modern cottage along the driveway and assumed it to be the home of Jamie's parents who laughingly called their new home, the gatehouse. He remembered Sydney had told him, when Jamie married about seven years earlier, the family had built the gate house cottage so his parents could enjoy a smaller modern home. They expected their only son would need the main homestead for their grandchildren. After Jamie had caught his bride in bed with the stock agent, and his inevitable divorce, young Finn had filled the grandchild role. As time went on Doris Dalton felt pleased Sydney had not married Jamie. Doris could see any schoolgirl crush Sydney had for Jamie had long gone and her big personality and bossy nature would have been hard for Jamie to deal with. Although George Dalton, Jamie's father, thought her to be just what his son needed. A strong woman with a kind nature who would organise him, and of course he imagined joining not only the families but also the land.

Years after Sara had moved on from her acrimonious divorce, Sydney had finally managed to get Jamie and Sara together. Doris and George were thrilled. Sara's daughter Olive, and Finn, being like siblings came as an added bonus. Today Doris cared for Olive while Sara worked in her little boutique in Martinborough. Normally she took the weekends off, but since Covid Sara could not afford to pay staff, so she shortened her winter hours to accommodate the situation. When Fletch stopped in front of the old homestead Jamie came out to greet him. Standing on the front veranda in his socks, he beckoned him in.

'Fancy a brew mate?' Jamie asked, as he shepherded Fletch towards the big farm style kitchen.

'Thanks, I need a sounding board,' he looked toward Jamie. 'To be honest it's been a hard few days. Perry has missed his window to return to New Zealand. There are no flights coming this way. Air New Zealand will fly from Auckland to Los Angeles, but they then fly on to the UK and there are no flights returning this way from California. I know, because I've been considering going back to the States.' Fletch acknowledged the shocked look Jamie delivered him as he took a chair around the huge old kitchen table with seating for a dozen people.

'Why the hell would you want to go back there? California's in a bad way.'

Jamie didn't need to tell him how bad; the TV news had been full of it. He'd been checking online regularly. It had been growing increasingly more difficult to speak with his old Dad, who lived in a private, aged care facility for veterans.

'At first, I needed to find Perry and sort him out, then I started thinking I should visit my old man just in case. The visa thing is out of my control.' Fletch raised his eyebrows and continued. 'My father the old soldier told me he didn't spend years traipsing through Vietnamese rainforests freshly sprayed with Agent Orange fighting Charlie, to have his only son get caught up in some Chinese manufactured virus. There is no talking him out of his belief this pandemic is a weapon of biological warfare.' Fletch grinned, 'I think the fact I told him about Sydney and Finn had something to do with it too.'

'Oh yeah, what exactly did you tell him about Sydney and Finn?' Jamie handed him a coffee.

'Not a lot, just the truth, I love them both and about how difficult it looked at present and so on. I told him honestly about the funding for the movie drying up, I grizzled I guess.' He shot Jamie a rueful look.

'There is an easy way out of this,' Jamie raised an enquiring eyebrow as though asking if Fletch knew what it might be.

'Not you too. I told Sydney it wouldn't work,' he watched as Jamie laughed.

'I don't know what you were thinking but I reckon Finn had the answer when he asked you to be his daddy. Although, my suggestion was you launch some kind of interactive video game.'

'Funny, the same thought crossed my mind, when I got the idea, we could animate Devil's Moon. I actually dreamed, this really vivid dream, where Devil's Moon turned out to be a kind of dystopian planet but the last habitable planet in our solar system.' Rubbing his three-day old beard, he thought for a bit.

'Yes, I imagined various tribes of creatures, including humans, fighting to live there and setting up alliances to make it happen. Then there could be battles between the groups who were at differing levels of evolution but even the most primitive would have special powers. I'm going to think about this,' he said with absolute conviction.

FLETCH ARRIVED BACK at Boar Gully Farm in the dark and on a high from his afternoon with Jamie. The time he'd spent with Doris and George Dalton had proved fun. He found them a fascinating repository of life in New Zealand over the past fifty years. The Dalton's had known Sydney and Perry's parents very well. After talking with them he learned the Daltons were a good fifteen years younger than the Martins. According to George Dalton, Sydney's father had been one of those people born old. Old before his time, he thought like an old man but had the good sense to retire from farm work and lease out the property. Mrs Georgina Martin, 'Luv' her husband called her, had always been very fey. A dreamer and Perry took after her. Mrs Martin's dreams were also very creative, but in the domestic arts. Cooking, sewing, knitting and while her daughter learned those arts, Sydney a good businesswoman, never feared being different. Never one to follow the herd she stood out, 'especially for a girl,' Mr. Dalton senior had advised, as though girls were less capable and had no business being smart.

Fletch had been fascinated by this attitude, especially as it did not equate to the expectations people put on her. The neighbours all offered help to Sydney, a woman on her own in the world. In the next breath they would actively seek her advice or opinion on some very worldly matter, like estate planning or investments. Regardless of what he learned; he had enjoyed their company. In this strange Covid world his mind raced ninety to the dozen with ideas about Devil's Moon.

As he entered the house via the back door he called, 'hi family I'm home.' Suddenly he laughed, having no idea where the greeting came from. They were not his family, and this is not really his home. Still, it seemed right to him, and they were all comfortable with it.

'In here, we're in here,' Finn called excitedly.

The family room felt toasty and something cooking smelled delicious. Sniffing and smiling he murmured something smelled good.

'Soup,' advised Sydney who sat cross legged on the floor. She grasped his hand and pulled him down just as he saw the little round bundle of sleeping puppy in a basket near the log burner.

'This is Spotty my new pup, he's cute, eh?' Finn said, resting with his back against the sectional settee as he sat on the floor with one hand on the puppy basket. 'He sleeps a lot. Mum says it's because he's a baby.' Finn stroked his new friend lovingly.

'New rules around here boys. Close all doors, don't leave anything lying about unless you want it chewed. Remember, he needs to be taken outside to pee regularly.'

Later when Finn slept and Spotty also slept in his crate in the laundry room, Fletch, bursting with enthusiasm, wanted to share his new idea. Now he thought of it as his idea. He had thought of it before Jamie. Anyway, he entertained Sydney with his online video game idea.

'You've got your mojo back,' she snuggled into him on the settee as he went on with gusto about his plan.

'I'll need at least four different civilizations and creatures. Tomorrow I'll get started, I'll have a hierarchy of classes and tomorrow night when Finn gets home from school, I'll get his childlike brain on the idea. Kids have amazing ideas. You too, tell me what you think when I flesh it out more for you...' She had moved her face closer to his and the light in her eyes filled him with renewed vigour.

'Can these creatures make love across the species?'

'Why do you think your Avatar will be a different species to mine?' His eyes glinted a dark flinty steel as his lips quirked.

'Mine will be smarter for sure,' she teased, him nibbling his lip.

'Mine will have secret superpowers,' Fletch said as she chuckled.

'Show me.' This time he stifled her chuckle when he claimed her mouth. Unravelling her plait with one hand and holding her face with the other, he kissed her till she moaned in delight. Hardly giving her time to catch her breath Fletch enveloped her in his arms and shifted his kisses to her neck, his breathing now ragged, his voice hoarse and gravelly.

'You want me to show you, right here?' then as if on cue the sound of a baby howling from the puppy crate broke the spell.

Chapter Twenty-One:

E very evening after Finn went to bed, Sydney and Fletch sat in horror as the news of the world played out, watching it from the safety of their living room in rural New Zealand.

Melbourne, Australia appeared to be in a bad way with around six hundred new cases appearing daily, with today's total now over seven hundred and fifty cases. Finally, the Government had insisted on a New Zealand style lockdown.

'Too late,' Sydney sighed, 'the horse has bolted. They still have too many opportunities to bend the rules and infect people.'

Only a matter of days later, the Premier of Victoria, Australia tightened the rules yet again. Now Melbournians had to stay home, unable to leave the house, even for exercise. The hospitals had over a thousand cases in the high dependency units, the health system was stretched to breaking point.

'I worry about my old father, when I hear stories and see the devastation on TV,' Fletch said in a low voice, after hearing the story of a woman with parents in an aged care facility in Victoria, Australia. The woman complained to the network news her mother had been unwell and she had been stopped from visiting her or her aging father diagnosed with Covid19. The staff were overwhelmed and could not give her updates about her father's condition.

'It's understandable their anxiety is running high at a time like this.' Sydney reassured him in her pragmatic way, 'but remember this report is hearsay. Families sometimes lose sight of the fact they are not the only ones in this situation, and they get demanding. I feel so sorry for the front-line workers.'

In rural Martinborough the week seemed like business as usual. Except Sara Corbet, Sydney's friend, and Jamie Dalton's new love phoned in a terrible state.

'I've just heard from my father in Britain. The little village they live in has been clear of Covid until now and a cluster has just broken out. Dad has been called back to help at the cottage hospital they have turned into an isolation hospital. He's staying with another doctor and not going home to Mum because she is asthmatic. Mum's not old, she's just sixty, but she's immunocompromised.'

'I'm sure your father's got everything under control. He'll keep her safe.' Sydney tried to reassure her friend who sounded distraught.

'To be honest, I'm more worried about Dad. He's the one confronting the virus. He's been putting in some very long hours and he gets tired. When you're a tired front-line worker you're more vulnerable,' Sara lamented. As soon as the women finished their call, Sydney phoned Jamie.

'If you care for Sara as you claim, you'll go to her right now' she told him in her bossy tone.

'Look Sydney, I can't go. I've got a stock truck arriving at four thirty in the morning, and the cattle are not in the stock pen yet,' he grumbled. Had she woken him?

'I don't care if you do need to get up at three in the morning to get back in time to meet the stock truck. I'll draft your bloody cattle if that's what it takes. You should be more organised. How come those cattle aren't in the yards already? Really Jamie.' Sydney didn't hold back. Finally, when Jamie did manage to get a word in, he contritely said, 'I'll phone you from Sara's if I stay over.'

Listening to Sydney's end of the conversation Fletch smiled to himself. Doris Dalton had been right about Sydney being far too bossy for the likes of easy-going Jamie. Fletch could handle her, he had commanded men in the army and for some unknown reason, she didn't boss him about, not since those first few days in lockdown when they came to an arrangement. What Fletch couldn't handle in a woman, would be a disorganized needy sort, of melting mood. No one could accuse Sydney of being disorganized or wimpy. He loved her passion and joy de vivre. Two hours later Jamie did phone back, just as Sydney prepared for bed.

'I've set the alarm for three am. you don't need to worry about my stock and Sara says thank you.'

FLETCH HAD MADE TWO new kites so he and Finn could fly them together and he joked, next time Tim visited, he would have his own kite.

'Don't you worry, son; I'll teach you how to cut the line on Tim's kite when it's in the air.' The pair had giggled at the thought of it.

A patient man, Fletch taught Finn and Spotty about basic puppy training. When Sydney asked him how come he knew so much about dogs for a city boy, he explained he had a neighbour growing up on base who trained military dogs and taught Fletch a good deal about them. 'Sometimes I would go with him and watch as he put young dogs through their paces. I learned from his patience and the way the animals trusted him.'

Before long Spotty would woof at the door to be let out to pee, he came when called and he understood what 'No' meant. One night, about two weeks after Spotty arrived, Sydney busied herself tidying the house before bed. Checking on Finn as she did, she noticed he had Spotty in bed with him. The pair looked cute together, but she took the pup to his bed crate in the laundry. On her return she told Fletch, who dropped his lower lip and pulled a face.

'I remember doing the same as a boy,' he said ruefully. Sydney gave him the side eye; this man who claimed to be a trained killer was a big softy.

As the visit to Wellington approached, Sydney built it up to create an excited anticipation. Fletch and Jamie were going to watch the rugby game, Wairarapa Bush versus Manawatu in Masterton. During the week Tim had faced-timed Finn so he could see Spotty. This, his second phone call to the boy in as many days. Fletch thought it a good thing. It showed the effort Tim is making to get closer to the boy.

Sydney appeared less impressed, simply because this new development made her anxious Tim had hurt her terribly and she saw no reason things might be any different with Finn.

TODAY, THE SECOND SATURDAY in August, she planned to drive over the pass to Wellington for Finn's visit with his father. The weather always a consideration, looked good, but rain threatened. Sydney had arranged she would be at Tim's Thorndon home at ten thirty in the morning. The pair set off after breakfast around eight thirty. Unsure whether she should leave the child alone with his father for the day, Sydney had discussed it with him, and Tim surprisingly suggested they should play it by ear. Although relieved she did not want to spend all day with the man if she could avoid it.

On arrival at the Thorndon address in good time, Tim greeted them enthusiastically.

Sydney could see there had been a great deal of refurbishment on the grand old villa. It must have cost a fortune, but he had money. Curiously, Tim watched as she checked out his home, saying nothing. It looked beautiful but not to her taste. The interior had lost all its character.

'How are you, Finn? Sydney?' he asked, 'Come in and you can tell me what you'd like to do first.'

'Good, thank you.' Their perfunctory reply in unison and he ignored it, determined to win them both over. They walked along the expansive hallway towards the open plan kitchen family room. Finn's eyes lit up with excitement when he saw a table and on it a train had been set up complete with a figure eight track, a bridge, a station, and houses with trees. It looked quite unique.

'I've had this since I was a boy. My mother insisted I keep it. So, it's been stored in the attic space.' He smiled at the enthusiastic child. Sydney felt overcome with a strange unfamiliar feeling. The feeling you get in your gut when you realise your sworn enemy of seven years is not all bad. An excellent judge of human nature, Tim recognized the expression on her face. It went hand in hand with the realization he was making progress and he planned to milk it.

'Make yourself a brew while I show Finn how this works.' He waved at the tea and coffee things set up on the counter.

'Thank you, what will you have?' she looked around the well-appointed kitchen with its white granite counter tops and upmarket appliances. Tim called 'coffee, thanks' but he didn't look up from teaching Finn the intricacies of his old Hornby train set. Sydney couldn't help herself. She had to open the elaborate chef's oven. There were two of them side by side. She opened the first and then quickly opened and closed the second. They had never been used. The accessories were inside and still wrapped from when it had been newly installed.

As soon as Finn got the hang of propelling the train along the tracks, he wanted to do it alone. Tim seemed pleased and sat down with Sydney, at the dining table nearby.

'He learns fast,' Tim mused, sipping his coffee.

While Sydney sat busy wondering, 'when did Amanda move out?'

'What makes you think she's moved out?' he pursed his lips, why was she asking?

'Well, there's not much in your fridge and remembering what you told me the first time you met Finn...' she shrugged.

'Perhaps I should have made myself clear. Amanda left me before I met Finn. I told you we had many issues.' Lifting his gaze, he watched Finn smiling and talking to himself completely engrossed in play.

'Where's the fat controller?' Finn asked. 'You have Sir Topham Hatt here, he's from Thomas The Tank Engine.' Finn liked Thomas the tank engine.

'I don't know where the little man came from. I found him in the box with the other characters. I thought he could be a passenger,' Tim explained.

'Don't you cook?' Sydney accused, looking around the pristine kitchen.

'Yes, I do, but on the stove top not the oven,' why did she doubt him? 'Amanda didn't cook' he informed her. Tim always loved his food, so this seemed like karma again.

Quickly she changed the topic. 'Shall I leave now while he's happy?' her voice sounded a little thready. Tim gave her a look of pure compassion, he understood how she felt. Well, if he didn't, he tried to. His concern showed.

'You don't need to go, I understand it's too soon,' his voice quiet then he turned to Finn.

'Do you want mummy to come to the zoo with us? You can play trains later.'

An hour later Finn stood in front of the otters' enclosure watching two young otters chasing each other under water. It had been years since they had visited the zoo, and he loved the whole experience. After a walk, he stood in front of the glass enclosure of the tigers' home and one strolled towards them and Tim, taking out his phone, photographed the scene. An older man surveying the scene offered to take a family shot of them all. Tim thanked him.

Handing over his phone and tapping Sydney on the shoulder, he put his arm around her.

'You're definitely a chip off the old block,' the willing photographer said to Finn, who frowned not understanding the expression.

'I mean you are so very like your daddy, but I expect people tell you all the time.' The boy said nothing processing the man's words, his expression confused. He looked from Tim who smiled, to his mother who stood silent.

By one o'clock all of them fancied lunch and Finn still bubbled away about the various animals when their food arrived. Corn fritters and bacon arrived for the adults and Finn had chosen pancakes with bacon and bananas, covered in lashings of maple syrup, his favourite.

'Is he right, the man who took our picture? Are you, my daddy? Fletch said you were a relation.' The child, at only six and a half seemed like an old soul. Both Tim and Sydney were put on the spot. They had known this moment would arrive sooner or later.

'Yes, it's true' Tim told him. Before Sydney could agree Finn boldly asserted,

'I want Fletch to be my daddy.'

'Yes, but Fletch also told you, you can't choose your relatives' Sydney pointed out.

'Yeah, Olive said that too.' he pronounced, peeved. 'But if I could ...' Finn stopped and naïvely looked up at Tim. Nobody spoke. Tim felt wounded and Sydney closed her eyes, she had always known this day would come but why did it have to be so hard. Tim carefully defused the situation talking about the placemats which were cartoon maps of the zoo. He suggested they keep a clean one as a souvenir.

After lunch Tim proposed they took a trip on the cable car and had a look around at the cable car museum at the top of the ride. Afterwards, they enjoyed an ice cream on the beach at Oriental Parade.

'We could go to Te Papa, but I don't think we have enough time to see everything. Except, see the apartment building over there? he pointed to a luxury low rise apartment building. 'You get a really great view of the city from there. We can ride in the lift.' The thought of riding in a lift grabbed the child's attention.

'The grandparents place, he informed Sydney.'

'When did they move out of Kelburn?' she asked, and he told her, a couple of years ago.

It must have been arranged they visit Tim's parents because they were ready and waiting for them. The afternoon tea table had been set up.

Catherine and Grant Winthrop were welcoming and knew better than to overwhelm the child with attention. After Tim had pointed out the view from the window, Sydney offered Finn her mobile phone suggesting he watch some Thomas the Tank Engine on U Tube while the adults chatted for a bit.

For Sydney, the atmosphere felt a bit stilted. Especially, given the vivid dream she had shared with no one. In this dream she became ill with Covid19. She remembered a nurse in full personal protective equipment telling her not to worry about her son as his father would look after him. Since her dream, the frightening and abhorrent thought started to worry it's way to the surface of her mind. If something happened to her, these people would become Finn's family. Sydney had little option but to acknowledge this and accept it. Still, she prayed it would never happen. She repeatedly told herself it would never happen but the only guarantee in life is death. She knew it was the truth, albeit a morbid truth. The Winthrops were a sound family and even if Tim had been spoiled and still acted with arrogance at times, it did not mean Finn would turn out the same way. Even as Tim tried to make his relationship with his son work and Sydney wondered had they married, how would Tim have treated his son. Well, she would never really know. Except she did know no man would ever treat her like a door mat. When she worked for Tim, he did treat her poorly at times unless she called him on it. Except for the few months they were 'together' but it ended abruptly, when he demanded she have an abortion and she refused.

Continually rehashing these thoughts made her more uncomfortable.

'Sydney, Sydney dear,' Catherine's slightly shrill voice brought her back to the present. 'I said how good you look and how well-mannered Finn is.' Catherine handed Sydney a cup of tea. 'He reminds me so much of Tim at the same age. I never wanted him to be an only child. You know we did have another child.' Catherine looked to where Finn his father and Grandfather were watching a windsurfer in the harbour, and she whispered,

'yes, another boy, Nigel he died at two, a mystery virus. Looking back, I think it may have been some meningococcal thing. It came on suddenly he developed a rash, the doctor admitted him to hospital, and he died overnight. The hospital told us there had been two other cases during that winter and two deaths.' She sighed and instinctively Sydney put out her hand and touched Catherine's arm, one mother to another.

'I know I became overprotective of Tim after Nigel's death. I spoiled him. We never did have any more children. Grant worked rather a lot too.' A weak smile crossed her face, as the men re-joined them for tea.

'I'm so glad you two were able to work together for the sake of this little one,' Grant referred to Finn. In his skilled way, Tim brought up some work-related matter, so his father's attention diverted away from them. Catherine had taken Finn off to the kitchen to watch her feed her cat, a large fluffy marmalade creature with a pushed in nose, reminiscent of Garfield.

'What do you call him' Finn asked.

'Ginger Spice, she's a girl cat' Catherine Winthrop explained kindly.

'Mummy said ginger cats are usually toms,' he said knowledgably.

'Usually they are, but not always. This one should have been used to breed.' Nana Cath said.

'Breeding female cats are called queens and female dogs are bitches.' He smiled; he liked using the word *bitch* knowing it to be a swear word too.

Sydney's phone rang and scrambling to retrieve it from the chair where Finn had left it, she excused herself to answer it.

'It's an American caller' she explained frowning. 'Oh my God is he alright? Who am I speaking to please? Grant and Tim could hear the alarm in Sydney's voice as she turned away from them. Grabbing her handbag, she took out a pen and note pad scribbling furiously. Saying 'I understand, I understand thank you for calling me.' Turning back towards the men she said firmly.

'My twin, Perry has been admitted to hospital.' she looked at her notebook, 'it's Dignity Health California Medical Centre. As a child he had asthma, but not badly, from memory.' She sat down and covered her face.

Grant sat down beside her reassuring her softly, 'now tell us exactly what the caller said and who called you.' he asked.

She explained slowly nibbling her lip as she considered her words.

'A nurse from the emergency room at Dignity Health called. It's nine pm yesterday over there. The woman asked if I had a brother called Perry Martin, and I confirmed I did. Then she said he had been admitted for tests and treatment after collapsing due to an asthma attack. She said he had been tested for Covid and would move to a quarantine facility until the results were known. If they were positive, he would be admitted to an isolation hospital because of his asthma.

I asked about his partner and the woman said she didn't know of any partner. I'm the next of kin on his medical records. Then she said somebody would be in touch in due course.'

Sydney's thick mass of long dark hair draped over her face like a curtain as she leaned forward.

'California is really suffering from what Fletch tells me. He is in regular contact. His father is in a private aged care facility for military veterans. I know he hasn't been able to talk to him for about ten days and had someone from Veteran's Affairs check on him and report back.' Tim moved quickly to her side. Crouching down beside her he said tenderly.

'I know you feel helpless. Worrying does no good, and it's not good for you. If there is anything I can do, I want to do it.' With his strong index finger, he turned and tilted her face, so they had direct eye contact. Seeing vulnerability in her face he wanted to protect her but aware it might be a minefield, did not hug her. When she looked into his vivid blue eyes she saw a different face, the face of Finn as a man and she wanted to hug him but the six-and-a-half-year-old version broke the spell.

'Mum Nana Cath has a Garfield cat called Ginger Spice,' seeing his mother's face he knew something had happened, 'what's wrong?'

'Uncle Perry's in hospital, he's got asthma.' She painted a smile on her face, but Finn recognized it as a cover up.

'Not Covid?' he had heard her talking to Fletch about Covid in California.

'No, but they have tested him as a precaution because asthma affects the lungs.' Looking around the room she decided they should get going back to the Wairarapa.

'But Tim said I could play with his trains.'

'Okay, but we should leave now, and you can have fifteen minutes playing while your mother and I talk,' Tim announced. They said their goodbyes and Finn hugged Nana Cath after a prompt from his mother.

Back at Tim's house he played with the trains while Tim and Sydney watched from their vantage point on the kitchen bar stools.

'Thank you for today. I could see my mother felt quite moved by Finn. She'll be weeping into her gin right now, I bet,' his voice quiet with a hint of self-deprecating humour.

'Yes, she told me about Nigel. I guess I understand her a little better now. does she blame you for not having had those formative years with her only grandchild?'

'She does, but I think she also blames herself for my behaviour.' This time a sardonic smirk crossed his face. 'Thank you again for helping me redeem myself. Our child is particularly bright,' he commented watching the boy at play. 'Are you worried about Perry?'

'No because he is a hopeless communicator. I'm not my brother's keeper.' she shrugged.

'Rubbish, we all know that's not true. All the time we worked together you were always the one who had to make the play, keep in touch, placating the parents. But you're holding back what's worrying you my little...?' he stopped short, before he called her mother mouse. Sydney nearly screamed.

'What worries me is I learned he has a serious girlfriend, a partner. They're buying a house together or they were about ten days ago. How come he didn't suggest the hospital authorities call her? Something is not right. I can feel it.'

'Do you want me to get an investigator on to it? he asked.

'No thanks, Ryan Murphy has a police officer contact over there, she found Perry once before.'

ON THE JOURNEY BACK over the Pass to the Wairarapa valley and then on to Martinborough, Sydney felt pleasantly surprised. She had enjoyed Tim's company today, apart from one patronising slip when he almost called her mother mouse. He seemed guarded and on his best behaviour.

Arriving home ahead of Fletch, she lit the fire and heated some spaghetti in tomato sauce with cheese on top as a quick meal for Finn.

Spotty danced about bouncing on furniture pleased to see them. He and Finn played until bedtime.

'When will Fletch be home?' the boy asked.

'Late I expect, they will have gone off for a beer and food after the game,' she advised him in her practical way.

After Finn had been put to bed, and as she tidied the kitchen Sydney found Fletch's mobile phone he had left home without it. Funny when he first arrived at Boar Gully Farm his phone had been a permanent attachment even though there was no cell coverage unless it happened to be a fluke. The thought amused her. While she enjoyed a cup of tea in front of the fire, the land line rang Tim of all people, phoned telling her how much he enjoyed their day and thanking her for making it straight forward for him to build a relationship with his son.

Chapter Twenty-Two:

Fletch had enjoyed an interesting afternoon with Jamie Dalton. Interesting because he gained a unique insight into the Kiwi male psyche, or so he thought.

Rugby, a passion with Kiwi men had gained almost religious importance. Jamie, being no different, gave him a crash course in the intricacies and basic rules of the game. It seemed so different from grid iron or baseball, but Fletch made the effort to take it in. Definitely a hard game and played by hard men.

Then he remembered young Finn saying he and Olive played in the same team, surely not.

'Do girls play this game too? I mean your Sara's daughter, little Olive and Finn play in their school team. Is it because they don't have enough kids if they don't all play?' Sipping his beer Fletch needed to get his head around this.

'They do, but if you're asking if Sydney played, no she didn't, well I can't honestly remember. The game Finn and Olive play is called ripper rugby. It's the kids' version and an age-appropriate game of no tackling.

'We breed them tough down under,' Jamie insisted. Fletch had come across a few of these guys when he served in Afghanistan. It would be wrong to say they were the same as the Australians because they were definitely different. Like cousins, part of the same family, in this case the Anzac family. Still, he noticed a difference the Australians were more like the Americans.

'If you must be more finite about it you need to compare apples with apples; breeding, schooling and social demographic,' Jamie grinned at Fletch, sipping his beer a little glassy eyed. 'But hey, I think they're a bunch of foulmouthed red necks mostly descended from criminals; my Aussie neighbour says I'm biased because they bleat us-s at every ...thing...' he started to slur his words.

'I think it's time I drove you home mate. No more beers for you tonight,' Fletch chuckled.

'And another thing the Aussies always steal our stuff, and our people. Pavlova, Lorde, Phar Lap, lamingtons the Aussies pinched 'em.' Helping him into the truck Fletch could see Jamie looked....

'I'm pissed.' he beamed up at Fletch, who wondered how the hell it had happened as he clicked his mate's seat belt secure.

FLETCH TOOK OFF HIS boots at the back door and crept slowly along the polished floor so as not to wake Finn or Sydney. The outside temperature had dropped to below freezing and he felt grateful the house exuded warmth. He backed up the log fire and stripped off to his undies while he waited for the logs to take up the fire so he could damp down the air flow to slow the burn. This way it would last all night.

All day, on and off, Fletch had agonized over the internal dialogue he fought, his very uncertain future, bloody Covid19 and his impending financial doom. Nothing to offer this little family he had come to love and consider as his own. Love, tonight he felt a need more basic and animal than love and he felt bad about it. Still, it didn't stop him from brushing his teeth and slipping between the warm sheets next to the woman he craved.

For a few minutes he lay there enjoying the warmth emanating from her, cosy and inviting. Making little kitten sounds as she slept Sydney looked so peaceful. He could see by the glow of Finn's nightlight in the hall, her eyes moved rapidly in REM sleep. For a few moments he watched her. Sydney's mass of dark unruly hair covered the pillow as he put an arm around her and firmly pulled her towards him. Slowly she turned snuggling in to him and sighed audibly.

'Mmm, my precious,' he whispered, watching a quirk of her lips.

'You have a good time today? she whispered sleepily.

'Not as good a time as I'm having now.' He tilted her chin up slowly, trying to kiss her awake. Nibbling teasingly on the full pouty lip she had pushed out inflamed his arousal. Even half asleep and totally defenceless in his arms, Sydney seemed full of mischief. Knowing he wanted her felt so good. She could taste his minty breath and smell his cologne and maleness. His maleness pressed up hard against her giving her a zing of desire. Her hands could feel the soft downy fuzz covering his warm rock-hard chest. Fully awake now, he helped her shed her baggy tee shirt and night knickers while he nibbled her neck.

'I missed you tonight,' her voice came out in little grunts, ragged and thready.

'Don't talk,' he kissed her hungrily. 'Just make love to me. I need you,' his husky voice barely a whisper. Stimulated by his nearness she felt totally awake, her breasts sending signals to her core, urgent and primal. She didn't talk not with her voice, but her lips and her body told him everything he had ever wanted to know.

IN HER OFFICE AT HOWARTH and partners, Sydney and her colleagues planned to listen to the Prime Minister's broadcast at one pm. New Zealand had been Covid free for one hundred and two days. The only cases had been intercepted at the border and were in government-managed isolation facilities. These were hotels leased under special legislation for the purpose of protecting the borders. They were not commandeered, instead the Government signed a mutually accepted arrangement with the owners. Some considered it most generous.

However, at ten thirty the previous evening a government electronic alarm blared out across the nation's well organised civil defence scheme via millions of smart phones, alerting the public to the fact a cluster of Covid had been diagnosed in the community. The cluster of four cases was being tracked and traced. This smart phone alert system had been set up to warn the public about earthquakes and tsunamis and other emergencies, like radical changes in the pandemic status.

All the team at Howarth and Associates were scurrying about trying to finish their work so they could take their lunchbreak at one pm. The boardroom had been set up with tea and coffee, and Ben Howarth had sent out for a tray of sandwiches. The receptionist switched on the television.

Sydney had been particularly busy with several cases all marital issues and custody matters. There had been a speight of new clients seeking legal advice on matrimonial issues and custody arrangements since the lockdown in New Zealand at the end of March. Psychologists believed they were stress-related situations. Emma Jacobson said she had experienced the same phenomena.

Sitting in the boardroom at one o'clock sipping their coffees and eating lunch the team listened in silence to the Prime Minister's report. She announced Auckland would revert back to alert level three and the rest of the country to alert Level Two. From there the Director General of Health outlined the plan to contain and eliminate the virus, saying by, 'going hard and early' hopefully they could move out of this level before it got out of hand.

'I bet they have to postpone the elections' Ben said, unsure where all this would end up. 'Thank God we're in Level Two, at least we can operate with caution.' The storm clouds of uncertainty were gathering.

'I feel like this virus is *our war*. I know some generations think we millennials have lived a charmed life of instant gratification; well, some might have. I must have missed it.' Sydney stood up, 'please excuse me, I've work to do.'

'What's eating her?' Ben asked, surprised.

'A certain custody case, the Lane family.' Emma explained, 'Cody Lane and his ex-wife Wendy,' she shrugged.

'The Cody Lane who was charged with the murder of Duncan McKenzie, the same guy Timothy Winthrop successfully defended?' Ben could see the picture. 'I hadn't joined the dots before. I knew she had Wendy Coleman as a client. I simply forgot Wendy married Cody Lane. The Coleman's are an old Wairarapa family.'

'Wendy Coleman Lane reverted to her own name and returned to the Wairarapa two and a half years ago, before Duncan McKenzie had been found shot dead. Back then Daniel, the youngest son had not turned three and his older brother, Drew started school in Greytown. Their father made no effort to be in his children's life but now he wants to coparent,' Emma advised Ben. 'The youngest boy had not turned two when his parents separated, and Cody hardly took any part in his children's life. In part due to the fact his mother had taken out a non-molestation order against him. He's a bully with anger management problems. But now he wants to be in the boys' lives and Wendy, their mother, is not happy.' Emma fixed Ben with a determined look. 'I offered to handle the case in Family Court. Cody's lawyer is Taylor Goodwin.' Emma twisted her mouth in an expression of disgust. Everyone knew Taylor Goodwin; the woman looked like a hard-bitten tart according to Sydney. The kind of lawyer men like Cody Lane hired to make them look like a teddy bear, a Pitbull in lipstick.

'Well Sydney can deal with her, she's the consummate professional, she will do what's right. Frankly, Wendy unwittingly chose the perfect person, wouldn't you say? She researched her own case from every angle and hard and all as it has been for her, she did the right thing for her son.' Thinking about Sydney, Ben added, 'I'm happy for you to help her with this case because I don't want it ending up in Family Court.'

'Good because I had told her I would do it.' Emma sighed, 'it's set down for Thursday this week and now we are back in Level Two we don't want any deferments.' Looking at her watch, she excused herself.

THE TELEVISION NEWS depressed everyone with continual stories of the re-emergence of Covid in the community. Ironically, even President Trump jumped on the situation talking it up saying,

'we don't want to be like New Zealand, they took their eye off the ball and the virus has come back big time.'

'Talk about a crock of shit,' Sydney groaned. 'I can't believe you people voted him in,' she accused Fletch as she 'tsked.'

'Yeah, well it's called, democracy,' he answered weakly. Today Sydney needed to represent her client in family mediation. It would be fair to say she sat on the edge of her seat for no reason other than Emma, who had agreed to present this case for her, had phoned her the previous evening. Her young daughter Gracie had become ill, with some routine winter cold quickly became a nasty cough.

'It's just croup I think, but the health helpline says because of her high temperature I may need to get her tested for Covid. So, I have to be the one to stay home with her and isolate her not Pete.' Sydney had reassured Emma she could handle the case and she could, so why did she have this anxiety in the pit of her stomach?

The meeting would take place at a neutral venue as approved by the parties. Sydney had booked a meeting room in the Carterton Events Centre. This state-of-the-art building had several rooms suitable for the purpose. Wendy Coleman agreed to meet Sydney in front of the building at nine thirty for their ten am meeting. They had ample time to get a coffee and psych themselves up for the proceedings. On entering the building, they scanned their where abouts with the Covid app. A Government track and trace program for pandemic safety, then after hand sanitising, they proceeded. The meeting room they were to use sat opposite the kitchen and had been sound proofed. Sydney joked with the venue's manager that sometimes there were raised voices and so they needed privacy. In truth, very often there were screaming matches, and they didn't simply apply to the parents.

Wendy arrived on time, and she watched Sydney arrive. She had walked around the corner from the offices of Howarth and Partners situated on the High Street. They agreed to get a coffee in the meeting room.

'God, I hope like hell Cody doesn't spit the dummy. Tell me, because I can't understand it, how can he suddenly decide now, after all this time he wants to be in the kids' lives? I mean when we were together not only did, he not give a shit he made my life hell.' Wendy studied her red-painted fingernails as she stood showing quite a bit of leg in her short skirt.

'Yes well, if the boffins are to be believed Covid is not just responsible for breakups but also for makeups, in this case with his sons. Believe me your ex is not the first and for the boys' sake we need to get it right Wendy,' she sighed bent head down bottom up to rummage in her capacious handbag on the floor, she heard a man clearing his throat.

'Sydney,' he said before she had even stood up, 'I knew you were here,' he grinned. I'd recognise that arse anywhere, he thought. Nobody could accuse this woman of being mousey anymore. Did he see some bare skin showing he wondered, as she tugged at her fine merino top?

'Good morning, Ms Martin, Ms Coleman,' he smiled at them both but only had eyes for Sydney. More than ten years had passed since Sydney first started work at Winthrop and Partners. She didn't even remotely look like the same woman. Her hair, her beautiful crowning glory fell softly around her shoulders, not pulled back in some tight matronly bun. Tim watched it bounce around and down her back. Studying her he noticed her outfit could never be considered school marmish. The short black skirt she wore made her black sheer hose appear as though her legs went all the way to her armpits, helped by those four-inch heels. When she offered her hand, and her Merino top rode up a little she made no attempt to hide her midriff.

Recovering his composure Tim noted Cody Lane appreciated her too.

'Where is Taylor Goodwin, your lawyer, Mr. Lane? I understood she would be here too.' Sydney really wanted to ask, "what the hell is he doing here?" as she looked daggers at Tim.

'Regrettably, Ms Goodwin is unable to attend but having heard of my recent success in these matters she agreed I should come instead,' Tim spoke up, grinning widely.

'Well, I must say for the record,' Sydney set her phone down on the table 'Mr Winthrop and I need to disclose the fact we are...' she swallowed hard.

'I believe Ms Martin is about to disclose we co-parent our child. Therefore, we are in an excellent position to be of help to you. I apprised Cody of the matter before we came over here,' Tim aimed his sanctimonious expression at Wendy. They had met during the murder trial and while she didn't like her ex-husband much, right at this moment she thought Timothy Winthrop the best thing since sliced bread. She happily allowed him to be present especially as he and Sydney were co-parenting their child.

'Is he the reason you wanted Emma Jacobson to be here today instead of you?' Wendy wanted to know.

Sidney paused for breath, 'I thought there may be a possibility albeit a vague one. But if you're happy let's get down to business.' Politely perusing her notes, she went on. 'I see you all have a copy of the points to be agreed. Are there any you would like to discuss?'

'Yes, but we should systematically go through them,' Tim said, taking charge. Sydney knew he would and if it had not been him then the rottweiler Taylor Goodwin would have, so she planned to keep her powder dry, ready for the points they would not budge on. Methodically they went through every point, agreeing, yes, the father must be in the childrens' life, yes, they were happy with the agreed maintenance.

Many realters and developers considered Cody Lane the best real estate agent and property developer in the greater Wellington region. Although his business took a hit while he languished in prison accused of murder, it had soon picked up again. His legion of minions worked tirelessly for him even while he stewed in prison waiting to be tried. Surprising as it may seem, real estate in New Zealand did not appear to have suffered from being caught up in the economic fallout of the Covid19 pandemic well not in August 2020. People believed it due to the housing crisis and the overheated market. The huge shortfall of housing stock had never really recovered from the Christchurch earthquakes ten years earlier. In fact, the lack of housing stock had grown, making Cody Lane a very wealthy man, getting enormous amounts of money for the properties he sold or developed. As he sat opposite Wendy in his smart suit, and spikey grey hair, he looked like a man used to getting what he wanted. Little wonder he and Timothy Winthrop appeared to get along.

The third section of the parenting agreement covered the frequency of visits as Wendy had been the main carer of their children. Wendy also in real estate, specialised in luxury housing in the small town of Greytown, seven kilometres from Carterton with a population of two thousand five hundred odd people. There were a great many Wellingtonians who either bought weekenders (better than the average family home) or they stayed in luxury accommodation and shopped in the boutique township voted New Zealand's prettiest little town.

While Sydney liked the town, she thought it 'twee' and not for her more pragmatic sensibilities. However, she continued to be surprised by the turnover of real estate in the small township as many Wellingtonians thought they would enjoy the daily hour and a half commute over the Pass so they might enjoy their rustic idyll on the weekends. Only the daily commute soon became too onerous for many, and properties were bought and sold regularly. A real estate agent worth her salt could make a good living, not as good as Cody Lane in the capital city, but Wendy didn't need the aggravation accompanying the income.

'Look Cody, you know I usually work most weekends by appointment. My clients come over from Wellington, so I don't see why we can't work out some visiting times during the week. It makes more sense,' Wendy told them. But both Tim and Sydney seemed uncertain. Thinking about it Cody had another idea.

'Don't be ridiculous. Daniel has school and in three months they will both be at school, and we'll be back here sorting this out all over again. We need a sustainable arrangement. Ideally, I'd like to have him a lot more of the time, every second weekend as a start. We could meet at the bottom of the Pass after school on a Friday ...'

'Oh, I don't know,' Wendy grumbled. 'The way you change girlfriends I need to feel confident about who will be at your place with the boys on these weekends.'

'Wendy, you are divorced. Who Cody spends his weekends with is no longer your business,' Tim said firmly then he looked at Sydney, who seemed surprised by his comment. Sydney wondered whether Tim was saying he understood Fletch had become a permanent fixture in Finn's life. Putting a reassuring hand on Wendy's arm, Sydney suggested,

'Cody's choices haven't all been bad, he chose you, remember?'

Cody warmed to her comments and told them, 'I had a lot of time in prison to think about my situation and I had counselling and anger management courses. I'm a different man.' He watched a frown cross Sydney's face. 'I never once hit my wife Ms. Martin in case you were thinking I did.' He narrowed his eyes at her.

'Be that as it may, bullying can be done by phone these days, and punching holes in walls kicking furniture and yelling is enough to frighten most people.' Sydney said. Then added 'since you brought it up making Wendy or the boys feel uncomfortable at drop off and pick up times would constitute bullying,' she pursed her lips.

'My client knows what constitutes bullying, but I warn you not to milk it or complain unnecessarily, because the courts and the police will take a dim view of it,' Tim warned. Each lawyer had suggested their client should record their contact with one another at pick up and drop off times should they feel uncomfortable. Tim, now well aware women could be just as menacing as men in domestic situations if Amanda had been anything to go by, her tantrums were legendary. He felt relieved to be legally separated from her.

'Regardless of your comments Mr. Winthrop, all of us here are familiar with the statistics on family violence. I urge both Mr Lane and Ms Coleman to speak nicely and be kind to one another in front of their children.' Sydney sat poised for a moment then added to Tim's surprise. 'Kindness to one another was something Tim insisted on in our case, because it is easy to snipe and forget kids absorb bad vibes by osmosis. You only need to watch the Justice Department's own U-tube clips of children in these situations to see the effect their parent's behaviour has on the child's mental health.' As she spoke about how she and Tim were handling their new co-parenting situation, Tim noted Sydney had gone from calling him 'Mr. Winthrop' with an edge in her voice to a softer 'Tim.' He realised she had come a long way even if she did have some way yet to go. He felt reassured by it.

As the time went on Cody Lane and his ex-wife Wendy were moving to a satisfactory resolution. They would avoid a costly trial emotionally, financially and time wise. Also, they were both aware the court would appoint a lawyer for their sons who would interview not only them and their children but also extended family and friends. Then there would be no secrets. The court would know how much they drank on a daily basis, and what they smoked, if they did. The medications they took and why. Their financial situation would be scrutinised. The intimate secrets they shared with friends and frenemies would be exposed. Their work situations and every detail of their private home life questioned. There would be no stone unturned. Neither of them wanted such scrutiny.

So, they agreed Wendy would continue to do the lion's share of the parenting. Cody would take the boys every second weekend till Christmas which they would both share with their boys. Then Daniel and Drew would spend two weeks with their father during the school holidays.

Suddenly Cody insisted he would be booking Drew into boarding school when he turned intermediate school age.

'I want to watch him play sport every weekend, she' he pointed accusingly at his ex 'she never does anything that might crack a fingernail, how's this going to work for Drew and Daniel? They need their father.' Realising he had raised his voice, Cody went quiet. Wendy sat fighting back tears then she lashed out.

'See what I mean he will change the goal posts and then he'll bully me.'

'Bullshit, you're such a frigging drama queen, by the time the boys get to intermediate age you'll probably be happy for them to be off your hands at boarding school. I bet there's a bloke somewhere in the wings. I'll find out' he narrowed his eyes threateningly and Sydney looked from him to Tim who sat swallowing hard when she caught his eye. Shit who would put up with this crap for a living, Tim wondered. Then he noticed Sydney's lips quirk, luscious and full she quickly pursed them to appear severe.

'Mr Lane, I suggest we confine our agreement to the next three years. You should re-evaluate your custody arrangements again after three years. Frankly, the way the world is at present even three years seems like a lifetime.' Sydney tidied the papers on the table in front of her.

Wendy seemed keen to wrap things up and they agreed on the pickup and drop off point being the café at the bottom of the Remutaka Pass on the Wellington side. By the time everything was settled Cody began turning on the charm thanking them for their time and patience. Wendy could not wait to be the first to leave, saying she would be in touch.

Hardly had she left the building, when Cody turned to Sydney 'I bet Tim regrets the day he let you out of his life.'

Sydney laughed out loud. Then packed up her capacious handbag smirking.

'Oh, you would be surprised at what he said to me' she flicked her hair in a calculated move.

Back in her office she had no sooner dumped the file on her desk when she heard Tim's voice at reception.

'Ms. Martin, please we have just been in a meeting, and I forgot something. Timothy Winthrop,' on hearing his name the receptionist went into a tizzy. Sydney, whose door stood open called 'Tim, come through.' As soon as he stepped into her office, she closed the door.

'How come you were standing in for the Rottweiler? don't give me the bullshit line you used before.' Standing with her hands on her hips glowering at him only served to get his blood pumping. Without answering, he sat down in one of the club chairs in front of her desk.

'I wanted to see you in action. Frankly I don't see you in this family law business. I think you would be far better as a criminal lawyer. I've worked with you remember. When my private detective told me you were a lawyer at Howarth and Associates, naturally I checked. I never for one moment imagined you in the role. This is the second time you have surprised me. Last time I said I wouldn't underestimate you. I knew you worked here of course. I made the mistake of presuming.' By now she had slumped down in her chair. What did the man want?

'At one point in this morning's proceedings I saw a smirk cross your face, what amused you?' he asked curiously. She laughed out loud.

'I read your mind; you were wondering how I put up with the amateur dramatics the parents display in these situations. See, I worked with you too.' He remembered his thoughts exactly and she had seen right through him. Suddenly, his face changed.

'How is your twin doing in California?' he wanted to know.

'Well, he didn't have Covid and he's staying there. If I have grey hairs, it's because of him.'

'No, your hair's beautiful. I'm pleased about Perry, is he still as vague as he used to be?' Sydney sat there, wondering what Tim's game was? He had been uber sweet to her since the first time he had met Finn. It unnerved her Tim always had an agenda and she needed to find out what his current agenda would be.

'Say do you fancy a sandwich or something for lunch?' she asked.

'Sure, I'd prefer the *or something,* but I'd settle for a sandwich today.' He flashed those twinkling vivid blue eyes.

Sitting opposite him in the Wild Oates café, Sydney decided to see if she could glean what Tim wanted from her.

'Finn had Fletch make two new kites, one especially for you.' She watched his expression soften, 'you better make out you're surprised because I don't know if I should have told you.'

'Finn is getting to me. You know my honest regret is I missed his early years. I often ask myself how I could have been so damned stupid.'

Thinking like a lawyer, she commented, 'well, you were over me, so I guess it is understandable we were an unwelcome package.'

'Don't be so hard on yourself, the first couple of months I was furious, even the first couple of years I didn't want to know. But slowly I began to wonder as my friends became fathers and all the girlfriends fell by the wayside. While our sexual relationship had only been a few short months, I remember you said once, that you had a claim to fame as the woman with whom I had the longest ever relationship, after my mother.' With pursed lips and smiling eyes he leaned across the table and whispered.

'You still hold the title, only now I know why.'

'Don't Tim, don't. It's all academic now.' she didn't want to hear this. The whole thing had been difficult enough trying not to resent the man. But he didn't see it, the only thing he understood was he had made a huge mistake and now he would move heaven and earth to prove what he felt for Sydney. It occurred to Sydney if she invited Tim's parents to come to the farm for the next visit, she would not be alone with him.

Chapter Twenty-Three:

With Finn tucked up in his bed Sydney regaled Fletch with the events of the day.

'I can't believe the man still doesn't get it. He's a bully. I think he expects me to understand his perspective and behave like nothing ever happened,' she harrumphed. Fletch lovingly squeezed her shoulder as he pulled her to him and kissed her.

'You will Sydney, you will behave like it never happened because you love Finn and until he's an adult and can decide how he feels about his father for himself, you are far too sensible a mother to colour his perceptions of his father.' Fletch sat playing with her hair. 'He is such a bright boy. It won't be long before he works things out for himself, and he has sufficient of his mother's genes to let Tim know exactly what he thinks of him.'

Several weeks went past before Tim and his parents could come to the farm. They came after a week in Court with Tim defending a woman in a weird case of Munchausen's syndrome. The woman had poisoned her child in a systematic planned and repeated effort to attract attention to herself. The authorities caught her on the hospital CCTV footage putting something into the child's drink. Despite Tim's best efforts she was found guilty and sentenced to more than ten years in prison, which the judge said could be commuted to half the time if she admitted her guilt and accepted treatment.

The case attracted a great deal of legal argument at both Howarth and Associates and at Winthrop Partners, so it came as no surprise when once again it came up during lunch at the farm.

'Finn, I'd love to see your horse and the chickens,' Catherine had suggested as the conversation moved to the case.

Fletch lobbed a grenade on to the table by saying, 'I don't understand how you can defend a person you know has committed a heinous crime against a child and is sane.' Amused, Sydney waited for Grant to explain every person is innocent until proven guilty and they are entitled to the best defence available. For the defendant, the best happened to be Tim.

'The condition is now called 'Factitious Disorder;' the label is not factual evidence this defendant has behaved in this way. The use of a label is prejudicial to fairness and a finding based on fact,' Tim told them firmly.

Fletch simply grinned, knowing he had wound Tim up. Standing up he said he would join Cath and Finn. On a cue from Tim, Grant also left. Tim offered to help Sydney clear the table.

'Fletch has already loaded the dishwasher, there are just a few dishes to add.' Sydney said, distracted. 'I needed to talk to you alone. I'm comfortable with you having Finn on his own for a visit now, but I suggest you tread carefully and ask him, test the water at afternoon tea.' She watched Tim's face soften in mild amusement.

'You pre-empted me. You're turning into a good lawyer.' Giving him a wry look, she smirked knowing she couldn't keep blocking Tim forever. Five months had given Finn time to get to know his father. They weren't best friends, but Finn accepted him, so things were moving along.

WORKING FROM HOME IN rural Wairarapa, Sydney listened to the national news every day.

At noon on Wednesday the twelfth of August, the greater Auckland region moved back into lockdown Alert Level Three. Four days later on the sixteenth of August, the total number of active covid-19 cases in New Zealand had grown to sixty-nine, including forty-nine from the Auckland community cluster. The following day, nine new cases of covid-19 were reported in New Zealand. Prime Minister Jacinda Ardern announced the General Election would be moved to October seventeenth. Now, a month later, they were back in Alert Level One. The borders were still closed but talk still came up suggesting a trans-Tasman bubble with Australia.

Fletch walked down to the mailbox at the end of their long driveway, he needed the fresh air. Feeling quietly optimistic about Devil's Moon, the video game, he had spent the last few weeks glued to his computer screen fleshing out the characterisation and plot of the big picture. He and Perry Martin along with Karl Thalburg, both working in California, had started drilling down to more individual situations. It was a chicken and egg thing to him. The movie came before the game, but a worldwide gamer's conference soon to be held virtually provided him with the opportunity to pitch his idea to the digi-techno's before the event. They had narrowed it down to three games with the winner launching their game at this first-ever virtual conference. There the world's best gamers could play the game, pitting themselves against each other. The conference, now a mere ten weeks away, he needed the game finished in six weeks. Then he could have four world class gamers play it for the purpose of ironing out the glitches before the big launch.

Breathing in the fresh damp air he felt the hint of spring, with new buds and fresh foliage. Full of optimism he opened the mailbox and took out a large bundle of rural mail, now only delivered twice a week. Walking back to the house he shuffled through the pile of newspapers, two magazines, a bundle of advertising brochures and some letters for Sydney.

Inside the house Sydney had started preparing sandwiches for lunch and looked up at him.

'Any letters for me? Not window jobs they're always bills,' she complained as he handed her the pile. Quickly she rifled through them. 'Ooh this one's for you, Immigration NZ.' She handed back the envelope. Hurriedly, he ripped it open.

'Great, the Government have decided my current visa will remain valid in the present environment due to Covid19. Basically, they are giving me time, understanding the difficult business situation.' Lifting his broad shoulders in a shrug he added, 'I'm still in limbo really.'

'We're all in limbo, it's the virus. Until there is a vaccine, or the virus disappears nothing will change.' Sydney set down the lunch things, with sandwiches and fruit on the table.

What could he say? He was fast running out of options yet, still wildly enthusiastic about his video game which hopefully, would not only provide income, but stimulate interest in their movie. Fletch resolved to work every option until they were all exhausted.

'I'm not complaining, I'm grateful your Government recognised the talent pool here and is so supportive of the film industry. I know Devil's Moon will be made. My gut says it's going to be better than we imagined,' he said, his enthusiasm palpable.

Tim rang on the landline at seven in the evening suggesting he and Finn might Skype.

'Well, it would be so much easier if we could face time or WhatsApp. Have you thought about getting a cell tower on the property?' he sounded irritated.

'It wouldn't work, it's the hills and deep gullies, too many black spots.' He knew the technical reason for the poor reception, why did he enjoy being so perverse? 'I know you're busy this weekend I didn't expect to hear from you.' What does he want, she wondered.

'I want to be in my son's life.' Could he read her mind? 'All fathers have to work for a living, I told you this is a lifelong commitment.' Sydney bit her tongue. As soon as Finn felt happy enough to spend time with him and without her, she would relax a little.

'I understand,' she said quietly. She would like to have reminded him she too worked, had brought up their child alone, until Tim had a eureka moment in lockdown and decided he wanted to be a father.

'I'm trying to walk the talk here Sydney, do the right thing for my son,' he said sighing.

She turned to watch Fletch staring at her, holding his hands out in a question.

'It's Tim, he wants to skype Finn,' she explained.

'Fine, tell him we need thirty minutes to organise things.' Fletch frowned. looking firm. She repeated his words to Tim who accepted he would Skype in half an hour.

'Why did you suggest half an hour?' she asked, hanging up the landline.

'Because hun, this way we give him what he wants but still on our terms.' He suggested to Finn he get into his pyjamas, and he'd read him a story in his bedroom. In half an hour Sydney called Tim on the family I Pad. When Tim appeared on the screen, she left Finn to chat. The conversation for Tim felt like pulling teeth. She listened at the bedroom door before retreating to the living room. Tim asked questions and Finn answered. Totally aware of the little nuances of family life he had missed out on Tim had become sensible enough not to react when Finn said Fletch had read him half a story and would finish it later.

'He's a good storyteller, he puts on cool voices. Look here comes Spotty,' smiling to himself, Tim felt grateful Sydney had arranged getting Finn the pup. It had been a stroke of luck he happened to be there on the day. It gave their child so much joy.

'Would you like to come and stay with me for a weekend? You can play with the train set. We could go to Te Papa the big museum again, if you like' he smiled.

'Only if I can bring Spotty,' he insisted.

'Sure, but I need to get the fences made dog proof. It's not like the farm, the city is a little different,' he explained, as Finn cuddled his little pooch.

'We want to keep him safe, don't we?' The conversation hardly lasted more than five minutes. Finn came out to the living room and practically dropped the I Pad on Sydney's lap. Tim confirmed the gist of their conversation and Sydney told him to email her the details so she could mark the calendar.

With Finn safely tucked up in bed asleep Sydney dropped a bombshell.

'I don't want to sleep with you anymore Fletch. I thought I could handle it, but I can't. The truth is I never wanted to be in this situation and since you don't see any future with me, I refuse to live like this.' Watching the look on his face change, he looked devastated, she added quickly,

'I don't expect you to move out in fact I don't want you to go, these past six months you have become a father to Finn, but...' her voice hitched, and she turned away.

'Sydney, what brought this on? I'm just weeks away from completing stage one of Devil's Moon.' He put his hands on her shoulders, 'What's happened to make you feel like this?' He had always been honest with her but lately, as Covid dragged on and he had made no moves to suggest a future with her or even to talk about staying in the country, she began to fear being hurt when he went back to California. At first, she pushed the idea of it out of her head, now she could no longer be detached. Now in too deep, she needed to encourage Finn to develop his relationship with his father.

'Look, I never planned to feel the way I do, but I can't go through it again.' She referred to her feelings for Tim when they had broken up and he knew how hurt she had been, it crushed him.

'Let me think about this,' he whispered. 'I'll move back into the spare room and think about how...' he sat flabbergasted. She had blindsided him and he needed to think clearly. Sleeping on his own would be a good idea under the circumstances.

Chapter Twenty-Four:

Tim had a big case due in Court in a few weeks, so he wanted Finn to stay with him this weekend. The atmosphere between Sydney and Fletch had been fraught since she told him how she felt. Although tense both tried to carry on as normal in Finn's presence but like all children, he soaked everything up like a sponge and he soaked up the strangeness.

Today Friday, Sydney had arranged to meet Tim at the café at the bottom of the Pass at six pm with Finn. Earlier in the day Tim had texted Sydney. Spotty couldn't come for the weekend as his boundary fences were still not secure. The tradesman had been a no show. Sydney would need to explain to Finn. She felt less than impressed, Tim always ensured someone else mopped up after him. Typical of him, he should have said 'no, when I get the fences secure, we can talk about it.' Instead, Sydney would need to tell Finn the dog could not go, and he would be most unhappy.

Friday would be the last day of school before the holidays and the six-year-old felt tired and his Mr Grumpy face appeared. When he learned Spotty couldn't go with him the child had a complete meltdown. He didn't want to go. Fletch offered to take him and Olive to the movies, to see "The War with Granddad" on the Tuesday. He suggested a lazy day on Monday. Still inflexible, Finn made it hard work for Sydney, trying to get him ready for his father.

'Can you drive me there please Fletch,' he grizzled in a half blub, hugging him frantically around his waist. The look Fletch exchanged with Sydney showed his pained expression. He noticed she chewed the inside of her cheek her eyes anxiously darting around.

'I'm happy to do it, honestly,' he caught her eye. 'With you of course.'

'Thank you' she managed before disappearing to Finn's room to pack his bag.

'Come on Buddy let's take Spotty for a walk. I'll look after him for you this weekend, promise.' The pair trotted off outside for a walk. 'You're not very happy today, what's troubling you? You can tell me we're good mates.' Fletch put a fatherly arm around the boy's shoulder.

'Don't you like mummy anymore? You used to kiss her all the time, now you don't.' out of the mouths of babes and sucklings.

'Oh, I thought you said it was yucky when I kissed her?' he chuckled. Finn cut to the chase just like his mother, 'but she liked it,' the six-year-old told him.

'Yeah, but I've been kind of busy and tired, I still like your mummy, a lot I just forgot.' Thinking about it Fletch, needed to talk to Sydney. Not usually one to talk 'feelings' he wondered if something else disturbed her. They had never really discussed why she wanted to distance herself from him. Did she need to spell it out? He knew Tim had hurt her badly and so she folded in on herself. She became self-sufficient a good mother and a decent lawyer. He had pushed her, wanting more from the relationship. A family had been a long-time dream and he enjoyed it. Although they lived a simple life here in New Zealand, this life had been provided by Sydney, her home, her inheritance. She had the steady job and the passive income of the farm lease. The more he thought about it, the more he understood his own traditional values and ingrained prejudices. Being the only child of a successful military man who provided the income, his mother was a stay-at-home wife and he and his father were her world. As a family they were definitely not poor, but neither were they rich. Fletch had watched as many of his friends had struggled with the financial strains of raising children, school fees, braces, extracurricular activities, college, and university funds. Now, he didn't honestly know whether the restrictions he imposed on himself about being wealthy were so he could provide well for his family or feed his ego. Perhaps they were simply an excuse for not being able to commit, afraid of being hurt again. Emily had hurt him deeply.

Fletch remembered the day back in December 2013 when he came across Emily's training diary. She had never hidden it from him, but he had never taken any notice of it so in fact it was hidden in plain sight. Reading it sent shivers up his spine. No way Emily could have physically kept up the regimen set down in her diary. The diary placed on her little desk, in a corner of their living room. He had put off going through her possessions and happily delegated them to her girlfriend Carrie, who had offered. It worked well but Carrie left the little writing desk saying it held personal papers, bank statements and financial things Fletch needed to deal with. After procrastinating for a year, he finally went through it and found all sorts of things he felt sure Emily never wanted him to find. Her last two bank card statements showed she stayed in a motel on the other side of town twice in her last month. During this time, he had worked on base and at home. At first, he felt sure there must be some explanation, but a photo of Emily and Gray, her personal trainer dressed up and leaning in together at some function made him wonder what had been going on. Emily's girlfriend found her, and her telephone had been smashed with the sim card missing. Fletch remembered the police thought it suspicious, but he had a watertight alibi.

Fletch had been away on a field exercise, hundreds of miles from home in the company of a group of men, somewhere at Fort Jackson in North Carolina. Carrie had discovered Emily's body. The ME believed she overdosed on sleeping pills and her note simply said, "The perfect end to my imperfect life" E. Fletch never totally understood those words and speculated on them. Her family decided she must have been depressed and he should have noticed. How could he? She functioned at a very high level and hid things from him.

Needing to understand he went to see Carrie and talk to her. Geoff, Carrie's husband, brought the coffee to them and casually asked his wife if she had told Fletch about Gray. Carrie did not want to betray her friend but seeing how cut up Fletch looked, Carrie's husband insisted.

'The man needs some closure; it might join the dots for him.'

Slowly they told him about this relationship Emily had been having for more than three years with Gray, an ex-military physical training instructor now personal trainer, a married man, and ten years older than Fletch. On the face of it, the man seemed like a harmless family man. Looking back, he had been in her running group the day of the marathon, but he had not been injured. Fletch thought him caring and helpful until he learned the truth then he wanted to rearrange his face and would have, had he known, doubtless, the reason no one had told him. Did Gray come to his house when he was away? No wonder Emily didn't want to live on base and pushed Fletch to buy a place away from Fort Bragg. Gray could easily visit the mess and friends on base without causing suspicion. He knew there were ways these things could be done but they didn't live on base the last two years of Emily's life.

Months went by and still Fletch had no closure until he retired from the Army. As soon as his house sold, he received a visit from Gray the personal trainer. The meeting started out under the pretence of a casual drop by to say goodbye and ended up with Fletch telling him he knew of his affair with his wife. The man, visibly upset, explained he carried a lot of guilt about the affair, because he would not divorce his wife. They had a son with cerebral palsy. He spent a lot of time helping with the boy's physical treatment and as a result the child's life had improved to the point he went to a normal school and his physical limitations had lessened. Gray worried if he didn't live at home with the boy, his daily exercise regimen might slip back and with it the child's mobility and health. In the end Fletch almost felt sorry for the man and left his face intact. Anyway, from the look of his nose, someone had beaten him to it he remembered, slightly amused.

Finn tugging at his hand brought him back to the present.

'You'll still be here when I get back, won't you?' Finn asked anxiously.

'Definitely, we're going to the movies next week remember?' he squeezed the boy's hand.

The journey over the Remutaka Pass seemed quiet. Strong winds could be felt hitting them sideways on the straights. The electronic wind warning sign flashed as they drove on to the Pass. Sydney started singing silly songs like "the wheels on the bus go round and round" and Finn and Fletch joined in. Then he sang "She'll be coming round the mountain when she comes" the song another travelling favourite to take the child's mind off the journey.

Fletch waited in the vehicle while Sydney and Finn walked towards the entrance of the café. Inside, Tim waited for them. Taking one look at Sydney he could tell something seemed amiss and presumed incorrectly that Finn's first weekend away from his mother caused her grief. After hugging Finn, he stood up and taking Sydney's arm he promised to take good care of their son.

'Would you like to join us for dinner?' he asked quietly.

'No thank you, Fletch is waiting in the vehicle,' her reply absent minded.

'He's welcome to join...'

'Thank you no,' she shook her head looking at Finn. Tim let it go knowing Finn really like Fletch. They agreed Sunday afternoon, four pm, same place for pick up time.

'We might stay for tea then,' she kissed Finn and slipped away not wanting a fuss.

While the father and son waited for their dinner to arrive Tim gave his son a brown paper bag with string handles. Inside he saw a colouring book and a box of felt tip pens. Colouring in had always been a favourite pass time of Finn's. His father surrepticiously questioned the boy while enjoying his company.

'Mummy looked a bit tired, has she been working hard?' he slipped in as he passed the red pen, not really expecting any reply, as he watched the boy think for a moment.

'I don't know, but Fletch said he's tired that's why he doesn't kiss her anymore,' definitely not the answer he expected but as an expert in cross examination he held up the green pen for Finn and casually asked, 'what else did Fletch say?'

'He said he's been busy, but he still liked her.' A strange sensation filled Tim, on the one hand he felt pleased there appeared to be trouble in paradise, but the look on his son's face hurt him and he realised he loved this little boy, and the child might get hurt.

'Is mummy sad about it like you are?' He wanted to fix it, so his son didn't get hurt. He thought about how another woman in his life might affect his child. It could get complicated, he didn't need complications, well not at present. His regret about the way he treated Sydney still haunted him. He knew he hadn't treated her well back in the day and now they might all pay for it.

'Yes, she tried not to cry when she packed my bag.' Finn's big blue eyes widened as though he had just thought of something. 'I think Fletch might be going back to America when he's allowed.' Tim murmured his understanding just as the server arrived with their food.

On their return journey neither Sydney nor Fletch spoke until they arrived in Featherston.

'Let's get some food in Martinborough,' he suggested.

'You don't need to stop for food,' she told him.

'I want to, even if it's just fish and chips in the square if we can't get a table somewhere.' Leaning over he touched her hand; she didn't pull away. 'We need to talk properly.'

'I don't know that we have a lot to say to each other. You made yourself perfectly clear months ago and if you change your mind now it won't be for the right reasons, so it won't work.' Breathing in sharply, she looked out of the window, ignoring him.

'Nevertheless, I need you to know a few things.' Aware he would be rehashing old ground, he tried to think how he could explain his feelings honestly. Now, surreptitiously sneaking a peak at him with a sideways glance, she wondered what he could say to mitigate this situation. Once he'd said he had 'feelings' for her, big deal, they had been living together in the biblical sense for the past six months. 'Feelings' were the least of her expectations, especially since she loved him so desperately. This time she would not put her heart on the line, it would be like self-flagellation. No good could come of beating yourself up.

'Gee, I think it might be fish and chips in the square, the town's pretty busy and besides, I'm not really dressed for dinner.' she complained as they drove down Kitchener Street and around The Square. Fletch looked around as he drove but said nothing. Driving past the cinema to the fish and chip shop he pulled up and climbed out, walked around to her door and opened it.

'Your usual hun?' he leaned in and kissed her while she sat captive in her seat. Groaning she responded. They were in a public street and so it wouldn't go far. Fletch determined to get over this glitch in their relationship. He felt sure she wanted him. He returned with a packet of food and two bottles of ginger beer. Handing her the packages he continued around the square and stopped at a picnic table. The wind had dropped, and it turned into a pleasant evening. Sydney set up the food and drink on the table.

'Thank you for coming over the hill with me tonight.'

'You're welcome. I enjoyed the singing,' he joked pinching a chip from her fingers just as it touched her lips.

'Watch it,' she swatted his hand, grinning and taking his chip in the same move.

'Watch it minx or ...' he grinned not wanting to verbalise his thoughts.

'Or what?' she teased, laughing and moving her food out of his reach.

'Or it will all end in tears,' he said. She laughed instinctively, watching Fletch mimicking Finn finger-waggling lips pursed. They fell silent for a minute or two then Fletch grinned, 'I just gotta share.' Fletch looked earnest, 'but you must promise not to say anything to Finn.' He beamed, and Sydney wondered what secrets those two shared on their regular afternoon walks.

'Finn worried because his teacher seemed less than impressed by his honest suggestion. Apparently, she had a pile of coins on her desk and asked the kids to identify them and also asked Finn what he would use to pay for a three-dollar punnet of strawberries. When he answered he would use his bankcard why bother with a pocket full of change, his teacher said his answer wasn't helpful.' Laughing Fletch added 'Then he said to me quite honestly, why do some people make life more difficult?' Fletch smiled and then he sighed, he loved Finn.

'He's a pleaser you know, but he struggles with it at times. How's your work going this week?' she asked, not wanting to have the conversation.

'It's full on.' He meant it had been difficult when his creativity had been suddenly sapped, by her relegating him to the friends' zone. 'I had a long talk with my old Dad today. He can't understand why the Trump administration aren't taking Covid as seriously as they should. There are too many layers of command and no nationwide cohesive plan. The old soldier was not impressed. The vets have a website and the numbers of old soldiers dying is alarming. Dad said they don't give cause of death but it's way higher than the same time last year. Of course, my dear father is a conspiracy theorist,' he smirked. 'Since Finn, I've thought about him a lot. He's a good man who loved my mother deeply. He's still lost without her, and she's been gone years now.' Sipping his ginger beer, he looked wistfully towards the mountains. He didn't want to have the conversation either.

'Let's go home and get a real drink,' he read her mind.

Sydney stood in her bedroom changing from her office clothes into comfy lounging trackpants and tee shirt, She never heard the landline when Fletch answered it.

'Is Sydney available, its Tim?'

'Sorry mate I think she's taking a shower.' She went to get changed. Can I have her call you?' he could hear Finn calling him in the background. 'Put him on Tim, I'll deal with it.' Not wanting to rock the boat, Tim put Finn on the line.

'What's up Buddy?' he asked, his voice firm.

'I can't sleep, it's not dark enough. But I still want the light on.' He sounded as though if pushed, he would burst into tears.

'Okay, I'll get Tim to fix it, but you must close your eyes and try to sleep. Count sheep in the paddock, promise me?' the boy agreed. Fletch told Tim the city light pollution might be too much and suggested a blanket over the window or blackout curtains in future plus a night light in the hall. About half an hour later Tim called again, and Sydney answered.

'He's fast asleep, it worked.' When she seemed surprised, he explained. Fletch had come to the rescue again.

The rest of the weekend went without incident and even the Sunday afternoon pick up and tea with Tim passed with ease. To her pleasant surprise the father and son duo were building a rapport. Tim charmed her at tea entertaining them both about his boyhood antics with the neighbour's pet rabbits, letting them escape inside the house.

'I can't have pet rabbits. Spotty would kill them. Terriers kill rabbits,' Finn told them in his simple pragmatic way.

Chapter Twenty-Five:

The next few weeks Tim worked extra-long hours to prepare his case and life at Boar Gully farm went on much as always, although more than a little stilted. The friends' zone didn't feel like a happy place for Sydney. Fletch now spoke openly about going back to America to attend to some pressing business. Perry and his girlfriend had bought a house together. Although he and Fletch spoke on Skype or Zoom meetings with Carl, Perry had little to do with Sydney. Almost as though he sensed the changed dynamic between her and Fletch and had given up on her ever holding on to a man. The old-fashioned patriarchal views he held annoyed Sydney, who felt sure he had married but because of Covid, kept it under the radar. Perry had always been the sort to need a big flash wedding, to go with his big hairy audacious goals as an Oscar award-winning movie director.

Perry had this image thing; the church with the best stained-glass windows, the cake with more tiers than anyone else. Fletch never discussed Perry anymore and the distance between Fletch and Sydney now ached like a vast gnawing cavern. One day when lunching with Sara, she spelled it out to her.

'I just can't do it anymore and I won't. No matter what I feel for the guy, I got over Tim and I'll get over Fletch. It's just more complicated because Finn loves him. The guy's a commitment-phobe what can I say?'

'These are strange times, Sydney. Have you ever thought you could be driving him away?' Sara didn't agree with Sydney's actions.

'Yes, but what else can I do? He is going to leave sooner or later. I thought I could enjoy him while he's here only I can't. It would be like prostituting myself. I do want him, but I can't do it,' she sniffed 'I'm sure he hates me. I mean he didn't like me at the start. I should have left it there, but we grew on each other. You know I proposed to him, and he refused me. I did it more than once, desperate eh?' Surprised, Sara thought they were a forever couple.

A couple of days later Sara agreed to pick up Finn from school. She arranged with Sydney to take him to the hairdresser with Olive to get their hair cut. Sydney had court in Masterton. Sara arrived with afternoon tea and after the children were fed, they went outside to play. Sara quizzed Fletch about Sydney. At first, he seemed annoyed Sydney had discussed their issues with Sara, but they were best friends, what did he expect?

'Why didn't you accept her proposal if you have feelings for her as you claim?' *Women,* Fletch sat gobsmacked.

'Because I'm forty-one years old and I have nothing to bring to this alliance. I don't even own a suit here.' Sara saw the hard edge some ex-military get after years of service.

'What do you mean? You're making a movie I know things are tight, but you must have assets back in the States,' she said, as though she thought him childish.

'I didn't think I'd be required to give you a statement of my financial position but as you're asking, I have my apartment on the market, but the arse has fallen out of the real estate market in California. It's not like New Zealand.' Sticking out his chin, he narrowed his eyes. 'Be honest with me Sara, would you marry a man with no assets because, my stocks and bonds are wallpaper at the moment. Technically I have no income the movie investors have gone AWOL, even my army super has gone down the toilet. To say things are not looking good is to paint far too rosy a picture, I'm broke.' The words were spat out and she looked shocked. He could see it on her face.

'But you have a flash four-wheel drive,' she spluttered.

'Bought before we lost the movie backers. I'll probably have to sell it to buy my air ticket back,' he exaggerated. Watching her horrified expression, he sneered, 'see I thought so, I don't see you as the sort who would marry someone in my position, I don't blame you, I wouldn't do it either.' After he said it, he felt better, vindicated somehow.

'I'm sorry, I didn't realise your situation was quite so dire,' she whispered, still very surprised.

I'm sorry it's none of my business.' Sara had lived a modestly comfortable life not unlike Sydney, but in an instant, she could see her friend was the better person. and she felt small and shallow but still held to her view.

When Sydney arrived home from work, she suggested they all take the horses out for a ride. She wanted to blow away the cobwebs after a particularly gruelling day in court. Knowing Finn would be keen if Fletch came she put on her best happy face. They headed across to the paddock with the bridles to catch the horses. Fletch ambled slowly behind. Finn ran ahead, Pickle always came when he called him.

'You look worse than I feel, lets open a bottle of wine when we get back,' she said, sounding much better than she felt.

'It's not Friday,' he replied.

'No, it's not, but sometimes you have to live dangerously,' her mischievous grin tugged at him, and he smirked. 'What have you done today?' she asked, noticing Jamie's tractor parked beside the shed. Finn called out to them irritated.

'Come on you old slow pokes, check my saddle please.' An adult always checked it for him, after a spill he'd taken because the straps were not firm enough and the saddle slipped around. Fletch checked it and the three of them soon set off. The gentle wind warmed and with daylight saving time the days were longer. Spring still offered fickle terms, but Sydney would take what she could get after a day like today. They rode in companionable silence and when they arrived back at the stable paddock Sydney opened up.

'A new partner joined the firm, he's been practicing on his own for years, but he hates conveyancing. Ben Howarth says we need his other skills so we can be more rounded. The new partner is Maxwell West. Max is about forty-five, quite suave and a very competent criminal lawyer, as small-town lawyers go.' She took off her helmet before dismounting and ruffled her hair. It billowed in the gentle breeze. 'The only problem is, Ben wants to promote me to be Max's assistant with a view to my doing more criminal work. I told him I'm not sure, but I want to make partner, so I'll have to suck it up.'

Fletch rubbed down Pickle and Trigger the mount he borrowed from Jamie Dalton. he now enjoyed these rides; they went out three or four times each week. He let Sydney ramble on about her day, but he felt more than a tad annoyed. The more he thought about his conversation with Sara the more it irked him. Back at the homestead they opened the bottle of wine. Fletch offered to cook dinner. He had prepared the meal earlier; a warm potato salad made with small gourmet potatoes, asparagus, spears boiled eggs, finely chopped red onion, and crispy pan-fried pancetta with a creamy mayonnaise. He slavishly followed the recipes in the Martin family recipe books, using coloured garnishes, like chopped peppers, sweet corn or whatever he had to hand. he enjoyed it and after six months had become competent. Angus beef steaks were always a favourite, and he would BBQ them just before serving.

Sydney noticed all sorts of small jobs had been completed; the washing folded up; the windows cleaned. When she went to put Finn's clothes away just before dinner, she once again noticed Jamie's tractor parked beside the shed. It had a rotary hoe attached to it and covered in fresh soil. Walking outside, she noticed all the vegetable gardens had been ploughed and planted. She felt sure Fletch had done it. Knowing where any comment about it might lead, she waited till Finn went to bed. Fletch stood and offered to make them tea.

'No, I think you deserve a rest, I see you've ploughed and planted my summer garden. I need to say thank you.' As she stood to move to the kitchen, he put his arm around her.

'Say it like you used to.' He bent to kiss her and sighing she obliged. He smelled so good tasted so good. How would she cope when he left?

'I need to know you'll be okay,' his deep voice sounded a little husky, 'in case I...'

'You plan on leaving us soon, don't you?' A hurt look crossed her features.

'I... er I don't want to, but I feel the need to try and save the remnants of my life.' Tucking a stray tendril of hair away from her face he whispered, 'I'm sorry... I'll come back.'

'If you can. When you'll be able to is a different matter' she sniffed and pulling away moved to make the tea. The landline rang. Picking it up, she heard a woman's voice with an American accent.

'Major Fletch Carter please Ma'am,' her tone business like. Sydney alerted Fletch to his call.

'Fletch Carter,' he said and whatever the woman said made him turn away.

'When did this happen?' he asked, then silence. 'He sounded fine when I spoke to him earlier in the day,' silence again. 'What are you saying, you know I'm eleven thousand kilometres away. May I speak to him please?' he sighed. 'Oh mercy, I'll be in touch. Please call me if there is any change of status, thank you.' He ended the call, then turned back to Sydney.

'My father has Covid, he had it when he called me earlier. He never told me, never mentioned it.' Raking his fingers through his thick hair she noticed he had more grey than when he first came to the farm. 'The nurse in charge of the isolation ward said he's taken a turn for the worse. I can't believe it. He sounded so full of life, sure he coughed a bit, but he smoked during the Vietnam years. They all did. Why didn't he tell me?' His pain almost palpable, Sydney went to him, hugging him.

'I think he wanted you to have a memorable, fun chat. Perhaps he knew things might get worse and wanted to give you something positive to hang on to.' Turning back, she picked up the mugs of tea and set them down on the coffee table, watching Fletch deep in thought.

'I need to be stateside. I must see him before...'

'I understand, drink your tea and we'll get online and make a booking. Within an hour the efficient Sydney pulled out all the stops and had Fletch booked on a flight to Auckland the next day, Friday, and then on a flight to Sydney, Australia and from there to Los Angeles. In her efficient take-charge manner, she helped him pack his bags and arranged to drive him to the airport. The departure time for Auckland was set for one in the afternoon. It was now ten thirty by the time everything had been organised. Finn would come with them to the airport, then Sydney would drop him off at Tim's home for the weekend.

As Fletch tried to sleep his thoughts drifted to his conversation with his father earlier in the day. Basically, when he had complained about his financial situation, his father dismissed it.

'Fortunes come and go son; you are never going to starve. Hold on to what's really important and don't be afraid to do things differently.' When Fletch had asked his father if he ever had any regrets, his old man really surprised him.

'I don't do regrets, but there were always things I could have done better, like spend more time with my family. A little less time spent travelling with Uncle Sam and more time spent with you. Kids grow up so fast, but you gotta have them first. Your mother and I would like to have had more kids, we lost a couple, early miscarriages,' he explained. 'Barbara had the rhesus negative factor and I had been deployed so much we missed our window, so, I guess it is a regret of sorts. She said there were no guarantees in these things. We both loved you so much.' How come he never knew his mother had been rhesus negative? He had always wondered why he had no siblings, his mother simply said, 'we weren't blessed with more.' Thinking about it, he only asked her the question when he wanted to become a father. Tossing and turning sleep evaded him when he heard Sydney's familiar footsteps on the wooden hall floor.

'Can't sleep?' he asked huskily. He felt her lift up the duvet cover and slip in beside him.

'Shush just hold me please' she snuggled up to him and they both drifted off to sleep.

At breakfast Fletch explained to Finn he had to urgently return to America because his father was ill in hospital.

'Is it Covid?' trust Finn to cut to the chase.

'Yes, and it's serious,' he whispered.

'You're not coming back, are you?' his big blue eyes welled up. Sydney looked away. This day had come much sooner than she ever imagined.

'I want to come back, but at the moment with Covid I can't promise when it might be,' his words were slow and considered. Seeing Finn's lip tremble, he frowned and turned his gaze away. Fletch put an arm around the boy. 'I'll Skype you from the States, okay?' Finn nodded.

After breakfast when Finn played with Spotty Fletch told Sydney.

'I've spoken to Jamie Dalton and the Ford dealer in Masterton, they'll deal with my vehicle.' When Sydney said he didn't need to sell it she could house it in one of the spare garages on the property, Fletch had solemnly shaken his head. He wasn't coming back she knew deep down in her heart.

Even Finn seemed in no mood for singing on the way over the Pass. Glancing over at him, Sidney sniffed back tears, he looked so completely lost. She glanced across at Fletch who turned taking in the sad little expression on the child's face. Fletch didn't want this but driven by duty and some other compelling force he needed to go. He remembered from back in the day when his father would say to him, 'just one more mission, son.' Of course, he never really believed him. It had been just something he always said. His mother would say 'Duty calls.' Somehow, he found 'duty' more believable. Duty calls is what he used to say to Emily whenever he deployed on some exercise. 'Duty calls.' It sounded so different from what Sydney had said to Finn by way of explanation.

'Fletch's daddy is all alone and sick, he must go, family come first,' Sydney's explanation felt more palatable for Finn to understand.

At the airport, waiting for his boarding call, they sat huddled together in silence. Fletch held Sydney's hand with his other arm around Finn drawing him into a hug.

'Take care of Spotty, and your mother of course,' he said. Hearing his boarding call, he hugged the boy and then he took Sydney's face in his hands and kissed her lovingly, tenderly ignoring the warm tears he felt run down her cheeks.

Dabbing them away she told him on a faltering breath.

'Contrary to what I may have said in the past, you're always welcome at Boar Gully, Fletch Carter.' Acknowledging her invitation with a single nod of his head, he had no voice. He would have cried liked a baby, so he turned away, cabin bag over his shoulder. He never looked back.

They had a few hours to fill in before Tim would be due home from the office. Thinking quickly, Sydney booked two tickets to 'Cats and Dogs Paws Unite.' Finn enjoyed the popcorn and Sydney couldn't remember anything about the movie except how bad she felt. In the powder room she freshened up, determined not to let

Tim see what a mess she felt inside. It was amazing what a fresh application of makeup and a good brush of the hair could do for a girl's morale. A quick spritz of fragrance and she smelt good to go. By the time she drove across town to Tim's house, the town buzzed with activity, a Friday night type of frenetic. They didn't get to his Thorndon villa until five thirty-five. Fortunately, he had arrived home from his office in plenty of time and greeted them warmly.

'Fletch get away okay then?' he asked, trying to appear sympathetic, although he felt pleased the guy had gone. 'Stay and have some dinner with us tonight,' he insisted.

'I can't I need to work all weekend, the practice has a new partner, Max West. Have you heard of him?' he said he had, and Sydney elaborated, 'yes, well Ben has me working with him, the idea being I expand my horizons doing a bit of defence work. I'm dying for a cup of tea.'

Finn made himself at home and asked if he could play in his room where Tim had set up the train set. They agreed and Finn went off to play.

'I believe you could be a brilliant defence lawyer.' Tim filled his electric jug and pointed to a draw for the mugs. 'If you ever need a second opinion, I'm happy to give it.' This news thrilled him, he could imagine working with her again. Enthusiasm filled him with thoughts about her future options. 'I'm really pleased for you; I've always thought family law is fine, but you need to have options.' The pair sat discussing the merits of this new situation and sipping their tea.

'My god look at the time' I better get going. It will be bedtime by the time I get home at this rate.' He pressed her again to stay but she insisted on going and went off to say goodbye to Finn. Finding his room empty she called out to him.

'Come on Finn, mummy has to get going. Finn where are you?' she called. Tim came out from the living area and taking the stairs two at a time, he said he'd find him. He called out as he went from room to room, 'Tim, Tim.'

Sydney called, 'did we leave the front door open? The front doors open Tim,' her voice at concert pitch now. The grim expression on Tim's face alerted her to the fact Finn had gone, nowhere to be found, he raced down the stairs.

'I didn't leave the front door open, in fact I know I didn't. I make a habit of locking it.' Glancing at his watch he asked, 'how long have we been talking?'

'Heavens, it's been forty-five minutes, maybe more.' Sydney felt distracted and anxious, Finn never wandered off at home.

'I'm calling the police. You wait here, I'll check the street too.' Tim pulled on his suit jacket as he spoke to the emergency operator. Turning back, he called to Sydney, 'I'll keep you posted.' Now out of sight, he could see darkness descending. The street previously overcast was now almost dark and it was getting on for seven pm.

'police, my name is Timothy Winthrop. I'm a barrister with Winthrop Partners here in Wellington. My six-year-old son is missing from home. He had been playing in his room while his mother and I talked after work and when we went to check on him, he had gone. The child is called Finn, Finn Martin, yes, I said my name is Timothy Winthrop. The boy's mother is at home in case he returns. I'm out on the street looking for him. He had on jeans and a sweatshirt. He's blond haired and blue eyed.' Tim felt puffed and filled with anxiety.

A marked patrol car rounded the corner of his street. Tim ran back towards it, to meet the police parking outside his villa. By the time he reached the house, Sydney who had invited them in and stood busy furnishing them with all Finn's details. She sent them a photo she took earlier in the day of Finn and Fletch at the airport. Sydney became alarmed when she saw how distressed Tim looked.

'Sergeant, I hope to God this is not relevant,' he puffed and panted, breathless from running, 'today I turned down a case requiring me to defend a paedophile. The man Colin Bert, has a string of convictions for paedophilia.' Tim's voice cracked. 'He rang me from Rimutaka prison, I turned him down. I couldn't do it. I couldn't look at my sleeping child and defend a man like him in all good conscience. I said I'm over committed, no capacity.' Tim sniffed sounding choked up, 'the thing is this man said to me, "I hope you won't regret your decision." To be honest, normally I would toss off a threatening remark. His sort are often trying to intimidate. Oh God, help me.' On hearing Tim's words Sydney started sobbing, immediately Tim went to her, trying to comfort her.

'I'm probably worrying needlessly here Sidney, but they need to know. I couldn't bear it if anything happened to him. Getting to know him has been a joy, I love him so much.' Now Sydney comforted Tim. More police arrived. The new arrivals were senior plain clothes officers. Recognising one of them, Sydney felt relieved. Detective Inspector Dan Parker often worked as a Police prosecutor. D.I. Parker, also a qualified lawyer lived in Carterton and travelled over the Pass, sometimes on a daily commute.

'Ms Martin, I'm running this enquiry.' Dan looked towards Tim, and then Sydney. 'We've met in the course of our work,' he sounded kindly, not forceful as she had heard him in court. The dog squad are coming, and they'll see what they can find.

'Call me Sydney, please,' she insisted. 'What's happening please Inspector?' she tugged at the bottom of her sweater. Everything seemed to be moving so slowly. The stats were frightening with missing children.

'I have a team searching the neighbourhood and talking to the neighbours, somebody may have seen something.' She noticed two people in white hazmat suits with toolboxes. Then seeing the word Forensics on the back of the suits she gasped, covering her mouth.

'Don't worry Sydney it's simply a precaution.' Now people seemed to be milling around everywhere. Turning away from her, D.I. Parker answered his mobile.

Tim walked outside to talk with another detective.

'Get Mr. Winthrop in here detective,' D. I. Parker called from the hallway. 'Sit down Sydney, I need to talk to you and the child's father together. There's a national TV crew just down the road waiting for a jury verdict at the High Court. My offsider says it will be hours away as they have just returned to the jury room after a question. I'd like to get them up here and have Tim speak to them, appeal to the public of New Zealand to help us.' He looked towards Tim, who seemed pleased to have something to contribute. 'We are taking this matter very seriously. He is not at your parent's home; they are staying put in case he manages to get there if he just wandered off.'

'He wouldn't just wander off,' Sydney said annoyed. 'We've always had rules,' she insisted. Ignoring her words, DI Parker casually asked if anything had been troubling the child lately. Then Sydney remembered Fletch, she would need to phone him.

'Well, my brother's business partner, Fletch Carter, stayed with us during lockdown. He's American from California and came here to make a movie. Then Covid hit. He lived with us for over six months and Finn loved him. Fletch went back to America today. We saw him off at the airport he flew out to Auckland at one o'clock.' Sydney went quiet, chewing her lip.

'But Finn's known he would return to the States for weeks, he told me so,' Tim elaborated. 'He's a stoic little boy, I'm not convinced Fletch leaving had anything to do with it.' Just then the television crew, a cameraman and female reporter, arrived at the door.

'Just a moment' Sydney said, grabbing her handbag and taking off down to the powder room. The Police inspector thought it was simply an ablutions call. In truth Sydney wanted to call Fletch. She needed his support. The call went to voice mail she left a message telling him Finn had gone missing. Looking at her watch he might have boarded for Australia, but with any luck he had not. Brushing her hair, she washed her face, swiped on some lip-gloss and spritzed her perfume. It always soothed her to feel fresh. Taking several deep breaths, she returned to the living room. Standing in the doorway she beckoned Tim; D. I. Parker followed him.

'Have the police sent someone to Rimutaka Prison to interview Colin Burt?' she directed her question at the police officer. Holding Tim's arm she whispered, 'I called Fletch. It went to voice mail his flight to America via Australia is probably in the air by now.' Tim could see her fragility and her strength. He stroked her face with his index finger.

'Don't worry about Colin Bert, the police will deal with him. And Fletch, he's gone I'm sorry. Let's do this interview in the formal living room, it will be quieter in there.'

They were seated on a brocade covered lounge suite together, with D.I. Parker sitting off to one side. Sydney said nothing, but Tim took her hand and nervously spoke from his heart.

'We are desperate to find our son. If you have seen him, or have any information please, we urge you to contact the police. We pray it didn't happen like this, but our six-year-old son Finn has disappeared from his bedroom at home.' Watching Tim, Sydney felt sick he barely managed to hold it together. 'He is a solid boy, tall for his age, and he speaks well. People often mistake him for being older, but he is only six years old.' When Tim's voice cracked Sydney squeezed his hand.

'Please,' her voice barely above a whisper. 'he's only a young child.' The camera panned her face as tears rolled down her cheeks and Tim put his arm around her. The camera went back to D I Parker who spoke of what the police were doing to locate the child. The dog squad returned. They had found a scent, but it ended abruptly down the road and around the corner from the house. DI Parker understood this had ominous ramifications. The Inspector now felt confident the child had got into a vehicle or been carried into a vehicle, but he would not share his thoughts with anyone outside his team at this point.

By the time the grandfather clock in the hallway chimed nine o'clock most of the police had left the property. The DI had a private conversation with Tim, where they prepared him in case, he had a call demanding a ransom. The phones were bugged with recorders and trackers. Grant Winthrop Tim's father had someone sit with Catherine. He arrived at his son's home with a list of cases Tim had worked on over the past year. He insisted the police call on Amanda Tim's ex, who now lived with her banker boyfriend.

'When I saw her in town, she didn't look pregnant so she must have had her baby. The woman has never been particularly stable,' Grant said. D I Parker wondered why no one had thought of her before. Immediately he took the Sergeant and went off to her home.

Chapter Twenty-Six:

Sydney looked worn out. She hadn't eaten since she sneaked a handful of popcorn from Finn's box at the movies, eleven hours ago. The thought Finn might be hungry and scared someplace completely unfamiliar to him, rocked her to her core. Someone had sent out for takeaways, pizza and some Chinese. Despite Tim's urging she didn't fancy any of it.

Tim's father, Grant, had always been well respected in law enforcement circles. Sydney felt sure his good reputation had motivated DI Parker to involve the press in the search so early. Also, she thanked God Tim's concerns about the paedophile were being taken seriously. The man had cohorts on the outside. Sydney hung on fiercely to the belief Finn was resilient and self-contained for a six-year-old. They both prayed there would be an innocent explanation., but for the life of her Sydney couldn't think what it might be, especially now the TV and radio stations had broadcast his details. Any sensible adult who knew anything, would have been in touch by now, surely?

Grant looked like an older leaner version of his son. He sat down next to Sydney and spoke kindly to her.

'The police have their best people on the case. You know Finn is a very knowing child, he's smart and this will work in his favour. You have done a good job with him Sydney. He's a bright child he might be hiding somewhere. He and I have talked about staying safe in the city.' Looking at him carefully Sydney noticed his hand had a slight tremor which he steadied on his thigh. 'I couldn't sit at home helpless. Catherine took a sedative, and the neighbour is staying with her.' Rubbing his face where a beard might grow, he added quietly. 'Poor Catherine, it's the reason she drinks you know.' Sydney frowned, wondering what he meant.

'We lost a child to meningococcal disease. Finn will be alright; I feel it quite strongly' he told her almost wishing he hadn't mentioned it. The memory of his lost son had plagued him for forty years. Grant had cherished Catherine and turned a blind eye to her sometimes-excessive drinking. He had felt guilty for not being there for her so often when the boys were babies.

D I Parker knocked on the bright red front door of the otherwise unremarkable suburban house in Wilton, one of Wellington's northern suburbs. A tall good-looking man in his late thirties wearing horn rimmed spectacles, dressed casually, answered the knock looking surprised.

'Sorry to disturb you at this hour sir, I'm Detective Inspector Parker. May I speak to Amanda Winthrop.' D I Parker held out his ID the man looked nonplussed.

'I'm her partner Inspector, may I ask what it's about?'

'And your name is?' D I Parker asked, lips pursed as he stood slightly stooped in the doorway, his suit rumpled as though he had been sitting for a while.

'I'm Dave Fenton,' he said not moving.

'May we come in Mr Fenton; this is important.' D I Parker moved closer to the man. He didn't have all night. 'It's about a missing child, her ex-husband's child to be precise, look time is of the essence sir. Still the man didn't move. D I Parker turned to his offsider, 'get the warrant from the car,' he the young officer with him.

Then sniffing DI Parker said, 'can you smell something Sergeant? smells like ... weed, do you smoke Mr. Fenton?' The Sergeant sniffed understanding what DI Parker alluded too.

'Yes, I can, is it...' he sniffed again.

'What are you talking about? I don't smoke and I've never even tried marijuana,' Dave Fenton protested.

'I need to speak to Ms Winthrop now.' As D I Parker spoke it dawned on the vapid Fenton, he meant business and he stood back to allow the police officers to enter the house.

'To be honest, Amanda and I just had a row, and she went to bed, I'll go and get her. Students live next door. I'm sure they smoke weed.' Dave Fenton ushered them into a comfortable lounge room and went to get Amanda, the Sergeant followed him, stopping short at the bedroom door.

'Amanda get up and make yourself decent, the police are here to talk to you. It's to do with Tim's child, he's missing.' A female voice could be heard complaining before Fenton griped, 'I thought you said Tim couldn't have kids. Hurry up Amanda the police said it's urgent.'

'Amanda Winthrop, it's the Police. Hurry please, this is a serious business.' the Sergeant commanded from the hallway. Fenton appeared in the bedroom door helping Amanda into her robe.

In the living room the questioning began in earnest.

'Where were you between five and six o'clock this evening? When did you last see Timothy Winthrop, your ex-husband? When did you learn about his child? Have you ever met the child? what do you know about the child?' She raised her voice, protesting and snarking about her ex, however it soon became apparent Amanda knew very little. Then from a spare room a child's crying could be heard.

'My son's crying,' Dave said, moving to the spare bedroom with the Sergeant following him. In the room there were two beds, a small boy about three was crying his father picked him up, soothing him. In the opposite bed lay an older fair-haired child. on closer inspection her long fair hair covered her face and the Sergeant smiled nodding as the two men looked at the sleeping child. 'Charlotte, she's my oldest, she's seven. In the hallway the sergeant asked if he could check the rest of the house and Fenton agreed.

From Amanda's sometimes flippant answers, DI Parker could see she knew nothing important. She behaved selfishly and lacked empathy. Fenton returned from settling his three-year-old son, Jack, to sit next to Amanda commenting he shared custody with his ex, as D I Parker dropped a bombshell.

'Where is your baby Ms Winthrop? Mr Grant Winthrop your ex-father-in-law said he saw you in town a week ago and he assumed you had given birth, what happened to the child?' Dave Fenton looked aghast.

'Amanda when were you pregnant?' Fenton questioned the woman. The police watched as Amanda looked around the room frantically.

'You were pregnant your ex-husband Tim, showed me the scan shot the radiologist sent to his phone. You were twelve weeks at the start of lockdown the estimated date for the birth would be the tenth October, three weeks ago.' They all looked to Amanda who shook her head, embarrassed.

'It was a joke, one of the IT guys from work sent him the picture, we downloaded it from the net.' She did not appear remotely sorry other than she had been found out. Fenton looked unhappy and annoyed. Convinced they had nothing to do with Finn's disappearance The police went back to the Criminal Investigation Office.

'Dave Fenton, what a wanker,' the Sergeant said aloud. 'Amanda would be a right pain in the proverbial... I almost feel sorry for him.' As the town clock struck midnight the investigation team regrouped, and D I Parker phoned Tim to update him. Regrettably, he had nothing to report other than the fact his ex-wife had never been pregnant.

'Nothing would surprise me; except I think it backfired on her. She thought I suffered a low sperm count. Not true I've been infertile for years as a result of an infection. Another reason Finn is so precious.'

Now eight hours since Finn had disappeared from his father's home the police began looking closely at more sinister outcomes. They agreed not to worry the parents with any grizzly scenarios until the morning. By then all Colin Burt's known associates would have been rounded up and questioned.

AT AUCKLAND AIRPORT Fletch Carter switched his phone to flight mode after checking it, he had missed a call from Sydney probably while being processed through the covid tests. Listening to her message and the sheer panic in her voice he needed to talk to her. Breathing deeply, he dialled the number. For the first time in many years real fear gripped him. The kind of fear you felt when a situation beyond your control unfolded, and anything could happen. Like when the enemy had you alone and unarmed with a loaded gun pressed up against your temple. The situation felt dire. Sydney had never been a drama queen. This must be serious. He felt helpless he loved the child and his mother, but he had never spelt it out to her because he didn't feel worthy, with nothing to offer her.

The call immediately went to voicemail. In these circumstances there could be any number of reasons she had her phone switched off. He tuned in to check on the news in NZ for the evening. The TV interview came up immediately. Watching Sydney's sad little plea, he zoomed in on her face as her eyes welled up. His gut wrenched. Tim looked cut to the quick but to his credit he comforted Sydney. That should be me, they are my little family, then he realised he had given them up and walked away. His father hadn't bring him up to walk away from a tough situation. He could hear his father's voice, 'I've had my three score years and ten plus some. You won't get a *third* chance son.' This had been his second chance, and he didn't recognise it, because he had been blind. Another of his father's sayings rang in his ears. His father often quoted things from the King James bible where this little pearl had its roots, 'There is none so blind as he who will not see.' He slumped back down in his seat as he remembered like an omen, the rest of the proverb, 'the most deluded people are those who choose to ignore what they already know.' How could he have been so stupid? Suddenly someone shook him, the flight attendant.

'Are you alright sir?' The words didn't register like she spoke underwater, and he didn't understand. She shook his shoulder again her voice louder this time. 'I think I heard your boarding call sir?' He blinked as the answer came to him.

'Oh, I've just had bad news from my family in New Zealand,' he explained, 'I need to get back to Wellington ASAP, I won't be going to Australia after all. Can I get a ticket back to Wellington?' The young woman fell silent for a moment.

'I'm not sure sir, I'll see what we can do for you.' As soon as the attendant left, Fletch once again called Sydney on her mobile. It went straight to voicemail. He phoned the veteran's aged care facility in the States where his father had been admitted to their isolation hospital. After speaking with the nurse managing the isolation ward, he felt devastated.

'I'm sorry to report your father is in a serious condition and now on a respirator, Major Carter.'

'Thank you, ma'am, I'm currently in Auckland, New Zealand. I have a serious situation within my family here in New Zealand. I don't know what will happen now, I need to get back to Wellington,' his voice strained.

'We are taking the very best care of your father sir; these are difficult times. I will personally keep you appraised of your father's status Major. God Speed.' Fletch thanked her and hung up.

Ten minutes passed and a booking clerk walked towards him with the flight attendant in tow.

'The flight attendant's been told of your situation, and she has seen the newsclip. May I check your passport and papers sir?' the clerk asked. Fletch handed them over. The woman commented on his American passport and asked about his visa to New Zealand.' You are very lucky you had not left the country sir, getting back in would have been problematic.'

'I understand, please just get me on the first flight back to Wellington. I'll do what it takes.'

AT TIM'S HOME IN THORNDON the police presence had thinned out with only two officers remaining; a female detective who had set up a system to monitor all the incoming phone calls, and D I Dan Parker who had chosen to stay because if this could not be resolved soon, he feared it could have a dire outcome.

Three am and still no word. Tim needed to talk to Sydney alone. She looked exhausted and felt nauseated saying she would lie down on the bed in Finn's room. He followed her in there and suggested he pull up the trundle bed to the same height so they could talk.

'I feel so bad this happened, and on my watch.' He lay down on the second bed although they now appeared like one. 'I'm sorry sweet, you let me back into your life after the appalling way I behaved, I don't deserve the gift this child is, he's grown on me and...' he covered his face with his hands and sat up sniffing, the back of his eyes stung, he breathed deeply exhaling audibly. When he opened his eyes, Sydney sat beside him, her arms around him gently reassuring him, in her caring loving way she did not blame him.

'There is no fault to be apportioned here. If a child is not safe in his own home playing while his parents talk in the next room, then god help us.' Thinking about it she tried to push the sick thoughts from her mind, but she burst into tears. 'Oh god Tim, we have failed him' she said weeping in violent racking sobs she couldn't control. He enveloped her in his arms and held her firmly until she fell silent. Slowly they lay down together in Finn's bedroom holding each other until sleep claimed them.

Two hours later the DI passed the open doorway on his way to the bathroom and felt relieved the pair seemed to be at peace. But by the time he returned to the living room, so had Tim, looking unusually rough, his face now covered in a scruffy stubble flecked with grey, his clothes rumpled, his vivid blue eyes bloodshot and rimmed with dark rings.

'At least Sydney's sleeping,' he sighed. 'Run the stats by me now Inspector, what are the odds after all this time?' His words hung in the air between them, neither wanting to verbalise the last part of the sentence, that Finn be found safe and sound.

'Let's not dwell on the negative Tim,' The DI said quietly. 'The good thing is there has been no ransom demand, which I'm sure would have been made by now if he had been kidnapped and money was the motive.' Tim poured himself a coffee.

'Yes, and we both know ransom demands are rare. Madelaine McCann's parents never had a ransom demand. How many children go missing worldwide each year? Millions and millions, who are never found.' Tim felt sick.

'Focus on the positive, what we can do as soon as daylight returns.' Although as he said it Dan Parker realised for Tim there seemed very little he could do. 'As soon as it's daylight we'll be sending a team to search each back garden, and nook and cranny,' Tim agreed, keen for something to do. Although Dan knew the dogs had it right. Finn had disappeared in a vehicle and there would come a point where the parents would need to be told. The police needed to eliminate all the usual suspects and they were working tirelessly to get there.

Two hours later after a quick shower, Sydney dressed, pulled up her hair in a high ponytail and started cooking breakfast for the two police officers and Tim. Thank god for good habits like the emergency grab bag she always kept in her car with clean underwear and toiletries. They were often useful.

In all the years she had known Tim he had never looked so rough. Even after long jury trials when the jury retired for the night and he'd been on his feet all day and half the night, he never looked this bad, but he had never been this powerless before. He hardly touched his breakfast. After two cups of strong coffee, he planned to join the neighbourhood search party. Dan Parker took him aside as he left the house.

'The dog handler is convinced Finn left in a vehicle on Murphy Street,' As a father, he felt ill telling Tim this. 'We only know the scent was strong and it stopped at that point.' Now thirteen hours had passed since the boy had last been seen by his parents. 'We are setting up sites around town using child mannequins dressed the same way as Finn. His picture will be posted all over town.' Tim hung his head; this was his worst nightmare. Just then D I Parker's mobile rang, and he answered, it turning away from Tim. Suddenly, he swung around.

'There has been a sighting in the Hutt Valley, the local police are following it up' he said pleased to have something positive to report. Tim's gut roiled.

'A sighting, what does that mean exactly?' he asked, DI Parker turned from him again, intently listening as he waved his hand at Tim for quiet. Finishing his call, he turned back to Tim wondering how to couch his words as this incident was still unfolding0 kilometres away in Lower Hutt.

'A woman has spotted a child fitting the description of your Finn in the carpark of Bunnings Hardware store, with a man.' DI Parker hesitated, not wanting to repeat what the woman had reported, "a man is trying to force the child into his four-wheel drive and the boy is shrieking and kicking furiously." DI Parker said nothing.

'It just after seven in the morning, what are people doing in the car park at this hour?'

'The store opens at seven Mr. Winthrop.' Before he had chance to say more another officer also in plain clothes, approached DI Parker and took him aside.

'We have had another sighting, this time across town we're checking it out,' the officer kept his voice low. DI Parker realised they would get many such calls. They all needed to be verified and chances were, none would be Finn. He stood on the street in front of the Winthrop villa thanked the officer and turned to Tim.

'Let's go inside and wait we have another sighting. The team will contact us as soon as they have something concrete. You look like you could do with a coffee, I know I could.' He shepherded Tim inside while still wondering about the child in the Bunnings' car park. Barely had the pair drained their coffee cups when more sightings came to light.

Outside in the street and neighbouring area a heavy police presence, along with volunteers, began the neighbourhood search. Tim went to change into jeans, preparing to join them and Grant kept Sydney company, to keep her from her dark thoughts. She knew the statistics in respect of these cases but something deep in her heart kept hope alive.

The land line rang, and Sydney answered it, before handing it over to DI Parker.

'The child in the carpark sir, we have verified he was with his father when he had a melt down over not going to McDonalds for breakfast. The father felt very embarrassed, he had taken the boy to the store early so his pregnant wife could have a sleep in. They had bought paint to paint the nursery. We verified all this sir. Kids, who'd have 'em, eh?' the reporting officer made light of an otherwise serious situation. DI Parker sighed, as a parent keen on DIY he could see the picture and only imagine the father's situation.

'Nothing there, I'm sorry Sydney. You appreciate we need to take time to thoroughly investigate every sighting. We can leave no stone unturned,' he said sadly. Sydney did understand but why her child, she loved him so much. She could not bring herself to phone people at home in the district and tell them the situation. Already Sara had texted her and Jamie Dalton and Ryan Murphy were in the process of gathering a group to join the search. Sydney suspected Ryan would more likely be holding them back at present as in the built-up city area a group of men from the bush would likely be a liability. It wa0s not like when Finn went missing on the farm she remembered.

Tim's kitchen had become a hub. Phones and I pads seemed to click, vibrate and ring constantly, while Tim himself had joined the local search.

'He's been found right across town in Kilbirnie,' a female officer called out. Everyone turned to her. The young detective beamed from ear to ear.

'He's fit and well, a bit hungry. He'll be here in twenty minutes,' she called.

Euphoric Sydney ran outside to tell Tim. The word soon travelled around the team and Tim ran back to the house. Sydney cried, hugging him.

'What happened exactly?' Sydney asked D I Parker, who only had sketchy details.

'It's him all right, Finn0 will be checked by a doctor and will be asked more questions only when he arrives home here to you.' DI Parker said relieved, 'he got onto a bus and basically rode it all the way to the depot. The driver didn't really notice him, thinking he had an adult with him. when all the passengers got off the bus, he stayed on un-noticed. The driver parked the bus and locked it until cleaning people boarded it this morning.'

When the patrol car arrived with Finn, he ran to his mother burying his face in her hug. Tim's arms enveloped them both.

'What happened, darling?' Sydney asked, watching the child's face run the gamut of his emotions. 'We've had a lot of worried people looking for you and Inspector Parker here needs to know. It might help him find other children who get into similar situations.' Sydney could hear her voice crack; however, she knew the police had pulled out all the stops. They had thrown huge resources at this incident and however relieved she, Tim and everybody else were, Finn had broken the rules. He had left the house by unlocking the door and he had walked off the premises and not said a word to anyone. He knew, it too.

'I'm sorry mummy, I went outside to see if my toys were in your car, but you had locked it. Then I saw a big red bus and it stopped, just a little way at the end of the street. The door was open, and the driver stood away from it having a smoke and talking to another man. So, I took a look inside, but before I had a chance to get out, the driver climbed inside and yelled something at the man he had been talking to. He sounded cross so I just sat there, not wanting to make him mad. Then some more people got on and the driver drove off. I didn't know where we were going so, I stayed put. I liked looking out of the window, but it got dark, and all the people got off, so I hid because I felt scared. The driver parked the bus in a big yard and locked the door. when he left, I tried to get out, but I couldn't, so I cried. I remembered what Fletch had told me when I went to hospital.' Finn noticed Tim had stopped smiling and leaned forward with his forearms resting on his knees like he pretended to be interested but Finn sensed displeasure. Sydney asked what Fletch had told him.

'He said, when you're scared think about something you like doing, like riding Pickle. He said really think about it and all the small things you love, like the feel of Pickle's lips on your hand when he takes a sugar lump and what Pickle's whiskers feel like when he nuzzles my neck and the wind on my face and all those things. So, I did, and I fell asleep. When I woke up, I wanted a wee, but I didn't want to wee on the bus, so I did it on the bottom step and it drained outside.' Tim noticed D I Parker's lips quirk, the boy showed definite smarts for six. 'I got sick of thinking about riding Pickle, so I thought about flying my kite and all the things Fletch had shown me to get lift and hold it.' He shrugged. 'It worked just as well I slept some more. I'm starving, the police lady gave me MacDonald's but I'm still hungry.' Sydney hugged him and Tim smiled. He planned on being the influencer in his child's life. Still Fletch had taught the boy so much. However, Fletch could no longer influence Tim's child. Well, he couldn't do much from America. Tim felt pleased.

The news reported the happy outcome showing the missing six-year-old being reunited with his frantic parents. Sydney rang Fletch. The call went straight to voicemail. She wondered if they were playing telephone tag. Still, she shared the great news her voice full of happiness. She apologised profusely for causing him stress when clearly, he would not be in any position to do anything to help her. D I Parker reassured them the outcome could not be better for one so young.

'Don't be too hard on him, he has a curious mind and it's a great thing.' However, Sydney felt loath to leave him with his father. Finn did not want to stay when she reluctantly said she needed to go home. Tim tried to persuade her to stay, but she had very little in her grab bag for a long weekend so there seemed to be nothing for it but to suggest Tim come and stay with them. Sydney had serious reservations about asking him. Finn seemed keen, probably because he knew his mother would not be close if she went home without him. Although he claimed to be brave, he clung to his mother after his adventure.

Chapter Twenty-Eight:

T he first plane back to Wellington turned out to be the third plane after the arrangements were made. It had turned six am by the time Fletch boarded his return flight. Although he'd had plenty of practice sleeping on a sack of spuds as he referred to the feel of his kit when he travelled with Uncle Sam, still he felt pretty rough, as though he suffered a bad hangover. The flight attendant felt sorry for him having heard his story and seen the news. Although Fletch needed to explain, 'Finn is my 'lady's' child and other personal stuff he never planned talking about with a strange woman. She turned out to be compassionate and upgraded him to business class for which he thanked her profusely before rewarding her with an appreciative smiles. As usual she read way more into it than he offered, but at least he had a half decent sleep on the return trip.

Sitting half asleep thinking about Sydney and Finn he felt emasculated, useless and so terribly miserable that he had made the wrong call, he should have been there for them. By the time he collected his luggage from the carrousel and boarded the bus into the city his watch read seven thirty.

Boar Gully, hell how he loved the place. The pace of life felt like another era. The folks were kind and Sydney, sexy as hell Sydney, had offered him exactly what he wanted. Only he couldn't see it for the material dream he had been caught up in. What did she call those materialistic people? 'Consumernoids,' she called them. Like any of it mattered when the shit hit the fan. The bus finally stopped at the railway station, he hailed a cab and gave them Timothy Winthrop's address. As he gave the address his phone buzzed a news flash on his Google alerts.

'The missing child Finn Martin, has been found alive and well.' The headline filled him with joy and relief coursed through him, any other result too awful to contemplate. He had known the odds and pushed them away. First, his mother died while he was on deployment in Iraq, then his best friend Mike had been killed in Afghanistan, then Emily, the love he lost. Finn was safe, he thanked god. Three minutes later the taxi parked outside Tim's grand villa. Sucking in a deep breath, he pushed his financial inadequacies to the back of his mind and paid the driver.

Pressing the doorbell, he stood back; unsure just how welcome he would be. Tim answered the door, his jaw dropped.

'What happened, you miss the plane?' he sounded ticked off.

'No, I came back for the most important ...'

'Fletch, mummy Fletch is here, Fletch is here,' Finn pushed past his father and hugged Fletch. Sydney heard the voices and came to see what caused the ruckus. For a split second they stood staring at each other. Then he held out his hand to Sydney and ruffling Finn's hair with his free hand he said he needed a few moments with his mother and then bent down and whispered something in Finn's ear.

'Excuse us Tim,' firmly gripping Sydney's hand, he smiled at Finn. 'Stay put with your Dad buddy. We'll be back in five minutes. Word of honour.' Fletch touched his heart with his open free hand. Sydney endorsed his 'stay put' command and the pair walked down the street. Stopping abruptly, he turned and knelt down on one knee.

'Sydney Georgina Martin, marry me please. I haven't got much but it's yours. We won't starve and who knows what the future holds. I know you made the offer, and I turned you down but...' The expression on her face was not what he expected. She had told him she loved him.

'What's changed Fletch?' her tone clipped.

'Aside from the fact when I saw the news clip with you pleading for Finn's safe return and I said to myself I should be there, there is the woman I love, what is wrong with me. Nothing is more important than the people I love, my little family. How could I be so blind? I couldn't see the obvious.' Standing now he wrapped his arms around her. Taking her face in his hands, he whispered. 'Forgive me I'm so damned stupid. My father kept telling me what my priorities should be and now I know in my gut I'll never get the chance to tell him, I finally got it. Marry me please?' he pleaded sniffing, as her breath hitched.

'If you promise to tell me often how much you love me,' she smiled, and he kissed her.

'Is there no end to your demands? I'll show you... every nigh...'

'Don't make promises you might not be able to keep.'

'Try me, but you get rid of Tim, and I'll have a word to Finn.'

As they left a somewhat peeved Tim stood on the doorstep holding Finn's hand as he cheerily waved them goodbye. On the trip back to Boar Gully she asked what he'd said to Finn.

'I said, I want to ask your mother to marry me. Do I have your permission as man of the house? If she says yes, we'll spend time together during the week.' Then Fletch laughed, 'would you believe what he said to me? she'll do it no worries, mate. See you after the long weekend. I swear the boy is an old soul, he's been here before.'

Epilogue

Two months later Christmas 2020

'Where do you want this angel?' Fletch stood on tip toes before looking to Sydney for his instructions.

'On the top of the tree and you're the tallest,' she winked, grinning at Finn. 'Hurry you two, you just have time to test the lights. I think I hear Jamie's truck is outside. I've got afternoon tea on the table and Olive will be the first to see our tree.' As soon as the room lit up with fairy lights, Finn felt satisfied. He ran to the door.

'Olive come and see our decorations. Mummy's made everything special this year.' Taking his little friend by her hand the pair stood holding hands and staring up at the Christmas angel. In an instant Fletch had his phone out taking pictures.

'Cute, aren't they?' he said to Jamie who agreed, standing in his socks complete with hay attached having left his work boots on the front veranda.

'This is for you; the new rural delivery bloke is running late.' Jamie passed Fletch a bundle of mail. The two men joined the women for afternoon tea.

'Do you kids want lemonade?' Sydney called from the family room. 'The mail's late' she said stating the obvious while watching Fletch slowly open a large manila envelope covered in American stamps.

'It's from my father's lawyer,' he swallowed hard, and Sydney covered his hand with hers.

'I'm sorry you were not there for your father.' What could she say? The old man had succumbed to Covid19. However, they both knew regardless of whether or not Fletch stayed in New Zealand his father would have been dead before Fletch boarded his plane. Any mercy dash would have been futile. The old Vietnam vet had told his son only days before his death he had not traipsed through rain forests drenched in agent orange looking for Charlie and survived to have his only child catch some Wu Hu Flu and die. Fletch smiled. His old man the red neck from way back, he felt proud of him and his service record.

'I had no idea the old man had property like this,' Fletch said, studying the papers his father's lawyer had sent. 'Well, they were my grandfather's actually he bought and never sold anything. Although they may not be as valuable as some, there is a house and a joinery shop, worth a tidy sum.' Folding the papers back into the envelope, he shrugged. 'Somehow you're right hun, it just doesn't seem important anymore.'

Sara agreed. 'Dad might have survived his bout of Covid, but he'll never be the same and his doctor will not clear him to go back practicing medicine. His heart has been affected.' Sara referred to her father in England, where a new more virulent strain of Covid had appeared. It had come from India where it wreaked havoc. They thanked God for being in New Zealand.

Sydney very deliberately got out a bottle of bubbly and poured them all a glass.

'Let's be grateful for our blessings here in God's own country, and pray we continue to keep safe, then you can check our wedding pics. Ryan Murphy's a pretty good wedding photographer actually, we won't dwell on what else he may have shot with his police camera. Also, we can toast Perry and his fiancée, he's American now and next time we talk I'll tell him it was a fair swap, one Yank for one Kiwi.' Laughing she started handing out the glasses of bubbly. Kissing her teasingly on the cheek, Fletch added,

'I'll say it is a good swap I even raised the IQ level of New Zealanders.'

'The cheeky bugger considers himself a Kiwi now. I think you still have to do the paperwork,' Jamie joked.

'And the time,' Fletch quipped, 'but Devil's Moon, the video game, caused sufficient interest in the movie and we're talking to new backers, so, 2021 looks brighter. It will be a long haul for America, but Perry's optimistic now they have a change of President and hopefully the Senate.

'Mummy, can I have three Christmases like Finn?' Olive asked as she sat at the table next to her him. Sara frowned and looked to Sydney.

'We're having an early Christmas on the twenty third with a few family gifts, games and a flash dinner. Then Finn is going to his father on the twenty fourth and he'll have Christmas there including Christmas day with his father and grandparents. Tim is bringing him back here on Boxing day afternoon. Then on the twenty seventh we'll have another Christmas with what Santa leaves under the tree here.' Sydney held up her open hands. 'Would you like to come here on the twenty seventh for Christmas lunch Olive, with Mummy and Jamie of course.' Olive beamed from ear to ear, a huge gap between her teeth showing a missing front tooth. 'It's settled then' Sydney offered her a creamed lamington.

'I'm not sure if you can have another Christmas with your Daddy, it depends if we are still at alert level one here and in Auckland,' Sara explained to Olive, who seemed resigned to the situation having been present when her mother skyped family around the world. But we can skype,' Sara advised as Olive, placated, smiled, with her nose covered in cream.

'Very generous of you to give old what's his name Christmas day,' Jamie indicated surrepticiously, in the direction of Wellington with his eyes, then he frowned. 'What will you two do then?' before he could invite them over to his farm Fletch laughed,

'We'll be so devastated I don't think we'll be able to get out of bed,' he winked.

THE END

About the Author

About the author:

Jenni Roussell is a naughty old tart with a wicked sense of humour.

She lives with her husband of fifty-Plus years and her latest canine side kick a spoiled miniature foxy called Zsazsa, because she can wind men around her little paw.

They all live in a tiny village in the Wairarapa with a population of less than two hundred residents who enjoy many secrets and stories.

www.ingramcontent.com/pod-product-compliance
Lightning Source LLC
Chambersburg PA
CBHW032040240626
47154CB00003B/1006